Praise for Serenity by D. Reneé Bagby

D. Renee Bagby distributed action, suspense, humor and romance throughout the tale that kept me entertained for hours.
—NeNe, Fallen Angel Reviews, Recommended Read

Serenity is a unique and well written compelling story of the power of love and the sting of rejection.
—Chocolate Minx, Literary Nymphs

Pick up Serenity if you're in the mood for strong emotion, a lot of crying, and a happy ending.
—Tina, Two Lips Reviews

The characters are wonderfully created, and the story brings laughter as well as tears.
—Susan Mobley, Romantic Times BOOKreviews Magazine – August 2008 Issue

A fantastic, emotional and heart wrenching read which will have readers on the edge of their seats in suspense, cheering for the romance, dabbing away tears and laughing with its humor.
—Danni, Nightowl Romance Reviews

If you are a big fan of fantasy romances, then Serenity might just be the next book you want to pick up.
—Tanya, Joyfully Reviewed

SERENITY

A GEZANE UNIVERSE NOVEL

D. RENEÉ BAGBY

Dedication

To Terez—I didn't change it, and I'm never going to, so there. Nyaaaah ;P

Author's Note

Please note as mentioned in the above dedication, I *still* didn't change it... or anything else for that matter. I promised myself that if I ever got the opportunity to re-release *Serenity* myself, that I wouldn't change it. No updating. No fiddling. I corrected a few typos and some punctuation, but otherwise the story is untouched. Why not "fix" it? Because this title, as it stands, is a time capsule for me to look back and see just how much my writing has changed. It's my job as the creator of this time capsule to put it back the way I found it so I can continue to look back at it and be amazed at my growth.

PROLOGUE

R HIANNON STARED IN SILENT HORROR as King Kiros, her father, was impaled.

"Run!"

She didn't know who had spoken or for whom his words were meant, and didn't care since her father had all her attention. He slid off his assailant's blade to the floor, blood spurting from the wound with every beat of his heart. He clutched at the wound to keep the blood from escaping, but it seeped through his fingers.

Rhiannon crawled to her father. She had to help him. He couldn't stop the blood oozing from his back. She could hold the wound. The mages would come and heal him soon.

"Rhiannon, stop!"

She screamed when someone grabbed her from behind and hauled her to her feet. The man jerked her towards him but she strained to keep her father in her sights. She had to help him.

The man shook Rhiannon until she braced herself on his arms to get him to stop.

"Wake up, damn you! We have to get out of here before Melchior arrives!"

Rhiannon tried to focus on the man. She blinked several times before she finally saw him. She whispered in confusion, "Wit?"

Her brother.

She hadn't seen him in over a year. On a whim, Kiros had moved the entire royal family to the Western Cheslav palace and only Wit was left behind. Her father said it was so Wit could petition the other kingdoms for aid in the coming battle. How Kiros had known war would break out, Rhiannon was never able to ascertain. But, break out it did. It took seven months before the battle reached the palace.

"Yes, it's me. Wit. Now, let's go," he demanded. He pulled her towards the inner throne room.

Rhiannon allowed herself to be pulled two steps before she balked. She gasped in horror as she realized what Wit was doing... or not doing, as the case was. She urged, "Father! We must help father, Wit. The mages—"

"The mages have fled, Rhiannon. Father is dead! Now—" His words choked to a halt and blood gurgled past his lips.

"Now you are dead, little prince," said Wit's killer. The killer jerked his blade sideways out of Wit's body. Blood and entrails painted the nearby walls. The killer smiled at Rhiannon. He brought the stained blade to his lips and lapped at the blood.

Rhiannon fell back with a horrified scream. She didn't freeze as when her father was killed. No, this time she ran. She didn't stop running until she had reached the inner throne room. Closing the doors took all her weight and strength, but she did it.

She wasn't quick enough with the lock. The rational side of her brain reasoned that no lock would have held against her brother's killer. He burst through the doors with a maniacal laugh and Rhiannon screamed in response.

The killer advanced on her with lethal intent. She couldn't take her eyes off his blade. Wit's blood left a trail marking the path the killer took.

He lifted the blade. With a final laugh, he charged her.

Rhiannon squeezed her eyes shut.

The blow never came. Instead, the sound of flesh meeting flesh then something heavy hitting the wall reached her. She made herself open her eyes and found her would-be assailant half embedded in the far wall. The one who'd put him there stood with his back to her.

"Melchior," she whispered.

He paid her no heed. Melchior had eyes only for the one he felled. "Guthr, you play with your life when you disobey my orders."

Rhiannon gasped and backed away. She moved slowly, hoping not to be noticed. Her destination was Kiros's throne and the secret passage behind it.

"She's just another human. What does it matter?" Guthr snapped. He picked himself out of the imprint his body made in the wall then flicked bits of rock and mortar from his bare shoulders. His manner was indifferent and a bit annoyed.

With a snarl of fury, Melchior snapped off Guthr's right horn. Guthr hissed with pain and moved his sword between them. Melchior roared. Guthr responded with a growl of his own but didn't attack and Melchior didn't reach for the battle-axe strapped to his back.

Guthr seemed to weigh his options then lowered the sword and backed down.

"Out," Melchior said.

Guthr grumbled all the way out of the throne room and slammed the doors closed behind him. Melchior threw Guthr's horn at the double doors. It pierced the left door, splintering the wood.

"Demon," Rhiannon said then slapped her hand over her mouth.

"Bhresya," Melchior replied, facing her. His dual-colored red and yellow eyes flashed at her and she ducked further behind her father's throne. He gave her a mock bow and greeted, "Queen Rhiannon, it is a pleasure to finally meet you."

"Queen?"

Melchior approached the throne. "Of course, Your Majesty. Kiros is dead, as are all of his sons, and your husband. That would make you queen." He smiled at her. "You seem surprised."

With courage she didn't know she possessed, Rhiannon abandoned thoughts of escape, came out from behind the throne and faced Melchior. "You mock me, *King* Melchior. You killed my entire family, thus making me queen, but my reign will last no longer than it takes for you to kill me."

Melchior stopped at the edge of the throne dais steps and looked up at Rhiannon. "I have no intentions of killing you, Queen Rhiannon. Of all the royal family, you alone will survive this day."

He jumped.

Rhiannon fell back against the throne with a gasp. Melchior landed a few feet in front of her and she held her hands out to protect herself. "Demons cannot lie. You said you wouldn't kill me."

Melchior laid a hand on her stomach, ignoring her attempts to get away from him. "You are right, Queen Rhiannon, bhresyas cannot lie. We are physically incapable of lying—unlike your father, and the rest of you humans." He smiled at her, showing fanged teeth. "You carry triplets from your late husband. You must be happy."

She stared at him in stunned silence.

She was pregnant? She had wondered... hoped, but the death of her husband three days ago had thrown all thoughts of children out of her mind.

"One of the three you carry is a girl. I want her," Melchior said, removing his hand and backing up a few steps.

That woke her up. She surged off the throne, confronting Melchior. "I would never give any child of mine to you, you beast."

Melchior laughed. "I find your words amusing considering your father had no problems giving you to me. Or, I should say, he promised you to me. When it came time to honor that promise, he changed his mind."

"What are you talking about? My father never promised me to you."

He nodded and his amusement vanished. "That alone is why you survive this day, Queen Rhiannon. You didn't know of your father's deception."

"What deception?"

Melchior indicated Rhiannon should sit. When she didn't comply, he said, "My story isn't long, but I don't wish you to strain yourself and hurt my future bride."

"Bride?" she asked, sinking back slowly.

"When your mother was pregnant with you, I approached King Kiros to stop the constant violence between our two peoples. I had only one stipulation—you would be my bride to cement the peace treaty."

"He agreed to this?"

Melchior pulled a folded sheet of paper from the pouch on his belt and held it out to Rhiannon. She took it and scanned the contents of the treaty Melchior and her father had signed. Kiros had indeed promised Rhiannon's hand in marriage to Melchior in order to ensure peace.

"You restarted this bloody war after nineteen years of peace because you couldn't marry me?" she asked incredulously.

"Don't flatter yourself, Queen Rhiannon. No human woman is worth this much blood. No, *you* are not worth this amount of carnage. My wife and three children are."

Rhiannon's hand went to her mouth as a horrible thought took hold. "What do you mean? What happened?"

Melchior clenched his hands. "Your father happened. He had my wife and children assassinated over a year ago."

That's how Kiros had known. Rhiannon bowed her head, ashamed that her father could do something so cowardly rather than simply accept peace. Kiros possibly wished to kill Melchior, as well. That was why Wit was sent to find allies against the coming war. A war only Kiros had known would start. She asked, "Did... Did you marry her when you couldn't marry me?"

"No. Asha was my wife of sixty-eight years. My youngest child was your age," Melchior answered softly.

Rhiannon had forgotten demons aged at a different rate than humans. Then how old would that make Melchior? She didn't think that question was appropriate at the moment, but another was. "You would have married me while still married to her?"

"You sound surprised at the concept of polygamy, when I know many of your human kingdoms embrace it." He pulled another paper from his pouch, this one rolled instead of folded, and handed it to her. "That time has come and gone, Queen Rhiannon. This is the future."

She read the paper. Her eyes went wide with astonishment. "This isn't a peace treaty. It's a war proclamation."

"You misunderstand my intentions." He turned and walked down the stairs. "So long as your daughter becomes my bride in nineteen years, war will be avoided. I shall not make the same mistake twice. I let Kiros renege on our agreement without punishment and he had my family assassinated." He turned and looked up at her. "I will remain with the living for another three hundred years or so. I can repeat this madness until one of your line decides to honor your word. Or, you can end it all with this simple bargain. Your choice."

Rhiannon read over the treaty again. She looked at Melchior and he watched her with a blank expression. "I cannot decide a peace treaty on behalf of all the kingdoms." She didn't want to decide a peace treaty at all.

She wasn't supposed to rule. That was for her brothers to do. She'd received no training. It was all too much too fast. She knew almost without a doubt Melchior had planned for her uncertainty and ignorance so he could take advantage.

"That's where you're wrong, Queen Rhiannon. Cheslav is the strongest of all the human kingdoms. The other kingdoms followed Cheslav into this war—and the original war. They will follow Cheslav out of it." He crossed his arms.

She shook her head, not wanting this responsibility. Fellen, her eldest brother, was supposed to rule after Kiros. They were all gone. Even her husband of six months was killed. That news had brought much grief when it reached her. They were childhood friends and had married because of love. Kiros had rushed the wedding, citing joy as an excuse for his haste. When in fact, he'd wanted her wed so the treaty he'd signed would be void.

Her mind wandered to the horrors she had seen just moments before. Kiros and Wit killed before her eyes and other scenes that would haunt her nights for the rest of her life.

No, this had to end.

She straightened, her resolve firming along with her spine. She held out the treaty to Melchior and declared in a firm voice, "I want something changed before I agree to this, King Melchior." She waited for Melchior to retrieve the treaty, but he didn't move. She shrugged and dropped the page. It floated and fluttered then zipped down to Melchior's open hand, eliciting a gasp from her.

Her surprise was stupid. All bhresyas possessed some magic. Melchior had already used his powers once when he told her about her pregnancy.

"What change do you wish, Queen Rhiannon?"

"I give you my daughter's hand in marriage and you give me Guthr's head. Both will be evidence of our—humans' and dem... *bhresyas*'—path towards peace," she answered then held her breath.

Would he agree to her condition?

"Because he attacked you?"

"No, because he is the stuff of nightmares. Of the entire bhresya army, Guthr is the cruelest and has the greatest bloodlust. The death of thousands can be laid at his feet. He even went so far as to try and disobey you."

"I agree. Such as he won't be needed in times of peace and he grows harder and harder to control. But, your daughter is not worth my most ruthless general."

"Then what is? I won't change my mind. Guthr must die."

"Not what. Who? Tiann. One ruthless general's death for another. Your daughter's hand for peace. Tiann's and Guthr's deaths for proof."

Rhiannon looked at his dual-colored eyes. A ring of red surrounded a ring of yellow with his black pupil in the middle. According to her father, all bhresyas had dual-colored eyes, but only those of the royal bloodline had eyes of red and yellow. She wondered if it was always red on the outside and yellow on the inside or if it switched. Her question would be answered if she'd seen Melchior's children. She'd bet Tiann knew.

"Tiann is father's top assassin as well as his strongest general."

"Yes."

Rhiannon's statement was more for herself than Melchior, but his agreement firmed her resolve. "My daughter's hand in marriage for peace. Tiann's and Guthr's deaths for proof," she said with a nod.

The change was made instantly and the page floated back up to Rhiannon. She signed it, let it fall back to Melchior, and he signed the document as well. A duplicate of the treaty appeared in his other hand and he sent it up to Rhiannon.

She looked it over to make sure nothing had changed then looked back at Melchior. "I won't be like my father. In nineteen years, my daughter will marry you. This war is at an end."

"This is only a ceasefire, Queen Rhiann. If the war restarts, you will probably find yourself lacking allies, as the other kingdoms will know the true reason behind the bloodbath."

"I don't understand."

"You have a copy, I have a copy, and I have sent a copy to all of the kings and queens of the other five kingdoms. They blame the bhresyas for the restart of this war. If you are more like your father than you want to admit, then the bhresyas won't be blamed again." Melchior pulled open the throne room door and exited, leaving the door open behind him.

Rhiannon slumped and stroked her flat stomach.

Triplets.

Thanks to Melchior, she knew she would have two boys and a girl. A girl whose life was decided for her already. Rhiannon hoped her daughter would forgive her.

She strangled back a scream when Melchior re-entered the throne room. He set a furry bundle on the floor. It looked like a puppy, but its fangs were too big for its mouth and its claws looked permanently extended and very lethal. It was also a very dark red, almost like clotted blood.

Melchior said, "A present for my intended. It is a thondi, a bhresya hound. They are extremely loyal."

Rhiannon didn't know what to say, so she didn't say anything. She stared at the puppy and it stared back at her. Melchior turned to the throne room door and pulled out Guthr's severed horn.

"So long as you are leaving presents, King Melchior, you could leave the horn," Rhiannon said. Her words were casual, as though Melchior had come to pay a social call instead of massacring her entire family. She descended the throne dais and crossed the room to stand next to him. The top of her head reached his chest... barely. She looked up at him with her hand held out.

She didn't know where she got the strength when her only desire was to hide in a safe place and cry for her loss. Someone else should have to deal with this mess, but everyone had fled. It was just her and she was queen.

Melchior laid the horn in her outstretched hand. "What will you do with it?"

The weight of the horn demanded she use two hands to hold it. It was flame red, like its owner. "I plan to give it to my daughter. It will be the beginning of a very long explanation."

"In nineteen years, Queen Rhiannon," Melchior said with a bow.

❧

Rhiannon's head lolled back against the bed. She felt the pressure of the babes inside her straining to be born but none of the pain. This didn't worry her as much as her inability to talk or move.

"Rest easy, Queen Rhiannon. I don't want to hurt you and I don't want to hurt your sons," the midwife said. "I only want the girl. She must die."

Rhiannon's mind screamed where her mouth couldn't. Where were her guards? How had she ended up alone with this woman? She didn't want her daughter to die. Melchior would restart the war!

Another figure entered the room via the window terrace. Rhiannon couldn't make out his face as he was hooded and cloaked. She only noticed him because the bhresya puppy, who stood beside her bed, growled at the man and bared his teeth.

The man ignored the puppy and snapped at the midwife, "What are you waiting for, woman?"

She spread Rhiannon's legs. "The babes come. You said only the girl was to die."

"Yes, yes. Hurry up." He looked at the doors then back at Rhiannon. "Don't worry, Your Majesty. No harm will come to your sons or you, but the girl cannot survive this day."

"Ah," the midwife gasped with pleasure as the first baby appeared. She cleaned the baby then bundled it up and placed it on the bed next to Rhiannon. "A son is born first. You should be proud, Queen Rhiannon. Luck comes to those who bear sons first."

The woman was mad. Rhiannon was drugged and helpless to stop her daughter's murder. How was that lucky?

The midwife smiled, oblivious to Rhiannon's distress. "You should thank me,

Your Majesty. Many women would beg not to feel the pain of childbirth as you are not. You simply lie still as the muscles of your body push the babes free of your womb." She ducked her head and helped the second baby into the world.

"Here she is!" The midwife cut the cord but didn't bother to clear the child's mouth and nostrils.

The puppy's growling became louder when the shrouded man came nearer to the bed.

"Shut up, you stupid beast," the shrouded man said, kicking at the puppy.

The puppy jumped back with a startled yelp.

"Ignore it," the midwife snapped. She handed the girl over to shrouded man. "Do it. I need to deliver the last child."

"Why did you let the beast stay in here?"

"It wouldn't leave. 'Tis a demon. I'll not touch any of their kind—not even to banish that hound from the room."

The shrouded man pulled his dagger. The baby in his arms cooed. She smiled at him and he smiled back. He rested the blade against her throat and whispered, "Goodbye, princess."

The man screamed in pain as the bhresya puppy latched on to his ankle. He dropped the baby in order to pry the puppy off his leg.

The puppy jumped away from the man, planting himself over the baby and growling.

Banging sounded at the door.

The shrouded man swore under his breath and tried to get around the puppy. He only got snapped at for his trouble. "Help me, you damn woman. The daughter must die."

"Queen Rhiannon! Queen Rhiannon, answer us!" Guards banged on the thick wood door.

The midwife picked up the blanket she would have used to swaddle the last baby and threw it at the puppy. Once it surrounded him, she snatched at the corner. Her actions gave the puppy a target and it buried its fangs in her throat through the blanket. It didn't release her until she stopped screaming.

The puppy shook off the blanket. He growled at the shrouded man in warning when he moved closer.

The shrouded man grabbed for the baby.

The puppy proved to be the faster of the two. It clamped down on the shrouded man's hand, tearing through flesh and bone until the hand severed from the man's wrist. The man fell back with a scream of pain. He wrapped his cloak around and around his wrist to stop the bleeding.

Wood splintered. The door to the chamber gave way under the assault of the guards, who took in the scene in horror.

The shrouded man used their confusion and fled the room the way he had come.

"See to the queen," ordered one of the guards. He gestured to a few men behind him and ordered, "Go after the assassin."

One guard knelt on the bed beside Rhiannon's legs then looked back at his commander. "The babe is crowning."

The commander pushed the man out of his way. He bent between Rhiannon's legs to assess the situation himself. "I'll deliver the babe. Get the girl off the floor." He caught the baby just in time. "Your other son is safe, Queen Rhiannon."

The guard that was displaced stood staring at the growling puppy. He looked from the puppy to the dead midwife.

The mages entered the room and cured Rhiannon of the enchantment the midwife had used. Rhiannon stumbled to her feet and almost dropped to the floor when pain knifed her insides. The mage nearest her kept her standing.

"Finish healing me," she snapped.

The mage who held her said, "My Queen, it is best if you heal naturally. Too much magic has entered your body this day. More mingled with—"

"Finish!" She shook the woman as best she could while being held.

The mage sighed then nodded to her associate. The other stepped forward and laid his hands on Rhiannon's stomach. Within moments she could stand on her own.

She shrugged off the mage who held her and walked towards her daughter.

"No, Your Majesty. The pup is crazed. He will kill you like he killed the midwife," pleaded one of the guards. He grabbed her arm to try and stop her.

Rhiannon glared at the man and he let her go. She knelt in front of the puppy and smiled at him then said in a soothing tone, "You know me. You've occupied my bed for the last eight months." She held out her hand to the puppy. "You may be her protector, but I'm her mother."

The puppy sniffed her hand. His jaws went slack, then he licked her fingers and gave a little bark. She scooped up her daughter. The puppy sat back and watched her.

Rhiannon stared at her daughter in wonder. Not a sound. She hadn't cried through the whole ordeal—not even when the shrouded man had dropped her.

Rhiannon ran her hands over her daughter's body to make sure the babe wasn't injured in the fall. The baby giggled and flailed her arms. Rhiannon stopped searching and stared. How could her daughter laugh? She was almost killed.

"She's so serene, Your Majesty. Who would think this bloodshed heralded her birth," the commander said.

Rhiannon stood with the help of a nearby guard. She signaled the commander to carry her sons and exited the room. She didn't want her chambers anymore. They were marred with blood that no amount of cleaning would ever erase. Just as she had moved to the Eastern Cheslav palace to escape the memory of her father's, brothers', and husband's murders, she would leave this room.

The puppy followed her, staring up at her and the baby.

She said, "You are right, Commander. She is serene and that shall be her name... Serenity."

CHAPTER ONE

"**S**ERENITY!"

The little girl groaned. She looked up from her tug-of-war with her puppy to her mother. She greeted with a smile, "Hello, Queen Mommy."

Rhiannon couldn't help returning her daughter's smile. Serenity's smile was, as always, radiant and ever present. It was hard to stay mad at her. Rhiannon made herself be firm in spite of her waning anger. "I told you to go to bed, young lady."

"Lorcan want play," Serenity said. She laid a hand on her hound's side.

He towered over the three-year-old Serenity. His shoulders came to Rhiannon's waist. At four years old, she had thought Lorcan would be almost fully grown. According to many of the palace guards who had seen other thondis, Lorcan had another foot to go before he was at his full height. The red fur of his youth had shed away, revealing reddish brown scales. It gave him an almost reptilian appearance.

The fangs and claws that seemed too big for his body as a puppy better fit him as an adult. His legs from shoulder to ankle and his tail from the base of his back to the tip were covered in short brown spikes. For those not used to him, Lorcan was a truly frightening creature to behold.

Rhiannon would have counted herself among the number of those to fear Lorcan if he hadn't lived in her palace for so long. He resembled any other hound to her after so much time. She almost forgot his affect on people until a guest of the palace reacted badly to his unexpected appearance.

At the moment, Lorcan only looked exhausted. He sat on his haunches and panted at her, as though he would wait to see the outcome of the argument between mother and daughter before he made another move.

Rhiannon put her hands on her hips. "No, Lorcan wants to go to sleep. He has to be tired after having you ride him all day and chase him most of the night."

"Pony!" Serenity exclaimed as she tried to climb onto Lorcan's back. One chubby hand grabbed the spike that grew out of Lorcan's left shoulder and used it to pull herself up.

Rhiannon plucked Serenity off Lorcan. She balanced Serenity on her hip and walked towards the girl's bedroom. "You can ride him tomorrow. I'm sure he will be more playful after he sleeps."

Lorcan fell into step beside her. Many of the patrons of the palace bowed nervously when the trio passed. Rhiannon knew Lorcan scared them, but the hound harmed no one unless they tried to hurt Serenity. Those few had died for their folly. Rhiannon had worried for Serenity's safety daily until she saw just how fiercely Lorcan protected her daughter. For his loyalty, she named him after her second eldest brother.

Rhiannon laid Serenity on her bed then looked back at Lorcan. He gave a good shake before he jumped onto the bed. He stretched his length beside Serenity and yawned. Rhiannon shook her head at the sight of such a scary beast sprawled beside her angel of a daughter.

She covered them both with the blankets then kissed Serenity's forehead and gave Lorcan a pat. "Go to sleep, Serenity." In a softer tone, she said, "The sooner you sleep, the sooner you can get up and play some more."

She watched Serenity snuggle into Lorcan's side and was satisfied that her daughter would finally go to sleep. Rhiannon walked quietly from the room and closed the door. She made her way back to her throne room, wishing she too could go to sleep. There were matters of court that needed her attention even though the sun had already set.

A soft thump from Serenity's room made Rhiannon stop walking with a sigh. Serenity was at it again. The girl had endless energy at night only to fall asleep at breakfast. When no other sounds came, Rhiannon figured Lorcan had shifted. She continued on to the throne room.

෨⸱ᕗ

In Serenity's room, the figure that had entered the room from thin air caught Lorcan's attention. He didn't move from his mistress' side but gave a warning growl.

The hulking figure approached the bed.

Lorcan's growling grew louder.

A tiny hand swatted at Lorcan from beneath the covers. "Bad puppy. Go sleep." To illustrate her command, Serenity burrowed deeper into the blankets.

"Princess Serenity?" inquired the deep, growling voice of the intruder.

Serenity sat up. She waved her hand over the illuminating stones and rubbed her eyes as the light filled the room. She blinked at the owner of the voice.

He started towards her.

Lorcan stood on the bed.

Serenity smiled. Her smile grew until she giggled with glee. "You're a bhresya," she proclaimed happily.

The intruder's steps faltered.

Serenity kicked off her covers and hopped out of the bed. "What your name? I'm Serenity. You know Melchior? He my future husband and he king of bhresyas. Queen Mommy say so," she babbled away happily. She looked up at him expectantly.

When she would have taken a step towards the intruder, Lorcan jumped off the bed and blocked her path. He bared his fangs at the bhresya while he shielded Serenity. She pushed at Lorcan's side and tried to get him to move to no avail.

The bhresya stared down at her. Confusion was plain on his face. He held out his hand.

Lorcan attacked.

᪥

"Queen Mommy! Queen Mommy!" screamed Serenity as she ran down the hallway. Many of the nobles and servants tried to stop her as she ran towards the throne room. Serenity dodged them and kept screaming.

Rhiannon burst from the throne room and met Serenity at a dead run. She scooped Serenity up and hugged her tight. Rhiannon asked in a soothing motherly tone, "What is it, Serenity? Did you have a bad dream?" She looked her daughter over for wounds. Had someone attacked Serenity again?

The guards surrounded them instantly. All waited with baited breath for the reason for Serenity's frantic state.

Serenity pointed a finger back the way she had come. She cried, "Lorcan bad puppy! He hurting bhresya. Melchior be mad. Make Lorcan stop, Queen Mommy!"

"Bhresya?" asked the commander as though he didn't recognize the word. "A demon!" He signaled his men. All of them ran down the hall toward Serenity's room. Rhiannon followed.

Lorcan didn't need to be stopped or helped. The bhresya lay on his stomach with his arms stretched out away from his body on both sides. Lorcan had the bhresya's right horn firmly clamped in his mouth. He would growl every few seconds but otherwise didn't move.

Rhiannon strangled back a scream. A large, burnt orange bhresya male lay on the floor of Serenity's bedroom. She couldn't tell much about him from his position. Like most bhresya males, he wore a simple dark loincloth and nothing else. He had no weapon that she could see but that didn't change the fact that he was dangerous and in her daughter's room.

Her arms clutched at Serenity as she realized the true horror of the moment. She hadn't seen a bhresya in almost four years. She had hoped she wouldn't have to see one—besides Lorcan—for another fifteen. How had this one gotten past the guards and into Serenity's room?

The guards surrounded the bhresya, drawing their swords and pointing them at him.

When the bhresya spoke, everyone in the room jumped, "My name is Chigaru. I was hired to kill Princess Serenity."

"You son of a—"

"Commander!" Rhiannon yelled, covering Serenity's ears and glaring at him. The man's look turned sheepish. She looked back at Chigaru. "Hired? By whom?"

"I do not know. We prefer anonymity and plausible deniability," Chigaru answered.

Rhiannon nodded. The person who contracted Chigaru's services couldn't be traced in case Chigaru was caught.

"We?" she asked.

"There are two others."

"Will they come if they find you have failed?"

"Yes."

Rhiannon asked the most pertinent question of the evening, "You obviously are good at your job. Your presence went undetected until Serenity called attention to you. Why didn't you kill my daughter when you had the chance?"

Chigaru's horns curved in a large arc in front of his face, so his face didn't actually rest on the floor but a foot above it. He shifted, sliding on his horns, so he looked at Rhiannon. Lorcan growled and kept a firm hold on his horn, but allowed him to move that little bit.

"She smiled at me. I expected her to scream—as all humans do. She is unafraid," he answered with an edge of disbelief and wonder.

Serenity sniffed and rubbed her nose on the back of her hand. Chigaru's gaze shifted to her. She blinked at him and sniffed again. Slowly, her smile returned. In true childlike fashion, Serenity had forgotten what she was upset about only moments before. She squirmed in her mother's arms. "Down. Want down," she said.

Rhiannon let Serenity stand. Before she could grab Serenity's hand and hold her at her side, Serenity dashed forward. When she got close to the circle of men that guarded Chigaru, she squeezed past them. One of the men reached for her to hold her back, but Lorcan released his hold on Chigaru and confronted the man. The guard jumped back immediately with his hands held in the air, looking at Rhiannon for help.

Serenity gave Lorcan a pat as she passed him, then stood next to Chigaru's head. She got on all fours in front of him, but he still didn't look right to her. So, she turned until the top of her head was almost flat on the floor then smiled. Now, he looked right.

She asked, "Not hurt?"

"No."

Serenity nodded awkwardly. "You're orange."

"Yes."

"Melchior orange?"

"No. King Melchior is midnight blue."

"I like blue." She nodded again. "Your eyes blue and gray. They pretty. My eyes pretty?"

"Yes."

Rhiannon couldn't wrap her mind around it. The bhresya... the *assassin* that had come to kill her daughter now lay on the floor and answered Serenity's questions as though it were normal. "You hesitated in killing my daughter this time. Will you escape to try again?"

"I will not flee. I will not harm Princess Serenity."

"Why?" she asked, not believing him but compelled to because of the bhresya inability to lie. It wasn't enough. Why the sudden change of heart? "You were paid to kill her. Isn't your honor at stake if you don't follow through?"

Chigaru shifted his attention to Rhiannon. "I know what happened in the past. I know how the war restarted. You did not know you were to marry Melchior. Rather than wait for your betrayal, I agreed to take the contract that would end the princess' life. But—" his gaze moved back to Serenity "—she knows."

"If I hadn't told her... Serenity is a baby! She doesn't know what marriage is," Rhiannon raged.

Serenity toppled back on her butt then looked over her shoulder at her mother.

"Do too. Marriage means mommy and daddy together. That what nanny say." She turned back to Chigaru and touched his horns. "I want horns."

"Humans don't have horns," Chigaru said.

"Why not?" She looked back at Rhiannon. "I want horns, Queen Mommy."

"No," Rhiannon said absently. She made up her mind. "I have to contact King Melchior. He will need to know about this attempt on Serenity's life."

The commander said, "You have not told Melchior of the other assassination attempts, why tell him of this one?"

"No bhresya has ever come to kill Serenity before tonight. King Melchior must be informed."

"My king would kill me," Chigaru said. There was no fear in his voice, only resignation.

Serenity's smile dropped. "No!" She got to her feet with her hands on her hips and yelled, "No kill Chigaru! He mine. He in my room. He mine!" She nodded at Chigaru. "Queen Mommy say stuff in my room mine. Right?" She looked at her mother for confirmation.

Rhiannon shook her head then explained carefully, "Chigaru isn't a pet, Serenity. You can't keep him."

"Mine!"

"Now, Serenity—"

"Mine! Mine! Mine! Mine!" She punctuated each word with a stamp of her tiny foot.

Chigaru solved the problem nicely. He said, "If I do not return, the others will come to finish the assignment. I can stop them."

That surprised everyone in the room.

"Why would you?" Rhiannon asked.

"She is my king's betrothed and she knows this. That makes her a member of the Nexian royal family. I am a subject of Nexeu. I belong to Princess Serenity, as she says."

Serenity smiled in triumph and patted Chigaru on the head. "Chigaru mine."

"Yes," he agreed.

Against the better judgment of Rhiannon's guards and advisors, Rhiannon allowed Chigaru to stay in the palace unmolested. She didn't contact Melchior, against her own judgment. True to his word, Chigaru protected Serenity from his compatriots when they came to finish his job. And like Chigaru before them, they became Serenity's as well.

CHAPTER TWO

CHIGARU STOOD WITH HIS ARMS CROSSED, staring impassively at the wall. His face showed total calm. No one would ever know a ten-year-old boy had spent the last twenty minutes screaming at him.

Joah, third born of the triplets, yelled, "Let me in."

The door to the room Chigaru guarded opened and Rhiannon came out. She nodded to Chigaru, who bowed to her, entered the room then closed the door behind him.

Rhiannon faced her last-born son with mild annoyance. She hated being mad at Joah. He was a smaller version of her late husband. She was sure Joah would grow to his father's height later in life and tower over her. Many had said her late husband had to be part bhresya to ascend to such a height when no other in his family was that tall. There was no way something so silly was true.

Joah's dark brown eyes flashed with their anger. His hands were fisted into the legs of his pants. It was a motion he must have done many times in the last few minutes because his pants showed several patches of crushed cloth.

He repeated for his mother's sake, "I want to go in."

"I have told you time and again, Joah, you cannot attend this class. These lessons are for Alric and Serenity only. They will join you for lunch."

"It isn't fair," Joah yelled. "Why does Serenity get to and I don't?"

Rhiannon laid a hand on Joah's shoulder only to have him jerk out of her grasp. Joah was an angry child—almost since birth. He was jealous of the attention Serenity received. Rhiannon had never explained to her sons about the many assassination attempts over the years, and she had told Serenity to keep them secret, as well. Joah mistook everyone's constant vigilance of Serenity as preferential attention.

"Serenity will be queen one day. She needs this training," Rhiannon said.

Joah looked horrified. "Alric won't be king anymore! When did that happen?"

"No, no, Joah. Alric will one day rule Cheslav, but Serenity will marry a king. As a future queen of another kingdom, she must be prepared to rule." She searched her son's face for understanding.

"If I marry a queen and become king, wouldn't I need training too?"

Rhiannon closed her eyes, not wanting to have this conversation. She hated treating her children differently, but Joah had to accept that he would never rule. Even if Alric was rendered incapable, Rhiannon would rather give the throne to another.

There was too much anger in Joah. She could never trust her kingdom to him.

She said, "All the other princesses are long betrothed, Joah. They are going to marry others when they are old enough, or they are already married."

"It isn't fair. I hate Serenity."

"Don't ever say that again, Joah. Do you hear me? Serenity is your sister. You shared a womb with her."

"I don't care. I hate her. And you can't make me not hate her," he yelled as he ran away down the hallway.

Rhiannon stared after him. She faced the door when Chigaru escorted Serenity and Alric out of the classroom. It was an unmotherly thought, but Rhiannon wished Alric was the one who had looked like his father instead of Joah.

Alric's attitude more resembled her late husband's. They were both mellow and slow to anger. When others would rush to act, Alric stood back and assessed the situation in its entirety before he committed to a decision. That was a good trait for a king to have. And yet, Alric's looks resembled Kiros's.

It was Alric's green eyes that did it. The trait was rare and was last seen on an ancestor from six generations ago before Kiros inherited them then passed them on to his grandson. Rhiannon didn't want people to remember Kiros when they looked at Alric. The two were nothing alike and she had striven hard to ensure that. But, Alric's eyes would be a constant reminder.

Serenity's eyes were a soft brown and always sparkled with hidden laughter. She smiled constantly. Years of assassination attempts had not driven the joy from her. Rhiannon was happy for that and prayed the trend continued for the rest of Serenity's life.

Alric said around a yawn, "That class gets more and more boring every time we go. Treaties this and diplomatic missions that. Can't I just let Joah rule?"

"No!" Rhiannon snapped. She softened her harsh denial with a smile. "I mean, you were first born, Alric, therefore this is your responsibility."

"But it's boring," Alric whined with a half smile.

Serenity laughed at his statement. "You only have to attend one class, my brother. After our lunch, I must study with Haige for another four hours. At least you can practice with the soldiers later. I must stay cooped up."

She looked out the window nearest them. It was a beautiful day. She could hear the sounds of spring over the clang of the sword practice that took place below. "Let's go eat outside today, Alric, Chigaru. It's pretty." She didn't wait for them to agree before starting away to act on her suggestion. Chigaru made a detour by the kitchen and informed the cook of the change in eating place. He brought Lorcan when he rejoined them.

Serenity smiled at her pet. Lorcan flopped contentedly beside her on the blanket one of the maids had spread for the royal triplets. In his usual fashion, Chigaru sampled all the food before the triplets tried any of it. As a bhresya, Chigaru's metabolism wasn't susceptible to any poison an assassin might use to kill a human, but he could still taste it if it was present.

Joah wasn't in the mood to eat. Instead, he lobbed one of his biscuits at Lorcan. The hound gave a short whine and licked the spot where the biscuit had hit him.

Serenity glared at Joah. "Food is for eating, not throwing, Joah."

"Fine." He ripped into his food. "I hate that thing."

"You only hate Lorcan because he doesn't belong to you," Alric said around a mouthful of bread and meat. He snuck a piece of meat from his plate to Lorcan.

The hound lapped up the meat quickly and licked his jaws. He looked between Alric and Serenity to see who would provide the next morsel.

"It snaps at me," Joah said.

Serenity said, "Lorcan only snaps at you because you always throw things at him. He's not as stupid as you think he is."

"No, but you are!" Joah picked up a rock and hurtled it at Serenity.

Chigaru caught the rock an inch in front of Serenity's face. She didn't even blink. He straightened with the rock in his hand and crushed it, letting the pieces drop through his fingers.

Alric sputtered in anger, "Are you crazy, Joah? Why did you do that? Apologize!"

Joah stood and kicked over the food nearest him. "You aren't king yet, Alric. You can't boss me around." He ran away from the picnic.

"Joah!"

"No, Alric. Leave him. He's angry," Serenity said. She wondered when Joah started hating her so much. She looked up at Chigaru.

He was silent, as was his wont. He showed no outward reaction to her brother's attack. She knew with a certainty he would have an opinion on the issue once they were alone together. Chigaru never spoke unless he and Serenity were alone. If his words were urgent enough, he would whisper to her.

"That's no excuse, Serenity," Alric said in an annoyed tone.

She just shook her head. "Joah doesn't want me around anymore, sister or not. In eight years, he'll get his wish. He'll be happier."

CHAPTER THREE

RHIANNON WAS DRAPED OVER HER THRONE IN TEARS. Every mother cried on her daughter's wedding day, but that wasn't Rhiannon's reason.

Someone had kidnapped Serenity.

Alric paced in front of his throne. Every few steps he stopped and looked at the doors only to shake his head and start pacing again. He stopped once more and looked at Rhiannon. "It's okay, Mother. They'll find her."

Rhiannon shook her head. Her tears continued in earnest. Would Melchior believe Serenity was kidnapped? Would he restart the war before they had a chance to explain? She had never told Melchior of the assassination attempts and she regretted that now. If he had known, this wouldn't be such a surprise. He might have sent more guards. Why? Why?

It was too late to regret the past.

Melchior had arrived.

Rhiannon cried harder at the sight of him.

"Queen Rhiannon, it is good to see you again on this joyous day. Prince Alric, it is good to finally meet you," Melchior said.

Rhiannon didn't question how Melchior recognized Alric. His place at her side marked him as the heir to Cheslav's throne. Alric glanced at her, but all she could do was cry. He turned a worried gaze to Melchior then slumped his shoulders in defeat.

"King Melchior, I wish I had happier news." Alric looked one last time to the door then back at Melchior and the bhresya males who waited behind him. Alric said in a flat tone, "Serenity was kidnapped."

"Lies!" Melchior roared. The males behind him put their hands on their weapons but didn't draw them.

Rhiannon surged off her throne and yelled almost as loudly, "It's true. And, it's all your fault." She pointed an accusing finger at him.

"My fault? How is your daughter's kidnapping my fault?"

"That!" Rhiannon threw the treaty at him. The paper waffled in the air with the force she put behind it, then it fluttered to the ground, landing on the steps. "That treaty has plagued her since birth. The midwife drugged me while a man tried to slit her throat. Only Lorcan's intervention kept Serenity alive." She sliced her hand through the air. "It didn't stop there. Almost nightly, Lorcan dragged dead bodies to lie at my feet. The blood still stains this floor with its memory."

Melchior's eyes closed to slits. "Who is Lorcan?" He recognized the name. He did not like that another male... another *human* male had acted as champion to his future bride and queen. Such actions would endear Serenity to the lad and make her transition to his wife all the harder.

"Lorcan is a thondi and Serenity's pet," Alric said. "Thank the gods for him, wherever she got him. Serenity would be long dead if not for him."

"Named after my second eldest brother," Rhiannon added dismissively. Horror shined in her eyes. Her tone changed from angered to concerned in one breath. "Lorcan! I had almost... You brought mages, King Melchior?"

Melchior couldn't follow this change of subject but nodded.

Rhiannon rushed down the throne dais steps. She grabbed Melchior's hand and pulled him in her wake. "You must call them. Our mages could only slow the bleeding. Serenity will be so upset if he dies. Please."

He didn't question her request, mostly because the woman seemed too frantic to give him a straight answer. He signaled for the mage he had brought to oversee the wedding ceremony to follow them.

She showed Melchior and the mage to Serenity's room.

Melchior took in his surroundings. It wasn't what he imagined a human female would have. All the furniture was oversized from the giant mirror on the far side of the room opposite the door to the bed. It was big enough to accommodate even Melchior's girth.

His attention returned to the mirror. It was plain and didn't deserve his interest but the multitude of varying colored bhresya horns did. Each horn was mounted on a wooden plaque then placed around the edge of the mirror as decoration. The red one at the very top of the mirror Melchior recognized as once belonging to his former general, Guthr.

Who did the other horns belong to and how had Serenity gotten them? And why such a vulgar display?

Melchior also wanted to know where the overwhelming scent of another bhresya male had originated. It wasn't a bad smell, and Melchior was sure the humans around him couldn't smell it. But, he could. A thondi wouldn't cause it.

Lorcan gave a baleful wail of pain. Melchior's gaze switched to him. Melchior walked over to the hound and watched the mage work. He would find out about Serenity's collection and the mysterious scent later.

"Who did this?" he asked.

Someone had stabbed the hound repeatedly. Melchior could only guess the attacker was human since the wounds were shallow. It took a lot of force to pierce a thondi's hide, since it was like armor. If Lorcan had fought his assailant, as Melchior knew he would have, then that would make the task of wounding him that much harder.

Rhiannon shook her head, ringing her hands, "We didn't see them. It was like Chigaru all over again. One minute she was here, the next Lorcan screamed in pain and Serenity was gone." She clasped her hands together in front of her face when Lorcan whimpered.

Melchior scanned the room again. He wanted to know the name of the bhresya male who belonged to the scent he smelled. He wanted to know why that male's scent was as dominant in the room as Serenity's. He assumed Serenity was the owner of the human female scent.

The more pressing matter was the location of his bride-to-be. He looked back at Rhiannon, finally believing her earlier claim of kidnapping. "If you are so concerned for Serenity's safety, why aren't your soldiers searching for her?" He had noticed none missing from the numbers that guarded the palace.

Rhiannon would have answered but Alric cut her off and said, "No one can track Serenity better than the Hell Hounds. We left it to them."

"Hell Hounds?"

"Five bhresyas. They are Serenity's bodyguards."

"I would know if bhresyas had entered Cheslav."

Rhiannon, who had knelt to be closer to Lorcan, snorted. She laid a gentle hand on Lorcan's side and he whined up at her. She said in a quiet voice, "Obviously you didn't, because three of them came to Cheslav with the intention of killing Serenity." Her gaze lifted and she met Melchior's gaze.

He could only stare at her in shock. This was the not the news he thought would greet him on his wedding day.

"Chigaru was the first. Then came Haige and Nym. Afterwards, Theyn followed and finally Mael."

"You never contacted me," Melchior said, once he found his voice. "I would have liked to be informed of bhresyas attacking my betrothed."

"She wouldn't let me," Rhiannon said. "She didn't want to trouble you."

"And, now she's kidnapped. How—"

Lorcan let out a loud, long howl, interrupting Melchior's question.

The volume of it shook the windows and Rhiannon covered her ears. The mage stepped back with a nod to Melchior to indicate the hound was healed, though Lorcan's display was indication enough.

Lorcan bounded off the mat and scented the air then took off running.

Melchior followed him. He yelled over his shoulder, "I go to retrieve my bride, Queen Rhiannon."

Rhiannon stared after him. "Bring her back safely, please," she whispered.

Melchior didn't spare an explanation for his guards and they didn't require one. They followed him without question and he followed Lorcan.

It wasn't long before they caught up with the Hell Hounds. All five bhresyas were mounted on lysidis—bhresya horses—and moved with a speed unknown to humans and their mounts. This amazing speed was attributed to the lysidis' third pair of legs. Like the bhresyas themselves and thondis, lysidis sported horns that grew from their temples and pointed forward.

Chigaru spared a glance for his king but kept his attention focused on the path ahead of him. He snapped the reins attached to his lysidi's horns, urging the animal to move faster. The other Hell Hounds were not so nonchalant.

Mael strangled back a scream at the sight of Melchior and nearly fell off her mount. "King Melchior!"

Melchior ignored her and pulled alongside Chigaru. His nostrils flared. It seemed he had found the owner of the scent in Serenity's room. He wanted to ask, but instead, he said, "I will hear your explanations after we have located my bride and returned her unharmed."

❧

Serenity couldn't see. That wasn't so bad. The worst part was the hard chair her captors had tied her to. Her butt was numb and her back ached from having her arms stretched behind her and bound. There was one light of hope—she knew only two held her and they were both male. She was also pretty sure one was human and the other was bhresya. Given that information, she had a pretty good idea of her captors' identities.

"I know you're still in the room. If you would be so kind as to move me to a bed, I would be grateful. This chair is most uncomfortable," she said. She waited a second. "Hello?"

The silence persisted.

"General Guthr and General Tiann, I understand your wish to see me dead as my marriage means your deaths, but couldn't a dying woman have a little comfort, please?"

The blindfold was removed, but she was left in the chair. Two smiling faces greeted her—one human and the other bhresya.

"You are too smart for your own good, Princess Serenity," Tiann said.

She looked at them both. A human and a fire red demon missing one horn—General Guthr. Rhiannon had given Serenity the horn on her eleventh birthday along with an in-depth explanation about the entire situation and its owner.

Serenity wondered if Guthr's viciousness was a result of his short stature and small horns. The male was a good head and half taller than her, but that was short compared to a normal bhresya male. And, Guthr's mounted horn that hung above her mirror looked child-sized. It was barely as long as her forearm. Serenity thought Melchior had only snapped the horn in half when he broke it from Guthr's head, but looking at him, she knew that wasn't the case.

His dark red hair looked as though it hadn't seen a comb or water in a few days… maybe even weeks. The hair went whichever way it pleased. His breechcloth and a sword were the only things he wore. It didn't look as though Guthr cared about his appearance.

Serenity met his gaze. That's when she saw the monster her mother told her about. His dual-colored purple and orange eyes held the promise of death and it made her shiver. She'd seen the look before, but never that intense or this close.

She looked away from Guthr to General Tiann. He was from Western Cheslav. His dark tan skin marked him as such. A vast ocean split the kingdom of Cheslav in half. Its occupants traveled freely between the two and intermingled, but the color of one's skin was an easy indication of which half of the kingdom they originated. Those of tan skin were from Western Cheslav, while those with brown skin—like Serenity—were from Eastern Cheslav.

Tiann was better kempt than his partner. He'd shaved his head bald and his loose shirt and pants looked pristine. Tiann and Guthr shared a height, which probably annoyed Guthr. But, whereas Guthr was a solid mass of muscle, Tiann was tall and lithe. He had the perfect body for an assassin. He'd had no problem slipping in and out of Serenity's room when he kidnapped her.

He was a former general of Cheslav and knew both palaces well. Rhiannon had rearranged the layout of the entire Eastern palace to guard against Tiann, but the secret passages remained. It was impossible to guard them all because not all of them were known. Serenity remembered stumbling across a few when she was younger. They made great hiding places, even if her bhresya guards could track her scent easily.

Serenity hoped the same held true today. She hoped they had noticed her absence quickly and would come to her aid. She also hoped they weren't too late.

The looks Tiann and Guthr gave her didn't bode well for her continued health. She looked away from Tiann's brown eyes. She planned to look at the ground but her gaze stopped halfway there and she received a mild shock.

Tiann's hand was missing.

"You tried to kill me when I was born. My mother told me Lorcan bit off the hand of the man who tried to kill me," Serenity said.

Tiann looked at his nub. "Yes, I must take satisfaction in the knowledge that today I did that damn mutt enough damage to kill him." He smiled at Serenity's look of horror.

"Lorcan," she whispered and bowed her head.

Guthr said, "Your death is not our goal, Princess Serenity. We merely plan to keep you long enough for Melchior to think the humans have tricked him again. He will restart the war, with Cheslav as the blame. Then, Tiann and I will return to our former jobs." He used his thumb and raised Serenity's chin so she looked at him. "If you don't behave and stop complaining, I will feel the need to kill you immediately instead of waiting for our employer."

He dropped her chin and turned away, signaling Tiann. They left the room and locked the door behind them. Serenity stared after them. She bowed her head again. This time in defeat.

This wasn't like the other assassination attempts. Lorcan was hurt, possibly dying, and the Hell Hounds would not suddenly appear to save the day.

Serenity shook herself in anger. She couldn't give up. She looked at her surroundings and noticed a window. She wiggled until her arms came free of the chair, thankful that Tiann and Guthr hadn't tied her to the chair.

Their mistake.

She stood, then promptly fell back. Her legs were asleep.

She waited for the feeling to return then made her way to the window. It took her a while to get it open. As loathed as she was to do it, she undid the latch with her teeth then spat several times to get the taste of rust and mold out of her mouth.

Her hands tied behind her back added a level of difficulty to opening the window, but she did it. It wasn't far enough to get through, so she wedged her shoulder in the opening and pushed.

The window was located on the fourth floor. She sighed, and mused to herself, "Well, if the fall doesn't kill me, they will." She leaned out the window, closed her eyes and let herself fall. Just as she braced herself for the impact, strong arms closed around her—strong *bhresya* arms.

She knew her plan hadn't worked. Guthr must have noticed her actions and caught her. She opened her eyes to the inevitable. A slow smile curved her lips when she saw whose arms held her. "You must be King Melchior."

Serenity looked at her husband-to-be. He was one of the most handsome bhresya males she had ever seen. True, her experience with bhresya males was limited, but her experience with males, in general, wasn't.

She'd seen hundreds of human males—servants, the palace guards, nobles, etc. And though many of her species would crucify her for such a thought, there was not much difference between the way bhresyas looked and the way humans looked.

Bhresyas had two ears, two eyes, one nose and one mouth—all in the same places. Their mouths sported long, sharp canines, their eyes had two irises of different colors instead of one, and their ears were pointed.

They didn't walk on hoofed feet or have forked tails—they didn't have tails of any kind. Their tongues were forked, but that was easily forgotten when faced with the true differences between bhresyas and humans—their coloring and their horns.

Bhresyas came in a wide range of colors, from purest white to darkest black and every color in-between. The horns, which sprouted from their temples, their foreheads, or their necks, were the reason most humans referred to bhresyas as demons.

Melchior's horns, only a shade of blue darker than his skin, came from his upper neck. They moved outward away from his body and then curved back so the two pointed ends met over the top of his head.

Serenity wanted to trace her fingers over the curve but couldn't. Partially because her hands were tied behind her back and because such an act was highly intimate, even if she wasn't bound. Only families and loved ones dared to touch another's horns. Only lovers touched another's horns the way Serenity wanted to touch Melchior's. Serenity was none of the above—yet.

As with Rhiannon before her, Melchior found himself nodding at Serenity's observation but unable to form an answer. His silence was for wholly different reasons. Rhiannon had confused him with rapid subject changes, but Serenity confused him with her total trust. She was completely relaxed in his arms and smiling at him.

He lowered her so she sat sideways on the saddle before him. He couldn't do anything but stare at her. Her wide brown eyes showed merriment. Whereas most females would scream and cry about being kidnapped, Serenity looked calm and happy.

A wayward strand of black hair from Serenity's long braid brushed against her cheek. Melchior smoothed it back in place with the edge of his fingertips. Serenity turned her face into his hand but held his gaze.

Movement from all around them snapped Melchior out of his trance. He watched the Hell Hounds and his guards rush into the house where Serenity was held. Only Chigaru and Lorcan stayed behind.

Chigaru approached Serenity's back. He pulled his dagger and cut her ties. This action brought Serenity's attention to him. She shifted on Melchior's lap so she faced forward on the lysidi in a side-saddle position and looked at Chigaru. "And here, I had started to worry. I should know better, right?"

He nodded.

"Did you have trouble tracking me?" Though she currently sat on his lap, her attention was no longer for Melchior.

Chigaru stepped aside to allow Serenity to see behind him.

"Lorcan!"

She jumped from Melchior's lysidi and fell to her knees in front of Lorcan. She didn't seem satisfied until she ran her hands over him fully to ensure he was unharmed. When her search turned up nothing, she threw her arms around his neck. Lorcan nuzzled her shoulder, whining with pleasure.

"Oh thank all the gods."

"Princess Serenity," Melchior said.

Serenity looked at Melchior with unshed tears in her eyes. She was about to thank him for Lorcan's health—she was sure he had helped somehow—when the Hell Hounds and guards returned.

"Nothing! I don't know how we missed them," Nym bit out in frustration.

Serenity looked at Nym. The rose colored female was visibly angry with her hands fisted at her sides. Normally, Nym was the picture of calm. Her graceful features hadn't known a frown in years, at least not one that Serenity had seen.

Nym didn't look the type to be a guard—or a former assassin. She was too dainty looking and Serenity teased her about it regularly. Nym was the shortest of the Hell Hounds, but still a head above Serenity. Her horns started from her temples and followed the curve of her head in the shape of a diadem. Whereas her horns were a shade darker, her shoulder-length ponytail was a shade lighter than her skin. It was a common theme amongst bhresyas, male and female.

Her delicate appearance made people underestimate Nym as a fighter all the time. Serenity had even witnessed the palace guards acting superior to Nym, which was stupid because even the weakest bhresya was naturally stronger than any human. But, Nym wasn't weak and proclaimed that with her clothing—a simple, long strip of light brown cloth with a hole in the middle for her head to fit through. The cloth was held to her body with a string of leather that crisscrossed between her breasts and around her stomach.

Serenity remembered the tales Nym told her of the ridicule she received from other bhresyas who had thought she wore the clothing to be defiant. She'd proved them wrong, sometimes dead wrong.

Nym didn't look for battle, though. She preferred, like Serenity, to spend her time quietly with friends and loved ones. Seeing the female angry enough that her yellow and green eyes flashed and she bared her fangs only intensified Serenity's waning apprehension about her near miss.

Serenity straightened with a shake of her head. "It's all right, Nym. We'll probably see them again."

Nym looked at Serenity in shock. "Again, Serenity?" Her gaze turned back toward the house then returned. "They have fled. It would be stupid of them to return."

"My captors see me as a very big threat. They will try again."

"Did you see them, my princess?" asked the malachite green bhresya in the back of the group.

Serenity turned her attention to Theyn. If Nym was the shortest, then Theyn was the tallest. His lean form towered over everyone present, including Serenity, who came up to his stomach.

His horns started at his forehead and went straight up for about a foot then curved back and down past his shoulders. Many times as a child—and sometimes recently if no one was around—Serenity had held Theyn's horns as he twirled around so her feet left the ground. She could never tell which of them enjoyed it more.

His height and horn formation meant Theyn had to constantly duck down when he walked through the doorways of the palace. It annoyed him, but he never complained since it wasn't in his nature to be in a sour mood. He loved to laugh as much as she loved to smile.

Like Nym, Theyn was mad. He'd already shoved his hand through his short hair five times since he exited the house with the others. That meant he wanted to hit something but couldn't. It was a habit Serenity had suggested to him as a joke because he used to pace and growl, which scared everyone. He took it to heart and she hadn't found a way to make him stop.

At the moment, she didn't care if he rubbed himself a bald spot. His question irritated her. That he didn't know, and couldn't guess, who'd taken her, when she had, only made her angry.

She said, "My captors were kind enough to take off my blindfold. However, I knew who they were before I saw them."

Melchior asked, "Who were they? They shall pay with their lives for their transgression against you, Princess Serenity."

"They will pay, but not right now. I was about to dress before they arrived and I would like to get back to it," she said in a voice that held no room for argument.

Theyn said, "We forgot Ines, Serenity. We were panicked when we found you missing—"

"I just bet you were," she said with icy undertones. Her smile was flat and she fisted her hand where it rested on Lorcan's head.

For the first time in as long as she could remember, she was afraid for her life... truly afraid.

Theyn jerked back a step. His purple and yellow gaze floated over his fellow Hell Hounds, who all looked resigned. Nym shook her head.

"I will ride with Chigaru." Serenity softened her look and smiled back at Melchior. "I hope you will forgive me, Your Majesty, but as we are not yet married it isn't proper for me to ride with you."

"Of course," Melchior said.

Chigaru placed Serenity on his lysidi and mounted behind her. She wanted to lean into his strength and take comfort from his nearness but didn't. If propriety dictated she couldn't ride with Melchior before their marriage, then it also said she couldn't seek solace in Chigaru's arms in front of her husband-to-be. Chigaru's arms surrounded her as he held the reins and that was enough.

The others mounted. Serenity waved Lorcan forward, who took off running with a howl. Serenity said over her shoulder to Chigaru, "With all speed."

Chigaru nodded then spurred the mount into its full speed.

"You do not find this pace frightening, Princess Serenity?" Melchior asked once he caught up with them.

Serenity shook her head. "I have ridden lysidis before."

The rest of the ride back to the palace was in silence.

Chapter Four

Rhiannon rushed to Serenity and hugged her tightly. "Are you unhurt? Did anything happen?"

Serenity laughed while trying to disengage herself from her mother. She knew the woman was worried, but Serenity's obvious good health shouldn't warrant such a reaction. "I am unmolested and unharmed, Mother. I am also running late. I need to dress."

Alric ignored her words and embraced her as well. He whispered, "You had us worried, little sister."

Serenity nodded at all the people that surrounded her. Their concern was heartwarming. She smiled to show she was okay and nodded in thanks to this show of emotion on her behalf, but it all annoyed her.

"Please! I must get dressed for the wedding. Please."

Chigaru stood straighter in his position beside Serenity. The concerned palace folk took their cue and returned to the wedding preparations. Serenity laid a hand on his arm in thanks. Her path was clear and she meant to return to her room and prepare for her nuptials.

Melchior stopped her. "You have not named your captors, Princess Serenity. Even if your... *hounds* do not hunt them now, my guards will."

"With complete respect to you, King Melchior, I don't know your guards and therefore I won't trust them with such a task," Serenity said.

"Serenity!" Rhiannon turned to Melchior. "You must forgive her, King Melchior. She speaks her mind no matter what it is. At times she insults without meaning to."

Serenity didn't care if Melchior would accept her mother's apology on her behalf or not. Her words and their meaning remained the same and saying it bluntly made them clear. "As for the names of my captors, that can wait until after the wedding. I want no more bloodshed on my wedding day. Understood?" she said as she looked around the room at those left. All nodded. She returned their nods with one of her own. "Then, I return to my rooms to dress."

She turned away and the Hell Hounds followed. She stopped short but kept her eyes forward. "Stay," she said quietly then continued on her way.

Nym looked at Chigaru. He had stopped walking. She shook her head in disbelief, then looked after Serenity with a look of horror on her face.

Melchior noticed this but said nothing. Something important had happened.

Mael ran after Serenity. "Please, Princess. Allow me to accompany you. You must be guarded," she said, kneeling with her head bent.

Serenity stopped, looked back at Mael, then continued forward. She said over her shoulder, "Only Mael."

"Thank you, Princess. Thank you." Mael rushed after her.

Rhiannon laid a hand on Chigaru's arm and said to him and the others, "She won't be mad for long. She is probably still scared—as she should be. It will pass before the day is through."

Melchior couldn't contain his curiosity any longer. The reactions of his subjects to this tiny human girl were unprecedented. "What is happening?"

Alric said, "Serenity doesn't normally restrict her Hell Hounds from accompanying her. It's too dangerous for her. On the rare occasions when she does, Chigaru stays with her. That he isn't with her now speaks volumes to her current mood."

"She's not upset, Queen Rhiannon," Nym said. "She's angry. We failed as her guards when she needed us most. Those kidnappers shouldn't have gotten her out of the palace, even if they got in undetected." She growled in frustration and clenched her hands.

Rhiannon led them all to one of the conference rooms that surrounded the outer throne room. "I'm sure King Melchior wishes to speak with you all. You will have privacy here. I must make sure the priest has arrived and that he and the bhresya mage are in accord with each other and Serenity's wishes for the ceremony. Alric, you will ensure the guards, both ours and Melchior's, are on alert as the Hell Hounds are not with Serenity."

The Hell Hounds entered the conference room after their king. Rhiannon and Alric departed for their separate tasks, closing the door behind them.

Nym looked at her king then away with a sigh.

Melchior asked the question that had plagued him since learning of them, "Why are you here?"

"To guard Serenity," Theyn said quickly.

Chigaru smacked him on the back of the head. Theyn's words were true but not the answer to Melchior's question.

Haige lowered his head as he said, "I am ashamed to admit Nym, Chigaru, and I were hired—more than likely by the ones who captured Princess Serenity today—to kill her."

Melchior looked at the dark gray male who was situated off in the far corner of the room. He alone sat while the others stood. Haige's elbows rested on the arms of his chair and his chin was propped up on his clasped hands. The pose made him look deep in thought.

A sad sigh escaped Haige. He reached up to trace the S-shaped curve of his horns. They started at his temples in an upward arc out from his head then dipped down to frame his face only to curve back up.

"When?" Melchior asked.

"Fifteen years ago," Nym replied.

"Fifteen years? When she was so young?" he asked in surprise. He thought they were new editions to the palace, not residents. How had he not known of their presence until now?

Theyn said, "Her first attack happened on the day of her birth, Your Majesty. Chigaru, Nym, and Haige were the first bhresya attackers. Many humans had attacked Princess Serenity before them."

"Yes, Queen Rhiannon said as much," Melchior said, though he hadn't believed it until the words passed bhresya lips. "And you, Theyn?"

Theyn shrugged. "Haige and Nym caught me while I raided one of the villages on the outskirts of Cheslav. I meant no harm. I only wanted to frighten the humans a bit and laugh as they ran."

"Mael?"

Nym said, "She was captured trespassing on Cheslav territory. We came across her when we acquired Ines for Serenity."

"Who is Ines?" Melchior remembered hearing Theyn mention the female earlier.

"Serenity's lysidi. A bribe for her not to contact you, my king." Before Melchior could ask, Nym added, "We tried to escape after we were captured. We were recaptured and Rhiannon thought to contact you. Serenity agreed. Haige offered the lysidi mare in trade for our lives."

"Who captured you?" Melchior had never heard of a human capturing a bhresya. Humans had a hard enough time fighting bhresyas successfully, capturing one was unheard of. Bhresyas were fast healers and stronger than most humans realized.

"Chigaru," Nym said. "He was sent first when we were hired since he is the best. After two months and he hadn't returned, Haige and I took up the assignment. He captured us for Serenity and then recaptured us when we escaped."

Melchior looked at Chigaru, waiting for the male to agree with Nym's words. He said nothing. "Why don't you speak?"

Chigaru continued in his silence.

It was common bhresya knowledge that a silent bhresya was a lying bhresya. Omission and silence were the only ways a bhresya could lie.

Nym said, "Chigaru only speaks to Serenity, when he speaks. He is the leader of the Hell Hounds, but he commands in silence. But, do not think his time here made him that way. His quiet attitude has existed for as long as I've known him. As second-in-command, I have learned to interpret for Chigaru over the years."

Chigaru nodded and his eyes said he wouldn't break his silence even if Melchior ordered it.

"Our escape attempt was the first time Serenity was ever mad at us. There was only one other. After that, we have courted Serenity's favor at all times," Nym said.

"The second?"

Haige answered, "Chigaru broke Prince Joah's arm. Prince Joah is the last born triplet."

Melchior frowned. "I knew of the triplets. In fact, I told Queen Rhiannon she would give birth to them. But, I didn't see another besides Crown Prince Alric earlier." He would admit he found it strange Prince Joah wasn't among the crowd of worried onlookers upon Serenity's safe return.

Theyn said, "You wouldn't, Your Majesty. Prince Joah was banished from Cheslav two years ago because he tried to kill Princess Serenity."

"Chigaru broke Prince Joah's arm when he disarmed him," Haige said. "Our princess was furious. Prince Joah has shown nothing but contempt for his sister since they were young, but our princess always wanted us to treat him with the respect due his station."

"Her own brother," Melchior said.

Everyone nodded.

"Serenity was upset her brother had tried to kill her. But, for Chigaru's violence, she kicked us out of the palace," Nym said.

Melchior gave her an incredulous look. Why should they care about the opinions of a few humans? They were bhresya—the first people.

Nym must have guessed his thinking because she said, "You must understand, King Melchior, we live among humans and we are tolerated because we are Serenity's. Once outside of the palace, the people of Cheslav treated us with hatred and censure. Though we were being punished, we couldn't leave Serenity unprotected."

"The palace folk live for the days when we are out of favor with Princess Serenity, so they can show us how they really feel," Theyn added with scorn in his voice.

Chigaru touched Theyn's shoulder.

Theyn looked at him and then Melchior. He mumbled, "Sorry, my king."

Melchior stood in silence for a time. This was all hard to believe. All this time, five of his subjects had lived in Cheslav and guarded his soon-to-be bride from those who—like some of them—came to kill her. Serenity was at ease with her bhresya guards. So much so that she commanded their total loyalty and—as their brown clothing that matched Serenity's skin perfectly proclaimed—their love as well.

"Your service is admirable, but why do they call you hounds? It is demeaning," he said.

Nym replied, "Not at all, Your Majesty. Serenity didn't give us the title to insult us. Though you might not have seen it, Serenity is a loving child. She is quick to smile and loves to be happy."

Theyn snorted and said, "Don't get her angry though. That girl can be a real bitch when—"

Chigaru smacked him again and growled.

Theyn held up his hands. "Sorry, sorry."

Nym rolled her eyes and continued, "Like I was saying, Serenity is happiness incarnate, but she has a temper. If someone came to kill her, we would capture them, find out who sent them and who helped them, and then Serenity would send us to kill them all. It was a complete slaughter—no prisoners and no survivors."

Theyn smiled devilishly and said, "People in the palace referred to Serenity as a demon from the fiery pits with five hell hounds at her side. After a time, Hell Hound became synonymous with Serenity's personal guards. The name stuck and we turned it into a title."

"When Princess Serenity looses the hounds of hell—" Haige started.

"—blood will surely flow," Nym finished.

Theyn nodded. "Gets to the point where we hope for an attack just to let some blood."

This time Chigaru knocked Theyn flat on his stomach. He planted his foot on Theyn's neck and added his weight. He didn't stop until the male's neck broke, then he stepped away.

Theyn coughed and sputtered, but he was paralyzed until his neck healed.

"You will have to forgive Chigaru's treatment of Theyn, Your Majesty. The past has proven that breaking his neck is the only way to silence the male. Theyn has a habit of talking too much," Haige said.

Nym added, "I'm convinced it's to compensate for Chigaru's habit of not talking at all."

Melchior was overwhelmed with all the information presented in the last few minutes. His bride surprised him. With his battle-axe—the physical representation of his right to rule—strapped to his back, he'd come to wed or wage war—and he would have started with Rhiannon. Instead, he had found his bride kidnapped.

What he thought was a ploy had turned out to be genuine. He went to save her and expected her fear of the coming nuptials, but was rewarded with her smile. She had no fear of bhresyas, which was something he had not expected. She loved Lorcan with her whole heart and had adopted her would-be assassins as her personal guards.

It was almost too much to take in. He had expected a frightened child. In her place, he found a confident and capable woman. He wondered if his bride would turn up any other surprises before the day finished.

Chapter Five

"Dame Mael, we accept you must guard Princess Serenity, but you are in the way," scolded one of Serenity's maids. She glared at Mael until the female went to a far wall and stayed there.

Serenity skimmed her hands over the surface of the bathwater. She tried to relax and enjoy her scalp massage. It irritated her to repeat her earlier preparations, but her kidnapping necessitated it. Showing up to her nuptials covered in dirt and smelling of mildew wasn't an option. Plus, she didn't want to spoil her lovely wedding dress. It had taken her maids the entire year to finish it.

The bliaut was white—as it should be. The floor-length sleeves showed off inner fabric a shade of blue the Hell Hounds had assured her would match Melchior exactly. When she saw him at the house, she was happy they were right.

A red and yellow braided belt to match Melchior's eyes and a white gossamer veil attached to her tiara finished the look.

The tiara was her prized possession as she had hand picked each of the blue, red, and yellow rubies that filled the design on the tiara. Those were Melchior's colors and she fully embraced them. Once she was given the right to choose her own clothing, Serenity had dressed in nothing but those colors. Her Hell Hounds encouraged her since doing so was a bhresya tradition.

She had wanted to be ready and perfect for her first meeting with Melchior, but was kidnapped. She looked at Mael, who stood against the wall. The female straightened.

"Princess?" Mael asked.

Serenity waved away the woman who massaged her scalp, then signaled the other women she was ready to get out of the bath. One of the women held a towel as Serenity exited. She dried herself rather than let the woman do it, while the other two maids dried her mid-back length hair.

"Where were you?" Serenity asked.

"Chigaru wished to ensure the palace security, so we searched the perimeter."

"It took all of you to do that?" She let the maids guide her to a bench where she laid on her stomach. The two maids who had dried her hair draped it over her head and combed it out. Two other maids massaged honey-scented oil into Serenity's skin.

"Nym wished it done quickly so you would not be left unguarded for long."

"So you all split up?"

"We were nearly finished when we heard Lorcan's scream."

Silence reined the room. The maids worked quickly. Some were as upset as Serenity at having to do all of the preparations all over again. Serenity flipped over when the maids finished her back. The massaging made the tension leave her body and she sighed.

She said, "Forget it, Mael. It is over. I will deal with the unfinished details after the wedding. For now, it is time to think of happier things."

"Are you scared, Your Highness?"

"No, I want to marry King Melchior. I was born to marry him." She rolled into a sitting position so her maids could dress her. Serenity sent one of the maids on an errand while the others finished her preparations.

The maid returned just as the veil was placed on Serenity's head. She admired her image in the mirror before she acknowledged the maid who had retrieved the perfume bottle she wanted. She sent all the maids except that one out of the room and beckoned Mael forward.

Serenity confided, "I am not mad with my Hell Hounds. I was merely scared and lashing out." She signaled the maid.

The woman took the cork from the bottle and dabbed it on Mael's wrists. She indicated Mael should kneel as the female was like all bhresyas and much taller than her. When Mael complied, the maid re-wet the cork and dabbed more on Mael's neck under each ear. The maid smiled at Mael and bowed, then curtsied to Serenity and left the room.

Mael sniffed at the scent. "It is much sweeter than what I would have chosen for myself, but it is nice. Thank you, Princess."

Serenity turned to the door, smoothing her hands over her dress. The motion didn't slow her heartbeat at all. A case of nerves overtook her once she stopped to think about what was about to happen.

Mael placed her hand on Serenity's shoulder. She smiled when Serenity looked up at her. "You always say Destiny put you on this path."

"She did," Serenity said. She patted Mael's hand. "It is time."

৵৽৽৶

Alric escorted his sister to the bottom of the steps of the throne dais. There, Melchior awaited her. He'd donned a long, white tunic vest to compliment the long white loincloth he wore. Serenity thought the color unbecoming on him, but he had worn it since it was human custom. Such regard boded well for their future with each other. Serenity was happy for that.

She placed her hand on Melchior's arm once she reached his side. Alric bowed to them both and continued up the stairs to his throne. He nodded to the bhresya mage and the human priest as he passed them. At the top of the dais, Queen Rhiannon sat on her throne.

Chigaru and the other Hell Hounds formed a semi-circle behind Serenity and Melchior. Rhiannon had objected to the formation as the Hell Hounds would block everyone's view of the ceremony. To this, Serenity had only nodded. She had no intention of making either herself or Melchior an easy target for an assassin pretending to be a guest.

Ten of Melchior's high-ranking nobles as well as his six guards were present for the ceremony. They made up the second semi-circle behind the Hell Hounds.

Both the mage and priest said their words over the couple simultaneously. Serenity was convinced she would grow bored if they had to do one version of the ceremony and then the other. Both officials had objected at first, but Queen Rhiannon had assured them the ceremony would be valid amongst both cultures if the words were said at the same time. The humans would listen to the priest and the bhresyas would listen to the mage.

Chigaru stepped forward at the appropriate time with the ceremonial silver dagger and handed it to Serenity. The mage sputtered his disapproval, "The dagger is supposed to go first to King Melchior, Sir..."

"Chigaru," Serenity supplied with a smile. She picked up the dagger and held her hand out to Melchior. He placed his hand palm up onto hers. "You forget, Your Excellency, we are combining ceremonies. In the human tradition, the bride must do everything first to show that she serves her husband." She placed the dagger over Melchior's palm. In one swift motion, she applied pressure and pulled the dagger down. Blood welled out of the wound. She handed the dagger back to Chigaru.

The mage frowned but allowed it, as he couldn't stop it now that Serenity had already started. The priest leaned over and whispered, "I have found it best to indulge Princess Serenity as she will always have her way, my equal." The mage nodded but still looked disapproving.

Serenity smiled at them both. She turned back to Melchior and cupped his bleeding hand in both of hers. Before her eyes, the wound had already started healing. She traced a finger over the wound, then she brought the finger up to her lips. She drew on the wound to make it bleed more, then straightened, smiling at Melchior. Over his shoulder she saw Haige rub his finger at the side of his mouth. She took the hint and smoothed her tongue over the corner of her mouth, catching the errant drop of blood there.

Melchior watched her tongue, mesmerized. Had Serenity distracted him this much when he saw her earlier? He came back to himself when Chigaru offered him the silver dagger. Melchior took the dagger and sliced Serenity's palm. Unlike Serenity, his touch was gentle so he wouldn't cut too deeply.

He brought the wound to his lips, but he watched Serenity. He expected her to flinch or at least show a little revulsion. She continued smiling. Nym was right. Serenity was a happy child.

The mage stepped forward and pressed their bloodied palms together. As he held them and said his words, the human priest stepped forward and wound a silver cord around their joined palms and said his words of ceremony.

"By bhresya custom, you are wed," pronounced the mage.

The priest said, "Your union is bound as your hands are bound when your lips have met to seal this contract between male and female."

Again, Serenity didn't wait. She reached up with her uninjured hand to the right side of Melchior's neck and latched on to the horn there. Her smile broadened at his surprised look. She pulled him down to her.

Upon learning that Melchior's horns protruded not from his temples but the middle of his neck, Serenity had wondered if she could pull on them. Nym had assured Serenity the doing of which would only entice Melchior, not anger him.

Their lips met in a chaste kiss—a mere pressing of lips—but Serenity didn't release Melchior until she was satisfied with the length of it. She dropped her hand away from his horn and he straightened.

"You are married," the priest said. He removed the silver cord and handed it to Serenity.

Nym stepped forward, removed Serenity's tiara and veil and stowed the tiara in a case she had carried with her. She retrieved the silver cord and placed that in the case as well.

The mage had the couple face away from him and he placed a golden diadem around Serenity's forehead. He announced to the crowd of observers, "I present to you the new bhresya queen, Queen Serenity. Long may she live, long may she reign."

"Long may she live, long may she reign," said the crowd in unison.

Rhiannon and Alric descended. The wedding was over but there was another bit of business to attend. Chigaru and Theyn, who had healed mostly but still walked with a limp as the nerves in his neck had not fully reconnected, brought the treaty forward on a wooden table. They set the table in front of the royal family.

Before anyone could sign, Rhiannon said, "Though I required it, I cannot fulfill the last part of the treaty. General Tiann fled Cheslav shortly after hearing the terms of the treaty I had struck."

"General Guthr has fled as well, Queen Rhiannon," Melchior said. "I had not expected him to do such a cowardly thing."

The mage held out the pen to Melchior. He quickly realized his mistake and changed his direction and presented it to Serenity. She held out her injured hand to him. The mage looked at her palm in confusion. He said, "You have not healed."

"I am human, Your Excellency. We don't heal as fast as bhresyas," Serenity said, her tone amused.

"Of course." He took her palm between his and healed the wound.

Serenity took the pen and held it out to her new husband. He signed the treaty, and then she signed. Serenity then handed the pen to the priest who passed it to Rhiannon. She signed, then Alric signed his name with a relieved sigh.

The mage and priest both gave their blessings on the validity of the proceedings even though the sacrifices were not present.

Alric shook his head. "Both of them cowards," he said in wonder.

Serenity smiled at her brother. "I wouldn't say that, my brother. They both had nerve enough to get into the palace undetected and kidnap me. It's not like they are too cowardly if they could accomplish that." She shrugged at everyone's stunned looks and slack-jawed silence. "As a matter-of-fact, it was General Tiann's second time sneaking into the palace and trying to do me harm. The first time being the day Alric and I were born."

The throne room fell into chaos. Serenity stood quietly as everyone ranted and raved. Melchior raged over the betrayal of someone he thought was a trusted general—if overly bloodthirsty, while Rhiannon swore painful revenge on Tiann when he was captured.

Serenity laid a hand on Melchior's arm and looked up at him. "I understand your ire at the situation I found myself in earlier this day, but it is time to depart."

Rhiannon looked at her daughter with confusion. "What?"

"It is time to leave. My bags were packed and sent ahead to Nexeu, facilitating an immediate departure."

"You don't wish to stay for the wedding feast?" Melchior asked.

Alric said, "Serenity... excuse me, Queen Serenity, there is no need to rush off. This is your wedding celebration."

"No, it's a departure celebration. The people of Cheslav and the other four kingdoms are celebrating an end to the warring not the beginning of my marriage. No one will celebrate with any great mirth until King Melchior, his guards, his nobles, my Hell Hounds, and I leave." Serenity bowed her head. "I accept that and we shall go." She patted Melchior's arm, then turned to leave the room.

She looked back at the Hell Hounds when none of them followed her except Mael. "Chigaru?" she asked.

Chigaru bowed and waved the other Hell Hounds forward, following in their wake. Nym breathed a sigh of relief, while Haige and Theyn nodded.

Serenity smiled and continued on her way.

CHAPTER SIX

IT TOOK HER AN HOUR TO CHANGE FROM HER WEDDING GOWN TO TRAVELING CLOTHES, and have her maids pack away the wedding dress for her future daughter's wedding. One of her maids cried and cried until Serenity promised to allow the woman to accompany her. Serenity was sure the bhresyas wouldn't accept her as their queen as easily as her Hell Hounds had and she would need a maid. The other maids showed no such display of hysterics. Their attitude was of mild disinterest.

She held no ill will towards them. In their eyes, she was as much of a bhresya as her Hell Hounds. She bid them goodbye and good health.

She was happy when she was able to meet the others at the palace gates. Melchior, his guards, the bhresya nobles, and the Hell Hounds were all mounted except for Chigaru and Nym.

Melchior made to dismount, but Serenity waved him back into his seat. He said, "Perhaps it would be best if you were to ride with me, my new queen. We wish to return to Nexeu with all speed."

"And I shall keep up, my husband, I assure you," she replied. She held out her hand to Chigaru and smiled wide when his large orange hand engulfed hers. "Call her for me."

Chigaru pressed two fingers from his free hand against his lips and whistled shrilly. From the direction of the stables came the thundering of massive hooves. A black lysidi mare burst around the corner and charged towards Serenity and Chigaru. The mare showed no signs of slowing.

Melchior dismounted.

Serenity knew he would try to stop her. She disengaged herself from Chigaru and stepped into the mare's path. The animal reared up on her two hind legs and skidded to a halt, pawing the air.

"Good girl, Ines," Serenity whispered with her hand outstretched.

Ines planted all six hooves on the ground and nuzzled Serenity's hand. The mare tossed her mane and gave an irritated snort after a thorough search turned up no treats.

Chigaru held out an apple to Serenity, who in turn gave it to Ines. That done, Chigaru lifted Serenity onto Ines' back and handed her the reins. Serenity turned her smile on all the stunned nobles and guards. "This is Ines, my lysidi mare. I have ridden her since I was six."

Ines tossed her head at the mention of her name. She dug deep furrows in the ground beneath her, showing her impatience to be off. Serenity patted the mare's neck. "Shhh, my beauty. Soon enough. We have one thing to attend."

She turned her attention to her Hell Hounds, looking at each of them in turn. "Tell me you are my Hell Hounds. Tell me my safety is foremost in your minds and keeping me alive is what you live for."

Melchior and the others exchanged looks but said nothing, only watched.

Chigaru stepped forward. Serenity leaned over Ines' back allowing him to whisper in her ear. She blinked her eyes to hold back the tears his words invoked. With whispered thanks, she laid a soft kiss on his cheek and he nodded and stepped back.

Nym didn't feel the need to whisper. She said her vow loud and clear.

Haige dismounted and gave his vow of loyalty on bended knee.

Theyn—ever the ham of the Hell Hounds—interjected declarations of brotherly love and undying devotion into his vow.

Everyone looked at Mael.

Serenity's smile turned icy—more a baring of teeth than anything else. "You don't speak, Mael. Why?"

Chigaru started forward but Serenity stopped him with a hand across his chest. "Mael, you suggested the others search the perimeter. I would even guess it was your suggestion to split up. Nym agreed because that would make the search faster." When Nym would have spoken, Serenity held up a hand for silence. "While the others searched, not only did you find General Tiann and General Guthr, you let them into the palace—or was it only one of them?"

Mael remained silent.

Melchior said, "You should answer your queen, Mael. Your silence only proves your guilt."

Mael gasped then coughed. The deep, wrenching coughs sent her to her knees. Blood passed her lips and splattered on the ground and her body convulsed.

Melchior blanched visibly.

"Poisoned perfume, Mael," Serenity said. "Your guilt was clear to me as soon as I bothered to think of it. You have never once said you were loyal to me. You always said you protected me because that was your job. Even donning my color did not say you were mine, as many of Cheslav's citizens are my same color. Or, perhaps it is the color of the one who hired you to infiltrate the palace. That person knew, as the generals knew, I was collecting bhresyas to better acquaint myself with the life I was to live once I married." She reined in her mount closer to the female so she could look down at Mael. She knew the poison caused Mael's throat to close and her heart to beat slower and slower.

The poison was slow acting and had lasted through the entire wedding—as Serenity had hoped. She didn't want to mar her wedding day, but knew her chances of getting close to Mael after the ceremony may be limited as the female would probably run.

"I loved you as much as I loved the rest of my Hell Hounds. You were a sister to me," Serenity said with utter disgust. She looked away from Mael then and faced the nobles. "You die knowing those who hired you will soon follow." She urged Ines into a trot towards the palace gates. The Hell Hounds mounted and followed after her.

Behind them, Melchior and the other bhresyas watched Mael take her final breath. Melchior looked after his bride. She possessed the poison that had killed his first wife and children. The poison King Kiros made and gave to his assassin for Melchior, but it was intercepted by his wife and shared—unknowingly—with his children. He'd watched them die in a manner similar to Mael's at the dinner table that same night. His last moments with his family were spent discussing affairs of state with advisors, instead of saying goodbye. He'd thought he had time. Kiros had cured him of that.

Melchior spurred his mount into a gallop after Serenity. The others fell in after him. He reached her side and said, "You will dispose of that poison immediately. It will not touch Nexeu soil."

Serenity turned a calm demeanor to her husband. "You mean, my husband, it will not touch Nexeu soil *again*, do you not?"

"You knew?"

"That it was the cause of your first wife and children's deaths—yes, I knew. My mother gave me the poison directly after Nym and Haige's attempted assassination. I insisted on keeping them and she insisted on protecting me." Her gaze shifted from him to the road. "You have nothing to fear. The poison is back in my mother's palace. I will not chance an accidental death because of paranoia. If I am to die in Nexeu, then that is my fate. Fear of the future has not driven me thus far. It will not start now."

Lorcan went streaking past them. Ines gave a baleful whinny and then growled. She looked back at Serenity then in the direction Lorcan had run.

Serenity laughed. "All right, my love. I know you have wished for home for so long." She loosed her hold on the reins and bent low over the mare's neck as Ines ran at her top speed.

Melchior spurred his mount to catch her. *The little fool will get herself killed*, he thought. War wouldn't be abated if Serenity died mere moments after wedding him. Queen Rhiannon would suspect foul play and the fighting would restart.

Threat of continued war had prompted Melchior into bringing some of his nobles as well as his guards. They weren't there for the beautiful ceremony and change of scenery. The nobles who attended him on this journey represented the best warriors Nexeu had to offer.

Melchior had come prepared to either protect his bride or restart the war. In the face of her foolishness, he wondered if he hadn't set himself a daunting task. He also wondered how the Hell Hounds had managed for the last fifteen years.

Chigaru and Theyn raced past the others after Serenity. Her laughter trailed in her wake. They caught up with her easily, but kept their mounts two paces behind Ines so as to give Serenity the appearance of freedom.

"There is no need to chase her, Your Majesty," Nym said as she pulled alongside him. "Chigaru and Theyn will not lose her."

Melchior slowed his mount but his worried gaze stayed on Serenity as she grew smaller in the distance.

Haige joined Nym and Melchior. "Nothing will happen to her so long as we draw breath, my king. She was our princess and now she is our queen. We accepted that long ago. The others of the kingdom will accept it as well."

"Is she always this reckless?" Melchior asked. He could no longer make out her or her guards. He'd be more nervous if not for Nym's and Haige's calm attitudes.

Nym answered, "Serenity was a prisoner of the Cheslav palace since birth. She and Ines both deserve the chance to run at top speed. Chigaru and Theyn will ensure no harm comes to her."

Was it as Rhiannon had accused? Had Serenity led a life of hardship because of the treaty he had proposed? The Hell Hounds could answer his questions easily, but a part of him didn't want to know. He wanted to believe Serenity was spoiled and privileged, not sequestered and guarded from every happiness.

Instead, he asked, "Is Serenity always smiling? I don't think I've seen her stop."

"Our Queen Serenity is a happy child," Haige said with a smile of his own. "Even when General Tiann held a knife to her throat at birth, she smiled—or so we were told by Queen Rhiannon and many others. It was how Queen Rhiannon knew to name her Serenity. She smiles easily. If there is ever a time she isn't smiling, then there is something truly wrong with the world."

Chapter Seven

MELCHIOR AND THE OTHERS WENT ON HIGH ALERT when they came upon Serenity and Ines some miles later simply standing. Theyn was beside her but Chigaru was nowhere to be seen.

"What's wrong?" Nym asked, scanning the area.

Serenity waved a calming hand at Nym. "Chigaru went in search of Lorcan. He noticed Lorcan's scent was no longer on the road." She stroked Ines' neck and cooed at her. The mare reared up and pawed the air. Serenity held her seat until Ines decided to plant all her hooves on the ground again.

Chigaru returned with a shake of his head. By then, the nobles had joined the group. Serenity, though still smiling, let a little frown crease her brow.

"Perhaps a song, my queen," Haige said, spurring his mount forward.

"Of course. How stupid of me. Thank you for reminding me, my teacher," she said then urged Ines after Haige. The others followed suit.

She looked up at the sky and let her voice carry over the land. She sang an old bhresya rhyme for children. Haige had used the song to lull her to sleep when she was younger.

By the looks on the faces of her companions, she had surprised them. Not only did she speak Nexian, but her accent was flawless. She attributed that to speaking it almost as long as her mother tongue.

She started the second verse just as Lorcan came tearing through the brush. He had a rabbit clamped in his jaws, his muzzle covered in blood. He looked pleased with himself. Serenity leaned over and patted his head. She finished the song and started another, since no one seemed to be complaining.

She liked to sing, it was the one thing—as a princess—she was allowed and encouraged to do. She had always wanted to dance, not the courtly dancing of standing in lines and holding hands with a partner as she walked in circles and wove in and out of other couples. Serenity wanted to learn the dancing of the court entertainers.

They danced with their whole bodies—hips swaying and bodies moving wherever the music took them. Their grace and the way their bodies moved—Serenity had loved it all. She hated that she couldn't learn to move like them. It was against all propriety for a princess and future queen to dance in such a way.

Since she couldn't have lessons, Serenity taught herself. She would watch the dancers avidly whenever they performed at state dinners and balls, then she would copy their movements once she was in private. In order to gauge her prowess, she danced for the Hell Hounds. They assured her she danced as well as any court entertainer.

It was a compliment only she would take, as her mother would have been scandalized. Serenity wondered if her mother and brother enjoyed the treaty banquet or if the celebratory atmosphere was dampened because they missed her, though she had just left.

"Something amiss, my wife?" Melchior asked in Nexian. At her startled look, he said, "Your song faltered just as we all started enjoying it."

Serenity ducked her eyes in embarrassment. "I'm sorry. My mind wandered," she whispered.

"To?"

"My mother and brother. I wondered if they missed me."

Theyn said, "As the sky would miss the sun should it suddenly leave in the middle of the day, my queen." He smiled broadly, showing his fangs.

"I have ever wondered how it is you can exaggerate in such a shameful fashion, Theyn, when no other bhresya can," Serenity said.

"It is all truth in my mind, my queen. So long as we believe and know it to be true, then we are able to speak it. And, I have only described the way I would feel if you were to suddenly leave me," he said in all seriousness. There was no hint of the usual mirth that graced Theyn's eyes as he made this speech. That spoke volumes since Theyn was rarely serious if he could help it.

Serenity blinked at him, her vision blurring with unshed tears. It was the second time one of her Hell Hounds had affected her this way. She wondered if it was the stress of the day that made her so emotional.

She pulled Ines away from Melchior so she rode alongside Theyn. She pulled him to her and whispered a thank you. With her cheek pressed to his, she said, "You are forever my joy, Theyn."

He nodded and she released him.

One of the nobles asked, "When did your guard become your guard, Queen Serenity?"

Serenity thought for a moment as she resumed her position next to Melchior. It was a hard question the noble posed her since she didn't have a clear memory of when the change occurred. "I'm not sure. Obviously, Queen Rhiannon wouldn't suddenly turn would-be assassins into bodyguards—with the exception of Chigaru." She smiled at him. Like Theyn, he nodded.

She continued, "Haige, Nym, and Theyn all started out as teachers. I wanted to learn all I could about my future life and they were a means to that end. Gradually, they went from teachers to bodyguards. I would be attacked and they would keep me safe. After a while, it was understood by everyone in the palace that the Hell Hounds were my personal guards."

Nym interjected, "It was a joyous day to go from distrusted prisoner to entrusted companion and guard."

"I knew you would make a good bhresya queen when the palace folk of Cheslav called you the demon princess," Haige said.

"They called me many other damaging things, my teacher. I chose to take them as compliments," Serenity said.

Melchior digested this most recent hint of Serenity's difficult childhood. He turned in his saddle and looked back at the small maid who had insisted on accompanying Serenity. Her short stature, even smaller than Serenity's, made her resemble a child. The full breasts that strained against the bodice of her dress and her round hips marked her as an adult.

She rode with one of Melchior's nobles because her horse would have slowed them down. Both the noble and maid looked mildly uncomfortable.

Melchior finally gave in to his curiosity. He had to know more about his wife if he would be living with her for another seventy to eighty years. He faced front and asked, "Why did you only bring one maid, my new queen?"

Serenity glanced back at her maid. "Alexa demanded it. She wouldn't hear of being left behind, even though bhresyas frighten her worse than anything else." She lowered her voice and said for Melchior alone, "Her father and uncle were killed in the war." Out loud, she continued, "My other maids were simply a necessity of my station. They served me because I was a princess of Cheslav and it was a privilege to do so, even if they saw me as a sacrifice and a complete waste of their efforts."

"Sacrifice?" asked another noble.

"As I said, the banquet wasn't in honor of my marriage. It was in honor of my departure. For all intents and purposes, the banquet was a funeral dinner."

"You're not dead," Melchior said with anger lacing his words. The humans continued hatred of bhresyas baffled him to this day. He wanted peace, why didn't they want the same?

"Not to Alric and my mother, but everyone else will treat the situation like I am."

"You've gone through the last eighteen years having people refer to you as a sacrifice?"

"Mother called it a marriage of state—something any princess must go through. Behind her back and to my face, others called it a ritual sacrifice."

"They never said such things while we were present, my queen," Theyn said with a loud growl. "I would have broken anyone who would have dared."

The other Hell Hounds growled out their agreement of this. Serenity said sadly, "You weren't around all the time, were you?"

"Serenity," Nym started. Her worried gaze scanned Serenity's face. "Had we known of Mael's treachery—"

"I don't speak of that," Serenity said with finality.

Melchior sensed Serenity's growing discomfort and decided a subject change was needed. "You disrespect your new queen when you drop her title, Dame Nym."

"Nym has never given me a title," Serenity said before Nym could answer. "It is not disrespectful... well, it was at first... but it isn't now. It is the way we are. My Hell Hounds are my closest friends and I couldn't keep barriers of propriety between us to make others feel better. My Hell Hounds and I are family. Nym is my aunt."

"Aunt?"

"Queen Rhiannon did not like when Serenity called me mother, and I refused to answer the title of grandmother," Nym said, wrinkling her nose. "I may be old by human standards but I am not nearly old enough to be considered a grandmother."

Serenity added, "Nym is... overprotective of me at times. It made me feel like I had two mothers. I could not call her mother, so I call her aunt. And, she is my aunt just as Haige is my teacher, Theyn my joy, and Chigaru my confidante."

"And Mael was your sister?" Melchior asked quietly. He didn't look at Serenity when he asked this. He wanted to speak of other things but the course of the conversation wouldn't allow it.

"I loved Mael as I love all my Hell Hounds. Her betrayal... no, it wasn't betrayal as she was never loyal to me. She was never mine. They were prisoners to my childish whims until they served me of their own free will. I assumed Mael was the same."

"What did your Hell Hounds teach you, my new queen?"

Haige answered for Serenity, "Bhresya politics. Queen Rhiannon would keep Prince Alric and Queen Serenity secluded away for three and four hours at a time each day learning the dynamics of human politics. I would then seclude Queen Serenity for another four teaching her bhresya politics."

"And, you are qualified to do this, Hell Hound Haige?" asked the noble who rode with Alexa.

"Supremely. I was an apprentice to Judge Furth for my first eighty-two years. I turned into an assassin for hire when Judge Furth chose Sakur—my constant rival in all things—as his successor. I didn't want to be part of a profession that would have one such as Sakur in its ranks." He didn't volunteer what he didn't like about Sakur and no one asked.

To get back to the original subject, Theyn declared, "I taught Serenity about bhresya life—history, entertainment, foods, and anything else we do to fill our days. I became an honorary chef when Serenity decided she should start gaining a taste for bhresya fare."

Haige added, "'Tis a wonder our queen lived to her eighteenth birthday eating your swill." For Melchior's benefit, he said, "Theyn's cooking was base and under-flavored and oft times inedible. We assured Queen Serenity she would receive better at the royal table."

At Theyn's huffy look, Serenity said, "I thought it was good."

"In that, you were too kind," Nym said. "I taught Serenity about bhresya death—the rites and rituals performed, how our people react to it that is different from humans, and our beliefs of the after life. Not only that, but I also taught her of other ceremonies, such as the marriage ceremony and the ceremony performed at birth." Before anyone could question her, she said, "I am the daughter of a mage and had planned to be a mage before turning my interest to assassination. As to why I did such a thing, that is between my mother and myself."

"It seems you were lucky in your choice of teachers, my new queen, considering they came to kill you," Melchior said.

"Destiny."

"Chigaru was the only one who acted only as your guard?"

Chigaru glanced back at Serenity with a raised eyebrow. Serenity smiled at him and answered, "Chigaru taught me about sex."

The whole party came to an abrupt halt. Actually, everyone else stopped because Melchior stopped. He stared at Serenity.

"You don't have to look that way, King Melchior. I am still as pure today as I was when I was born. Chigaru only explained some of the differences between human males and bhresya males."

"Like?" Melchior growled, glaring at Chigaru's back. The man faced forward and hadn't bothered turning back when the group stopped. Melchior was happy for that. He would gladly rip the man's throat out for having dared to touch his future bride.

Melchior wasn't sure he believed Serenity's words. The heavy presence of Chigaru's scent in her rooms back in Cheslav's palace spoke of more than words passing between them. And yet, her scent remained her own. That proved nothing. Chigaru could have copulated with Serenity many times, but never marked her, since he knew of her impending marriage and that such an action would be considered treason.

Serenity rode up to Melchior's side and placed a hand on his thigh. She waited for him to look down at her. "You'll find out what I learned from Chigaru tonight." She winked at him before spurring Ines back into motion. "If we keep stopping we'll never get to Nexeu. How far is the palace from the border of Cheslav and Nexeu?"

"Only three hours journey, Your Majesty," said one of the nobles.

"Good."

CHAPTER EIGHT

SERENITY'S JOY AT GETTING TO HER NEW HOME was quickly squashed in the face of her new subjects. Not one of them looked happy to see her. In fact, they all looked downright angry.

When her leg bumped Melchior's, she looked up at him in surprise. When had she moved Ines so close to his side? She didn't remember giving Ines a signal to pull alongside him and yet there she was. It was then she noticed her Hell Hounds, the guards, and the nobles had closed ranks around her and Melchior, shielding them from the mean-looking crowd.

She forced herself to smile in the face of this hostility. She couldn't look afraid. If they thought her weak, they would never allow her to rule them. Not that she had any delusions of grandeur on that front. Serenity only hoped the people of Nexeu would acknowledge her as their queen. She was pretty sure without having to ask, in Melchior's absence there would be a regent who would oversee the running of the nation, not her.

A gasp rolled over the crowd. Serenity looked around for the cause and came face to face with a dagger flying towards her head. She blinked at it in surprise.

Melchior jerked her to the side just as Lorcan jumped up and caught the blade in his teeth. He landed and chewed the dagger to pieces then spit it out. He whined up at Serenity.

Serenity sagged into Melchior's solid side, unable to move. If not for Melchior and Lorcan, she would have died. That was the second time today she'd come within moments of death.

"I'm fine," she said, though no one asked.

No matter how many times someone had threatened her life, she couldn't get used to it. It wasn't something she wanted to get used to either. She thought she would have no more worries once she was married, but this latest incident proved her hope was premature and misplaced.

Melchior situated Serenity on Ines before he looked in the direction the dagger had come. "Who dares?" he demanded loudly.

Chigaru signaled Theyn. They streaked off their mounts and through the crowd. When they returned, they had a male held between them. He was a white bhresya with eyes of two shades of blue and horns that curved from his forehead over the back of his head and rested on his shoulders. The male struggled, but Chigaru and

Theyn held him.

Melchior looked at Serenity and asked, "What will you do with him, Queen Serenity?"

Serenity looked at Melchior in shock. He wanted her to... She stopped her thought and looked at the male.

Why was she daunted? This situation was no different than any other assassination attempt. She turned a calm gaze to Theyn and commanded, "I want one of his horns."

Theyn reached over and snapped off one of the male's horns without hesitation. The male roared in pain. Haige took Theyn's place on the male's right so Theyn could present the horn to Serenity.

She took the heavy horn from him. It could be mistaken for some unknown animal's fang, it was so white. She handed it behind her, knowing Nym was the one who took it. Nym had mounted Guthr's horn and several others for Serenity and she would do the same for this one. Serenity wondered how many horns would be added to her collection in her lifetime of living in Nexeu.

"I also want his head," she said.

Chigaru held out his hand. Haige pulled his blade and handed it to him. Chigaru decapitated the male before he could bother to protest. Haige let the body fall. Chigaru laid the head at Serenity's feet. The male had a permanent look of surprise on his face. The people who stood closest to the royal entourage mirrored his look.

"She commands bhresya guards, but that doesn't mean she can rule!" came a male voice from the crowd.

All attention turned to a yellow-green bhresya male with forward curving horns that stood on a nearby rooftop.

The male continued, "She is an outsider. Don't welcome her. She could be here to poison us as King Kiros poisoned Melchior's first wife and children."

Serenity looked at Melchior and he nodded. She only had to point. Lorcan took off running with Theyn following. Lorcan brought the male off the roof, then Theyn dragged him before Serenity.

She smiled at the male and said in a sweet voice, "I do believe you have invited yourself and your entire family to be food tasters at the palace for me. And, given the mood of the people of Nexeu, I don't think one of you will survive the night."

The man looked horrified. He turned to Melchior. "Surely this human doesn't speak for you, my king?"

"*Queen* Serenity has passed judgment, so shall you heed it. If you live past this night, you shall learn to hold your tongue," Melchior said. He turned a deaf ear to the male's pleas and stared at his wife. She looked too sweet to be so harsh. It seemed she had prepared well for her new life.

∽∾

Melchior was to find out how well that night.

The banquet in their honor was blessedly uneventful. Even Serenity's food tasters had survived. Unfortunately for the food tasters, Serenity had determined they were uniquely qualified for the task. A single male had doomed his father, wife, two sons, aunt, and cousin to a life of complete uncertainty as a royal food taster. That the family was now a guest of the royal palace and should be treated as such softened the sentence somewhat.

The true reason for Serenity's tasters making it through the night was Serenity's withdrawal half-way through the meal. She had complained of fatigue and left. Melchior had spent the rest of the banquet assuring his nobles and advisors Serenity would perform as queen nicely.

He returned to his chambers two courses after Serenity left and was shocked at finding her in his rooms dancing. He hadn't expected her, since they had separate rooms with a wide hallway dividing them. Melchior thought it best that he give his little human bride a chance to hide from him since he hadn't expected her ready acceptance.

He hadn't expected her to greet him with a dance, either. She wore a sheer, blue nightgown that came to her knees. One thin strap had already drooped off her shoulder thanks to her movements. Her naked body was clearly visible.

Serenity didn't falter when Melchior entered the room. She smiled and danced towards him.

"Serenity?"

She said nothing, only moved past him to close the door and turn the latch. She trailed her hand along Melchior's back as she made her way to his front. Her fingers ran over corded muscles that flexed at her touch. She balled her hands into his vest and dragged it in her wake. She danced away. Melchior allowed her to take the vest with her.

He asked, "How do you know how to dance like this? I know it wasn't part of your training." His gaze never left her and he felt his body reacting.

Serenity did a tiny spin and raised her hands over her head, dropping his vest. "I watched the court entertainers and then taught myself. Mother would never approve, you're right." She leaned into him and placed a kiss near his heart, then looked up at him with a mischievous smile. "So, I never told her. Only the Hell Hounds know." She danced away from him with a small leap, then gave a graceful bow that opened into another turn. "And, now, so do you."

"You're not scared of what we must do to make this marriage binding?" His gaze followed her every movement but he kept his body still so he wouldn't startle her. The telltale tightening of his loins was something he knew she couldn't have missed, even beneath his long loincloth. Her dancing aroused him and not her as a human. A human female could never arouse him.

"Terrified." She performed three kick steps that landed her in front of him again. "But, I'll get over it." She laid her hands on his chest. "I'm your wife and this is part of my duties."

Melchior lifted his hands above Serenity's shoulders but hesitated. He didn't know how to hold her. Humans were more fragile than bhresyas and he didn't want to hurt her carelessly.

Serenity interpreted his hesitation as uncertainty and decided to get things started. She reached up to the horns on either side of Melchior's neck much the same way she had at the wedding ceremony. Instead of bringing him to her, she pulled herself up and planted her lips square over his, staring at his surprised expression.

She planted her knees on his hips, thus taking her weight off her arms.

Melchior put his hands on her waist, giving her even more support.

She closed her eyes when he responded to her kiss. His lips parted and she slipped her tongue into his mouth, seeking out his. Once they touched, the two edges of Melchior's forked tongue wrapped around hers and she sighed.

Her first true kiss with her husband was how she imagined it would be. She relaxed against him and wrapped her arms around his neck, under his horns. Likewise, she wrapped her legs as far around his waist as they could go. She tilted her head to the side and the kiss deepened.

Melchior broke away while he still had coherent thought. Serenity's eyes were heavy-lidded and she wore a somewhat dazed expression. "Where did you learn to kiss like that?"

"Chigaru and Haige," she answered huskily, kissing his bottom lip then trailing kisses to his neck.

He allowed his eyes to close. The news that she had practiced kissing with her Hell Hounds should anger him, but he couldn't bring himself to care as he focused his attention on the feel of her lips against his skin. "Not Theyn?"

She shook her head, sending tiny puffs of breath up to his ear and back to his collar. "Theyn said he couldn't practice such as this with me because he would never be able to give me up to you. Discretion over death."

She bit his ear and he bunched his fingers into her gown, trying not to grip her too tightly. "They seem to have left nothing out of your education."

"They only practiced kissing, and only because I commanded it of them. All else they explained. They did not teach. That is for my husband to do."

Melchior walked forward and lowered her to the bed. They couldn't do this standing up and clothed. Well, they could, but Melchior didn't want to be so base with Serenity's introduction to sex. He pulled the nightgown over her head, leaving her bare before his eyes. Though her deep brown skin was a shade most often seen on bhresya males, Melchior couldn't think of it as anything but beautiful and feminine at that moment.

He drew a hand over her breasts and she shivered. Her shiver turned into a start of surprise when he bent his head and took one of her nipples between his lips. She gasped and he slid one hand under her back while he massaged her other breast with his free hand.

Serenity arched into his mouth, grasping his horns and pulling him closer. Instead, Melchior pulled away and trailed his tongue down her stomach to the juncture of her thighs. He lapped at her and then made three lazy strokes before focusing on her nub.

Melchior smiled as he watched Serenity struggle not to cry out. She clenched at the bed and gritted her teeth, but the movement of her hips beneath his mouth told him that she enjoyed his teasing. He pressed a single finger into Serenity's passion-slicked depths. She cried out, her inner muscles clenching around his finger.

She was tight. He would have to take his time or else he might hurt her. He moved his finger forward and came up to some resistance. Something inside him unclenched. She truly was a virgin despite the knowledge she possessed, and she hadn't lied about Chigaru's and Haige's teachings. He didn't know why this pleased him, but it did.

"Something's wrong with me," Serenity said in a frantic, breathy voice. She tried to turn away.

He stopped licking her and pressed her back flat against the bed so she remained open to him. Serenity's fear mingled with the scent of her lust as he continued moving his finger in and out of her. He soothed, "Nothing is wrong, little Serenity. Let it come."

Melchior could tell that Serenity held back her release because she was uncertain, and knew what to do to help her along. He bent forward over her body and took one of her nipples into his mouth, suckling gently on the taut bud. Meanwhile, he stopped his in-and-out motions and curled his finger in an ever-repeating beckoning motion.

It only took a few seconds before Serenity let out a loud gasp. She released the bed and clutched at Melchior's shoulders, holding on to him as her body rode out its first climax.

Serenity's first release left her feeling dazed. She released Melchior slowly and lay back against the bed. Her breath came in pants. As much as she wanted to revel in the experience, she couldn't. Melchior's finger remained active inside of her. She rocked her hips forward, eager to feel the sensation again.

Melchior added another finger to her depths. He moved his fingers back and forth in a scissoring motion inside of her.

Serenity cried, "Oh! More!"

"As you wish, my queen," Melchior said with amusement. He removed his fingers from her, which made her whimper at the loss, and replaced them with something considerably larger.

Serenity wiggled against the pressure of this new object and tried to relax as it entered her body. She wanted to look down the length of her body and see what Melchior had placed between her legs but decided against it. Chigaru had explained this and she understood... at least she thought she had, but her fear had returned.

She moved her hips a little forward in hopes that the motion would reignite the pleasure she had felt moments before. Melchior sucked in his breath. She stopped and rushed out, "I'm sorry, Melchior. I didn't mean to—"

"Don't apologize," he rasped. He bent and pressed his lips to hers. "Never apologize for pleasure given."

"I pleased you?"

He nodded and said, "Move again."

She drew back then rocked forward. This time she and Melchior moaned in appreciation together.

"Again."

Serenity moved.

"Again."

She complied.

Melchior didn't have to tell her a third time because she caught the rhythm. He held himself still as she availed herself of his rock hard need. He wanted to move and it took all his control not to.

He waited until Serenity was close to another climax, her breasts pressing against his chest and her hands clawing at his shoulders, before he nodded. It was time.

He grasped her hips and stopped her movements. A question formed in her eyes, but he looked away. A simple forward push and he sheathed himself almost to the hilt.

Serenity gave a pained cry and shook her head. She pushed at his chest and tried to move away. He held her.

Ignoring her protests to leave her, Melchior held himself still to accommodate the pain she felt. Her inner muscles continued moving around him. His nobility wouldn't last long with her body welcoming him in such an exquisite manner. He needed Serenity compliant again. Slowly, he moved his hands up from Serenity's hips to her breasts. He cupped the twin mounds, bent his head and paid homage to them both.

A little squeak of pleasure from Serenity and Melchior's arousal jerked in response, and then Serenity yelped. He smiled at the sound. He made his manhood jerk again and lifted his head so he could watch her reaction.

Her mouth opened on a silent gasp and surprise was plain on her face.

Melchior urged in a quiet voice, "Move again, little one."

Serenity drew back her hips and then moved forward. Her movements were hesitant since she expected to feel more pain, but it didn't come. The sensation was wholly different from what she felt before the pain. She felt full and somehow she knew that was what her body wanted. She drew back, farther this time, and then pushed her hips forward.

She moved twice more before Melchior grasped her hips, almost painfully, and held her as he moved. He thrust into her over and over. Soon, Serenity met him and moved to the rhythm he set. She grasped his horns and pulled him to her waiting lips. She forced her tongue into his mouth, only to pull away a few seconds later and cry out.

Melchior returned his mouth to her breasts. He liked their softness. He went back and forth between the twin mounds. It didn't feel right giving one breast more attention than the other.

Serenity climaxed for a second time, her whole body drenched in sweat, and Melchior's release came only seconds later. He spilled his seed onto the covers and was happy Serenity hadn't noticed. His reasons would only hurt her feelings.

He looked down at his new wife. Her eyes were half shut and she looked moments away from sleep. He backed away from her then scooped her off the bed. Serenity curled into his arms and the position reminded him how small she was compared to a female of his race. He barely needed one arm to hold her and she weighed next to nothing.

His gaze went to her hands where they rested on his chest. He remembered the way she clutched at him. There was no way she had marked him—not in any way that could be considered permanent—not like his first wife had.

Melchior pushed thoughts of his first wife out of his mind as he carried Serenity to the bath that was prepared for him. He yanked on the bell pull before he shut the bathroom door. While he cleansed Serenity of sweat, the maids changed the sheets.

Serenity relaxed against Melchior's body once they were in the tub. He trickled water over her skin then smoothed a soapy sponge over her body. The contact made her shiver. She wanted Melchior to touch her again as he had before. Her body was tired but she still wanted more of the sensation.

It wasn't to be. She allowed herself to be pampered, since she couldn't move to do it herself. And, Melchior's gentle touches spread glowing warmth from every point of contact. Her head lulled back against Melchior's chest and she closed her eyes. She could get used to this.

CHAPTER NINE

THE NEXT NIGHT, Serenity sat at the head of the banquet table fully rejuvenated and anxious for the night to come. She had awakened that morning and found herself in the middle of Melchior's giant bed alone. Melchior had already gone, leaving Chigaru standing guard outside with Alexa beside him. Serenity had reasoned Melchior had things to do since war was averted and she left it at that.

She'd spent the better part of the day touring the palace with Nym and Chigaru. She hadn't seen Lorcan since they arrived at the palace, but she wasn't worried. Other thondis roamed the palace and Lorcan had probably gone to get acquainted with his own kind as the hounds at Cheslav had avoided him out of fear.

Theyn had gone to visit his family and Haige had found a willing palace maid to spend some quality time with—no one had seen him open the door to his chambers for the last seventeen hours. Serenity had only giggled at that news. She had urged Nym and Chigaru to get reacquainted with their homeland. Chigaru had merely shaken his head while Nym explained her family was in no particular hurry to see her and declined to follow Haige's example either.

In direct contrast with the reception Serenity had received yesterday, the nobles of Nexeu were happy to see her. She was the proof that the war was over. Many of the nobles had heard of how she dealt with the would-be assassin and found her handling of the situation to be truly bhresya-like.

Serenity winked at Haige when he finally joined the others in the dining hall. Theyn said something she couldn't hear but she assumed was inappropriate since Haige smacked him on the back of the head. She laughed out loud.

No one understood Theyn's sense of humor. Even if she didn't truly understand, Serenity found Theyn funny. His amusement at his own jokes was enough to make her laugh along with him, but she was alone in her consideration.

"What has you so jovial this evening, Your Majesty?" the noble seated on her right asked.

"I merely find the antics of my Hell Hounds amusing, my lady," she said with mirth in her voice.

"I must admit I find your... guards to be a marvel," said the female's husband. "To think they have lived in Cheslav for fifteen years, it is amazing."

"Thank you," Serenity said genuinely. She didn't miss how the male hesitated on the Hell Hounds' title.

"Here, here," piped up another noble. "Sir Theyn—"

"Hell Hound Theyn," Serenity corrected. She smiled and took a sip from her cup when the noble looked at her. "My personal guards are called Hell Hounds, my lord."

Some of the nobles at the table murmured disapproval behind their hands to one another.

"I do not insult them when I call them that. It is a point of honor for them to be known as my Hell Hounds."

Haige said, "Yes, my queen, it is an honor, a privilege, and not something I would ever change." He bowed to her. Theyn did the same then blew her a kiss.

She toasted them both.

The noble corrected grudgingly, "Hell Hound Theyn reminds me of King Melchior's second son Likos." He smiled at the memory and nodded. "Yes, I remember the lad was in trouble almost constantly. His sense of humor was his own and he was always a happy boy."

The mood of the room turned instantly somber. Serenity looked up at Melchior and saw his grim expression. She reached out to put a hand on his arm, but he stiffened before she could touch him so she pulled away. He wouldn't want the granddaughter of the man who had caused his first family's death comforting him.

The noble continued unaware of his king's change in mood, "The entire dining hall was moved to the other end of the palace because of the tragedy that befell that night. Such a shame it will probably be another seventy or so years before royal heirs will grace this hall again." He shook his head.

"You say too much," Melchior said in a low voice.

The male looked up at Melchior surprised. "I thought—"

"You thought wrong, Lord Halm."

Serenity looked between the two males. "I would be happy to bear my husband's heirs." She thought that would solve the problem nicely. If it were possible, Melchior stiffened more and the mood of the entire room dropped below freezing.

She felt, rather than heard or saw, Haige and Theyn move until they stood a few paces behind her chair. Chigaru and Nym left their posts at the dining hall doors and moved towards her as well. Their manner let her know her words hadn't had the desired reaction.

How stupid of her.

She laid her fork and knife onto the table and dabbed at the sides of her mouth with her napkin. "Am I to guess though you approve of my presence because it signals the end of the war, the idea of Melchior and I having children is out of the question?"

She looked at Melchior for some kind of support, but he stared straight ahead. "You've been without heirs for nearly twenty years. Are you truly going to wait?" she asked him.

He didn't answer.

"Or were you going to wait the required ten years before marrying another and having heirs with her?"

More silence.

"No, that wouldn't do. Someone with a robust appetite such as yours couldn't be expected to wait. I suppose one of your concubines could mother an heir or two. You do have concubines, I presume?"

Melchior's gaze jerked in her direction, though his body didn't move. She couldn't read his look, but knew part of the emotion in his eyes was anger. Good, because she was angry, too.

"I do have concubines, but no royal heir can be illegitimate. I would think you would thank me for having concubines as they would turn my attentions away from you."

Serenity wanted to scream at him for his words. They were newly married and his attention should only be for her. She wanted more of his touch and had hoped they would engage each other that night as they had the night before. She had spent her whole day looking forward to it.

The night before played through her mind as she tried to remember any word or movement that had made Melchior think she didn't want his touch. Her body flushed with the memory.

A thought occurred to her. She nodded as the thought suddenly made sense. "Just as you thought I would like separate rooms, correct?"

"Yes."

Serenity hadn't given it a second thought when Melchior showed her the rooms that would be hers. They were directly across the hall from his and many royal couples—many couples, period—had separate rooms. In fact, the royal couple of Lev had separate palaces, so Serenity hadn't taken offense at the arrangement. In hindsight, she should have.

She considered the people who sat around her. Some of them showed the same disapproval she faced when she first arrived at the palace gates. It was stupid to think they would accept her. The time with her Hell Hounds had colored her view of life.

Though Chigaru had accepted her from the start, it took a few years before Nym, Haige, and Theyn thought of her as they did now. She had forgotten about the time before they were her friends—the time when Chigaru's constant vigilance was the only thing that kept them at her side.

The next course was served. Her food taster, the wife of the male who spoke out against her, stepped forward. Serenity held up her hand, stopping the female. "Haige, have this female and her family escorted back to their home."

"My queen?" Haige asked.

Serenity looked over her shoulder at him. "I don't need them anymore. They have learned their lesson and I need not torture them further." Besides, she had lost her appetite. The rest of her thought wasn't voiced as no one else needed to know how hurt she was at this new development.

Haige nodded at Serenity's command and let the female rush past him. He didn't follow her as Serenity bade him but stayed watching the nobles at the table with a hard look.

Serenity allowed him that small disobedience since she knew he wouldn't leave her side until he felt she was safe. She turned her attention back to Melchior. He stared at the far wall and she cast her gaze to her plate.

"So, while I am in the assuming mood, am I to presume I am allowed a lover? It is only fair," Serenity said. She didn't like having this conversation in public but some part of her knew she had better have it now or not at all.

"No human would willingly come to Nexeu, *my* queen," Melchior said.

"I didn't say I wished to have a human lover, did I?"

There were some shocked murmurs at the table and a few of the nobles looked at Chigaru, Haige, and then Theyn. Serenity saw where their attention went and didn't care. The nobles and servants would think what they wanted about her request. They wouldn't be far off the mark.

"You have someone in mind?" Melchior asked.

"It's only a matter of asking."

Melchior looked at her. "I will consider this request."

Serenity rose and Chigaru moved the chair out of her way. She inclined her head to Melchior. "You do that. I find I'm no longer hungry." She turned away from the table and her Hell Hounds instantly surrounded her as she left the room.

Conversation erupted from everyone the second the dining hall doors closed. She ignored it all. When the Hell Hounds tried to comfort her, Serenity silenced them.

Nothing could comfort her. Her husband was waiting for her to die so he could marry a real queen and have full-blooded bhresya heirs. A third wife could give him heirs but she wouldn't be queen if Melchior married her while Serenity lived, not even after Serenity died. If a wife was taken *after* Serenity's death, then the title of queen could be hers—just as Serenity was queen, though she was Melchior's second wife.

However, if Melchior declared Serenity an unfit queen, then his third wife could be declared queen regardless of Serenity's presence. As a human, no one would argue she was unfit to rule at Melchior's side.

Destiny had played a cruel joke on her.

Serenity bade Chigaru remain once they reached her chambers and she had dismissed the others. No one protested. Haige took her hand in his, went to one knee and placed it on the curve of one of his horns. She almost snatched her hand away then changed her mind. With slow movements, she traced one horn from tip to base and then the other.

Haige smiled up at her. "For comfort, Serenity. Remember that."

She nodded and he left, closing the door after him. Serenity gave vent to her tears and Chigaru's arms surrounded her. Of all the Hell Hounds, Chigaru was the only one who'd ever seen her cry. That was because, of all the Hell Hounds, Chigaru was closest to her.

To others it may seem that Haige and Theyn held the same place in her heart as Chigaru but they and she knew better. She and her Hell Hounds were close and the normal rules of propriety didn't separate them. The inhabitants of the palace may misinterpret their physical and emotional closeness, but in Chigaru's case it wasn't completely untrue.

"Stay with me tonight."

Chigaru took Serenity in his arms and rested his chin on her head. "King Melchior has not given his permission, Serenity."

"Only to sleep. Like we used to do." She clutched at his vest, needing desperately for him to say yes. "Please." She couldn't stand another denial.

Chigaru nodded then released her long enough for her to change. He took her back into his arms as they lay on the bed.

Silent tears tracked down Serenity's face and soaked into Chigaru's vest. She wanted him to remove it. She wanted him to remove all of his clothes and hers, but didn't ask.

The time when they could lie naked together had ended when she turned twelve. Rhiannon was furious when she had learned Chigaru slept in Serenity's bed without the barrier of clothing. She didn't care if sleeping nude was a habit of bhresyas, Rhiannon didn't want Serenity doing it. She had barred Chigaru from Serenity's room for a month. Only Serenity's pleas and a mage's assurances that Serenity remained a virgin made Rhiannon rethink her judgment.

Weeks passed before Serenity grew used to the feel of a nightgown. It took months of restless nights before cloth between her skin and Chigaru's felt normal. On rare occasions, she had convinced Chigaru to shed his vest, at least. He wouldn't do more because he hadn't wanted Rhiannon upset needlessly.

This wasn't one of those occasions. Serenity wasn't sure she wouldn't demand Chigaru do more with her... to her. They were alone in her room—on her bed. Her pain and embarrassment made her want to forego Melchior's permission and take her lover.

She curbed the idea, not wanting to play with Chigaru's life in such a way. She simply took comfort in his presence and left it at that.

ࣟ

Melchior left the dining hall shortly after Serenity. Hearing the nobles speak plainly of their disgust at the idea of a half-breed heir had ruined his appetite. He was glad Serenity wasn't present to hear what was said.

He paused in front of Serenity's rooms before he continued on to his. Nym stood guard. She bowed to him though her manner was cool.

He asked, "You disapprove, Hell Hound Nym?"

"It isn't my place to approve or disapprove of the actions of the royal family, King Melchior."

Melchior noted Nym hadn't addressed him as *my king* like she had so many times before this moment. He ignored it in favor of another annoying fact. "I smell Chigaru." There was a question in his tone though he didn't want there to be.

"He is inside with my queen."

Sides were chosen and Nym was on Serenity's, but he knew that already. "I haven't given my permission for her to take a lover."

"They are sleeping, King Melchior. In Cheslav, Chigaru habitually shared Serenity's bed. He surprised several assassins that way."

"He could have slept on the floor and achieved the same effect," Melchior said in a heated rush. He noticed his instant anger and worked to hide it.

Why did he care so much where Chigaru had slept in the past or where he slept now? Melchior had made it clear Serenity wasn't welcome in his bed.

"Serenity prefers Chigaru in her bed. It seems that hasn't changed now that she is married."

The conversation stopped when Theyn came down the hall with Lorcan following close behind him. Nym opened the door and Lorcan entered. The sound of Serenity's tears reached them before Nym closed the door again.

Theyn left only to return with two chairs. He set one on either side of the door. Once he was seated, he said, "Goodnight, King Melchior."

It was a dismissal. Nym flat out ignored him, busying herself taking down her braid. She pulled her fingers through her hair with a contented sigh.

Melchior didn't have the energy to pick this fight. He would concede the Hell Hounds truly belonged to Serenity and no other—not even him. He quit their presence and went to his rooms. It would be a long seventy or so years.

CHAPTER TEN

SERENITY WAS ALL SMILES THE NEXT DAY. She took breakfast in her rooms. And though she showed no concern for it, Nym insisted on having a passing maid taste all of Serenity's food before she ate it. The depth of the Hell Hounds' paranoia revealed itself when yet another random servant was pulled aside to taste Alexa's food, as well.

That sent Alexa into a fit of tears. Serenity spent her entire breakfast soothing the woman between bites of food. In the end, she assigned Theyn to watch over Alexa instead of herself. There were obvious objections to this, but Serenity would hear none of them since she felt Alexa's safety was important and it was Serenity's fault Alexa was there.

Through all this, Serenity's mood stayed upbeat. Finally, Haige inquired as to why.

"Because, my teacher," Serenity said, "after crying my eyes out all night, I came up with a plan. I will seduce Melchior into impregnating me. He cannot harm the child once I am carrying it. He wouldn't dare. An heir will be born—"

"And have to deal with the same threats you endured as a babe, Serenity," Nym finished.

"I know that, but this is about my relationship with my husband. I also knew I would bear his children, even if the doing of it might kill me. I know Melchior wouldn't let harm come to any child of his loins—half human or otherwise."

She wouldn't be dissuaded from her plan since she knew it would work. Melchior's arousal on their wedding night meant he had felt something for her. And, he had said she gave him pleasure. She might be discouraged had Melchior not told her that.

Serenity stayed at Melchior's side the entire day. She sat in on meetings of state and, though no one asked her opinions, interjected suggestions here and there as she was trained to do. The nobles and advisors grudgingly admitted the validity of her statements and she felt better for having voiced them. Proving her worth would better ease the bhresya people into seeing her as their queen.

"Your insight is astounding for one so young, Queen Serenity," said one advisor.

Serenity smiled at him and said, "Humans don't live as long as bhresyas, my lord. We must learn fast or be left behind."

"True, true."

Melchior sat back in his seat. "Your advice in the matters of Nexeu is valid and appreciated, Serenity. However, your presence is not needed here. I thought you would tour the palace with your Hell Hounds this afternoon."

He'd dismissed her. She tried not to show how upset that made her. With a slow nod, she rose and excused herself. The advisors and nobles bowed to her as she exited the room and she closed the door behind her.

Chigaru and Nym waited outside the room with questioning looks. She shook her head at them. "Melchior doesn't wish me to be there," she said quietly. She walked away from the meeting room with no destination in mind except to escape her shame.

"Queen Rhiannon would be infuriated if she knew the way your education was being wasted," Nym said in dismay.

"My mother can't help me with this," Serenity said. "I'll just have to meet him in his rooms as I did on our wedding night."

Nym exchanged looks with Chigaru. Serenity was happy when Chigaru quieted whatever protest Nym would have voiced with a shake of his head. Nym gave Serenity a helpless look, but she ignored it.

Negativity wouldn't solve her problems with Melchior. She had to prove to him she wanted his touch and entice him into wanting hers. Once he remembered their physical compatibility, Melchior would soon grow to love her. His love and acceptance would encourage his people to follow suit.

༈

That night, Serenity waited in Melchior's rooms. She didn't dance. Instead, she sat on his bed naked and waiting. The situation embarrassed her but her predicted outcome made it worthwhile.

Melchior stepped into his room then stopped short.

Serenity stood and declared the obvious, "I was waiting for you."

He entered the room fully and closed the door behind him. "I can see that. Why?"

Her gaze lowered from his, her embarrassment building. She answered in a low voice, "I wanted to sleep with you again. I... I enjoyed it." She clasped her hands in front of her. Her idea to seduce Melchior hadn't seemed so difficult when she had thought of it a few hours ago.

A knock sounded at the door. Melchior didn't let Serenity hide herself before he opened to the knocker. A pink bhresya female stood on the other side, smiling at Melchior. Her gaze went to Serenity and her smile dropped.

The female rushed out, "Oh, forgive, Your Majesty. I didn't realize you and Queen Serenity were—"

"We're not, Mistress Keran," Melchior interrupted. He ushered her into the room. "Queen Serenity *isn't* staying."

Serenity took the situation like a slap in the face. This wasn't happening. She looked from Melchior to Keran. Melchior's expression was grim while Keran's looked smug.

The female was slender and delicate and her coloring made those traits seem more pronounced even though she shared Melchior's height. Her dark pink hair was a riot of curls that cascaded down her back and brushed the top of her thighs. Even her horns curled, spiraling from beneath her ears and forming a pink halo over her head.

Serenity wanted to rip that halo from Keran's head and add it to her trophy wall. But, the female wasn't to blame. Melchior had shamed Serenity, not Keran.

She grabbed her robe and didn't speak until she tied the sash in a tight knot around her humiliation. "Does this mean I can take a lover then, my king?"

Melchior moved aside so she could leave. "No. If you became pregnant, it would be a disgrace to the kingdom and me."

She walked past him out of the room. "There are ways to prevent pregnancy."

"Ways that are unseemly for a queen to be implementing. Goodnight, Serenity." He closed the door in her face.

Serenity turned and found Chigaru waiting for her when he wasn't there moments before. She reached out to him and he caught her before her legs gave out.

Chigaru carried her to her rooms. He waited for her to dress in a nightgown before taking her to bed. He held her as he did the night before.

Serenity didn't cry. She was numb to the situation. Her husband, the male she thought she would love and cherish, was an uncaring, insensitive jerk. He hadn't even bothered hiding Keran. The anger she felt at having his concubine know he found her, his wife, distasteful was more than Serenity could bear.

She shook with her anger. Chigaru's arms tightened around her. She pushed on his chest but he only held her tighter. Squirming out his grip didn't work either.

"Nym!" she screamed.

Nym burst into the room and Haige followed. Both had their swords drawn but hesitated when no danger presented itself.

"Serenity?" Nym asked, approaching the bed hesitantly.

"Remove Chigaru from my rooms immediately," Serenity commanded in a near frantic voice.

Nym's eyes widened at the command. She looked at Chigaru helplessly, but he kept his back to her. "Serenity—"

"Now!"

Haige stepped forward when Nym's hesitation continued and touched Chigaru's arm. Chigaru released Serenity. He tried to meet Serenity's gaze, but she wouldn't look at him. He sighed and left the room. Haige bowed to Serenity and followed his leader, closing the door.

"How did Chigaru anger you, Serenity?" Nym asked.

Serenity sat, shoving her hair out of her face. "I am not angry with Chigaru, my aunt," she admitted after a long silence. She got out of the bed and paced. "I cannot be comforted by him now. He is a male and cannot understand the shame... the horror..." she ended her sentence on a growl.

Nym pulled two chairs into the middle of the room and forced Serenity onto one of them. "Her name is Keran, Serenity. She is the head concubine in Melchior's harem. She has been Melchior's... favorite since the death of his wife."

Serenity's hands bunched on her lap. She'd already figured out that information and having it confirmed hurt more than she thought it would. She whispered, "She is beautiful."

Nym nodded and agreed, "She is. I wish I could tell you something that would degrade the female, but nothing I have learned about her could be construed as negative. I'm sorry."

"Defaming her won't mend my wounded pride. It was stupid to think I—a *human*—could seduce Melchior. Seeing Keran's beauty made me realize that fact."

"You are beautiful, Serenity."

"By human standards, not bhresya."

"By any standards. Your features and shape are pleasing. Chigaru, Haige, and Theyn prove bhresya males find you attractive despite the male coloring of your brown skin."

"It isn't enough! I don't want their favor. I want Melchior's." Serenity bounded out of her chair then fell to her knees and put her head on Nym's lap. Nym stroked her head as she normally did when Serenity was troubled. Unlike the other times, there was nothing Nym could say or do to help her through this ordeal.

"You shall have it in time. You are yet a child, Serenity," Nym said soothingly.

Serenity snorted in an unladylike manner. "I dream of children, Nym. I knew having a half-breed would be dangerous, but I had hoped..." She shook her head then leaned away from Nym with a sigh. "I am the idiot Joah took me to be."

"Do not think that, Serenity. Joah was only jealous of your future."

"He's welcome to it. Melchior doesn't want a bride. He wants a treaty. I could have stayed in Cheslav. I should have stayed in Cheslav," she groused. She gasped and her gaze went to Nym's face. "I'm sorry, my aunt. That was selfish. Of course I had to come here. This is your home. If not for myself and my marriage, then for you and the others to be comfortable again."

Nym stroked the side of Serenity's face. "Our comfort is with you, Serenity. Wherever you choose to live is where we will be. You know that." She smiled when Serenity turned her head and kissed her hand.

Serenity sat back when Nym stood and went to the door. She opened it and smiled at Haige and Chigaru. They both sat facing the door, waiting. Nym nodded and they stood. To Chigaru, she said, "You should probably retrieve Theyn and Alexa for tonight."

Chigaru grunted in agreement and left while Haige entered the room. He helped Serenity to her feet then embraced her. She traced her hands over the curves of his horns from within his embrace. "For my comfort," she whispered.

"Always," Haige whispered back. He kissed her neck then let her go.

She looked to the doorway as Chigaru entered with Theyn and Alexa. Theyn carried pillows and Alexa wore a confused look. Serenity smiled at the woman and said, "I could not leave you without a guard."

While she spoke, Theyn and Haige left the room. They returned with the mattresses from their beds and laid them on the floor, forming a giant square.

Theyn shrugged out of his vest and then started undoing his loincloth. Alexa gasped loudly and covered her eyes.

Nym demanded, "What are you doing?"

He stopped and looked at the females. Alexa had her back to him, Serenity looked amused at Alexa's actions, and Nym had an annoyed look with her arms crossed. He said, "I'm preparing for bed. I always sleep nude. We all do."

"Not tonight," Nym said.

Haige agreed, "If Serenity were not present, then there would be no problem. We will not tempt fate and Melchior's temper by sleeping nude with our queen, though we have done so in the past."

"Queen Rhiannon didn't mind. She even understood," Theyn said. "Melchior is bhresya. He knows we all sleep nude."

Serenity said, "Oh, Mother did mind, quite a bit actually. She never said anything because Nym and Mael were present whenever we slept together. Every other night, she made sure Chigaru and I were fully clothed before we retired."

Theyn sighed in frustration and redid his loincloth.

Serenity grabbed Alexa's and Nym's hands and walked to the center of the giant bed. She lay down on her side with Alexa to her front and Nym at her back.

Alexa asked, "Won't we need blankets to ward off the cold, Your Majesty?"

Serenity chuckled. "Not with these four heating us." She put her arm around Alexa's waist and gave her a squeeze. "Alexa, as we are the only humans and you are destined to become very close to all of us, you should start calling me Serenity."

"I—"

Nym laid a hand on the woman's shoulder, cutting off her protest. "It is better to agree than try to argue."

Alexa nodded stiffly then stiffened more when Theyn laid down facing her. He smiled at her and she smiled back tentatively. Chigaru lay above their heads while Haige was curled against Nym's back.

"Alexa, relax. This is the safest you will ever be, surrounded by the Hell Hounds. I would sleep like this after every assassination attempt," Serenity said happily. Her voice subdued somewhat when she added, "You have taken Mael's place in the circle."

One by one each of the Hell hounds placed a hand on Serenity's shoulder, arm, or head. She looked at them all in turn then placed her hand on top of Chigaru's. To him, she whispered, "I'm sorry for earlier. Tomorrow I shall speak of our situation to Melchior again."

He nodded.

Silence filled the emotionally charged room and they all fell asleep.

CHAPTER ELEVEN

MELCHIOR CLOSED THE DOOR, blocking out Serenity's stricken face. Her timid confession had set his blood surging through his veins even as he denied the reaction. He hadn't meant for her to see Keran, but that was more Serenity's fault than his. She shouldn't have been in his rooms.

That excuse seemed childish considering she'd waited in his rooms two nights ago. Though after his earlier dismissal, he didn't think she'd want to see him again.

"That was mean," Keran admonished with a laugh. She pressed her breasts against his back and smoothed her hands over his shoulders then traced his horns. "You are usually more considerate to the fairer sex, Melchior."

"Silence, Keran."

For some reason, her voice grated on his nerves when it never had before. He also didn't like the feel of her hands on his horns. She rubbed his horns whereas Serenity had stroked them, trailing her fingertips lightly enough to tease and entice.

Melchior growled and yanked Keran from behind him. He threw her towards the bed, angry at himself for his thoughts, but taking it out on her. He had summoned Keran to his room to take his mind off Serenity and all he could do was compare the two.

Keran laughed at his treatment. "You are so eager this night. Has your little human queen left you so unsatisfied?" She reached for him when he neared her and he knocked her hands away.

"Don't touch me."

"Why ever not, Melchior? You love the way I touch you." She tried to touch him again.

"I said do *not* touch me!" He grabbed her wrist in a crushing grip and forced her back against the bed. "If you cannot heed my words, Keran, I will send for a female who can."

"Of course, Melchior," she said, her laughter vanishing. "I didn't mean to make you angry."

"Be silent while you're at it."

Keran's worried look only made him angrier. He wanted to send her away and summon another, but knew the other females would annoy him the same. Rather than see to the need himself as he did the night before, he would suffer her presence.

Try as he might to avoid it, his mind slipped back to his one and only encounter with his wife. The memory wouldn't be denied so he closed his eyes and let it have him. He recalled the creamy feel of her pleasure-scented skin and her hesitant cries of fulfillment while in the throes of her first climax.

Even as he regretted her inability to mark him with the strength of her passion, he reveled in her demanding urgency. He'd wanted to have her again while he bathed her but felt it was too soon and she needed time to heal.

Having her follow him all day had tested his control. He'd thought she would pout and subject him to her anger after their disastrous dinner the night before, but she'd greeted him with a smile and a warm look.

Caught unawares by her sanguine manner, his body reacted instantly. He'd wanted to know how she'd react if he had lifted her skirts and pressed her into the common room wall with his hard need. He wanted to bury himself deep inside her—as deep as she could take—and listen to her screams as she...

"There! Oh, Melchior, yes! Yes!"

Keran's screams of pleasure wrenched Melchior back to the present and his true partner. His daydream hadn't hindered his performance if Keran's cries were any indication.

Since he didn't scold her for talking, she continued. Melchior found his earlier passion halved and his enjoyment of the encounter waned until he wished for a quick release.

He couldn't get away from Keran fast enough when his body finally obeyed his silent urgings. She didn't notice his haste or let his expanse of back, which he presented to her when he rolled away, deter her from hugging him.

"That was wonderful, my king. I've never felt you so gentle before."

"Leave, Keran. I've no more need of you." He shrugged off her hands and left the bed. He needed a bath. If Keran was smart, she'd be gone when he returned.

Anger seethed over and through him as he scrubbed his skin clean. He shouldn't see Serenity as anything more than a means to an end. In the morning, he would make that clear to her and then she would leave off following him... tempting him.

৵৽৶

Melchior was somewhat relieved the Hell Hounds didn't guard Serenity's door when he ventured across the hallway from his room to hers the next morning. He wanted to talk to her without their interference. There were things she needed to understand about her situation in this household.

The words died on his lips as soon as he witnessed her sleeping arrangements. Serenity slept on her stomach, half draped over Chigaru's stomach. Nym hugged Serenity's back and used it as a pillow while Haige was cupped around their feet. Alexa was wrapped in Theyn's arms and almost made them seem separate from the group except Chigaru's arm curved around Theyn's back.

The scene could only be described as highly intimate. Melchior felt like he had intruded. He stared at them for a long while as he tried to understand his anger at the situation. As a queen, Serenity shouldn't sleep on the floor in a puppy huddle with her servants, but that wasn't the root of his anger. He refused to dwell on the true reason. It made him angrier that something other than Serenity's lack of propriety had him in such a foul mood.

Serenity whimpered in her sleep. Nym rubbed her cheek against Serenity's back, Haige stroked her leg and Theyn reached around Alexa and placed his hand on her side. It was an instinctual thing, none of them were awake.

Chigaru's movements drew Melchior's gaze. The male stroked the top of Serenity's head, threading his fingers through her hair with each stroke. Melchior looked up to the male's face to find Chigaru staring at him.

Melchior stiffened. His reaction was telling and he knew Chigaru had seen it. Melchior was guilty of nothing, but why did he act like it?

Serenity turned her face into Chigaru's hand with a contented sigh. Chigaru watched Melchior in silence, his eyes betraying nothing of what he thought. Melchior withdrew and closed the door silently. His conversation with Serenity would have to wait for a later time.

An hour later, Serenity came down to breakfast and was all smiles. She took her place beside Melchior at the table but ignored him totally. She spoke only to Nym, who had accompanied her to dine. The nobles who tried to strike up conversation with Serenity were given short and direct answers that left no room for further elaboration or discussion.

Serenity's manner wasn't insulting but it was obvious to one and all that she only wished to speak to Nym. She didn't see the need to entertain the people who waited for her to die. She was a passing novelty to them. A novelty that had decided to stop performing for everyone.

Nexeu was no different from Cheslav in that Serenity was an outcast. She couldn't leave the palace for fear of an attack and the inside of the palace wouldn't be much safer, if past experiences were any indication. It didn't matter. She was happy in Cheslav and she would be happy in Nexeu.

When she was finished with her meal, Serenity rose to leave. She continued chatting with Nym as they walked to the door. They were two steps away from the table when Serenity remembered she needed to speak to Melchior. She went back and placed her hand on his shoulder only to have him jerk away.

Serenity pulled back her hand slowly then looked to see if anyone else had noticed his reaction. Not only had everyone else noticed, the nobles and servants whispered about it behind their hands. Some of the servants chuckled to themselves and gave Serenity pitying looks.

She straightened her spine at this. It was the same. Human or bhresya made no difference. Scorn was scorn.

She stepped deliberately closer to Melchior. All she had to do was inhale deeply and her body would press against his arm. He held himself rigid and she half expected him to move away from her, but he didn't.

"I have need to speak with you when you have a moment, my king."

He gave a curt nod.

She turned from the looks of amusement and preceded Nym from the dining hall. When the door closed behind them, she growled in frustration, "He could at least try to hide his disdain for me. His behavior is humiliating."

Nym agreed.

Serenity made a decision. She stopped and whirled on Nym, who only missed running into her by dodging to the side. "Get Haige and Chigaru, we're going riding." She frowned a little. "Where is Lorcan?"

Nym smiled and answered, "I shall find him for you." She escorted Serenity to Alexa's room where Theyn entertained the woman with a juggling act and then left to get things ready for Serenity's ride.

Alexa looked embarrassed when Serenity entered. Theyn winked at Serenity, which made Alexa hide her face. Serenity hadn't missed the way Alexa and Theyn were wrapped around each other that morning. Alexa had run out of the room stammering nonsense. Theyn gave her ten minutes before he followed. Serenity had warned him to keep his teasing to a minimum. He'd only smirked at her in response.

Serenity smiled at both of them, but took pity on Alexa. "If it makes you feel better, Alexa, I have woken up in some pretty compromising positions before as well."

"Truly?" Alexa squeaked out hopefully.

"So has Nym."

A knock sounded at the door. Serenity answered it before Theyn or Alexa could think to. She didn't know why Nym didn't just enter. When she opened the door, Serenity got her answer.

Melchior stood on the other side of the threshold, looking mildly annoyed. He clipped out, "I would expect, in the future, Serenity, to find you in your rooms if you wish to hold council with me so I do not find myself having to hunt for you."

Serenity returned his cold stare with one of her own. Her tone matched his when she said, "Since I thought you would put off our conference until later in the day, I did not feel the need to seclude myself in my rooms." She looked past his shoulder to Nym and the others. Lorcan sidled up to her and bumped his head against her leg. She smiled down at him, giving his head a pat. To Nym, she said, "I shall meet you at the stables." To Melchior, she said, "Do you wish to carry out our discussion in the hall or would you like to speak in private?"

Melchior had turned to look behind him when Serenity looked over his shoulder. None of her Hell Hounds greeted him. Truth be told, they looked upset he was there. It was on the tip of his tongue to send them all to the dungeons to be punished for their obvious lack of respect. He settled on glaring at Chigaru. Nothing would be gained if he showed his anger at their treatment of him.

He stepped back to let Serenity leave the room. Chigaru returned his look with a blank stare. Though he didn't turn from Chigaru, Melchior said to Serenity, "We shall speak in my study."

As they walked away, Alexa called out, "I shall prepare your riding clothes, your... uh... Serenity."

Serenity smiled at the woman then looked at Melchior. He knew his annoyance was plain on his face but could do nothing about it. She asked, "You have a problem with my maid using my given name without a title, my king?"

"None." He led the way to his study. Ten paces behind them, his advisors followed but he ignored them. "I do have a problem with you leaving the palace without my permission."

"I wasn't aware I needed your permission."

Melchior held the door to his study for Serenity to precede him. He slammed it shut against the intrusion of his advisors. This was personal, not a matter of court.

He said, "You are in danger outside of the palace, Serenity. I thought your past experiences would have made that abundantly clear."

"The Hell Hounds will be with me," she said in a dismissive tone. "Not to mention, my past experiences have proven that I am in constant danger whether inside the palace or outside of it." She sat in a seat nearest the windows.

Melchior's study overlooked a beautiful garden. Serenity would have to make a point of visiting it. She didn't have to worry about matters of state or anything else. Her lack of responsibilities demanded she adopt a hobby.

When she was younger and back in Cheslav, her studies had occupied her time. Now, her studies were finished and all for naught. No, a hobby wasn't just a happy notion, it was a requisite for her continued sanity.

Speaking of losing her mind...

"You have not given me your answer about my lover," she blurted out.

"You forget, Serenity, I said no," Melchior replied smugly.

"You said no because, as a queen, I shouldn't use the contraceptives of the common people. Propriety is already lost on me, Melchior. I dance like the court entertainers, I sleep with my bodyguards on the floor, and I ignore nobility to engage in conversation with servants. What is one more transgression? No one cares but you."

She got up and moved so she stood before him. "I would prefer to occupy your bed as is my right and duty, my husband," she whispered as she reached out to touch him.

He backed away from her.

She clenched her fist between them. "It is unfair for you to have release when I cannot. I will not remain celibate while you wait for me to die. You ask too much." She glared at him as she added quietly, "If you wanted to avoid this topic, you should have never touched me. No one needed proof of my virginity if there was never a chance of children. I could have remained in my ignorance. But, now... now I wish to take a lover."

"No." He grabbed her arm and hauled her up against his chest. "I will not have this discussion again, Serenity. You will take no lover. After this moment it will be considered treason if you do."

She jerked her arm free of his grasp and was surprised he let her go. She hadn't wanted him to release her. It was the first time he'd touched her since their night together. Even if it was to grab her, the contact was welcome.

"It would be ever so convenient if I was put to death for treason, wouldn't it?" She turned from him to leave. Her hand was on the knob when Melchior's voice stopped her.

"There is a ball in your honor, tonight. You *will* be there."

Serenity turned back, ready to tell him just what she thought of him and this entire situation. What stopped her was her mother. Rhiannon had raised her better. Serenity wasn't the rebellious type. She had accepted her lot in life up until this moment and that shouldn't—and wouldn't—change because her husband had introduced her to the carnal side of life.

Just thinking it made her inner calm snap back into place. Slowly her regular smile returned without having to be forced. This was her life, only the location had changed. If the bhresyas awaited her death, then she would live as long as she could to spite them. She would live happily just as she had before.

Serenity dropped a curtsy to Melchior. "As you wish, Your Majesty," she said in quiet submission. It surprised her to realize she meant it. She meant her subservience and she meant her show of respect. Melchior was her king before he was her husband, and she had to start acting like it. She didn't rise from her curtsy and she wouldn't until he dismissed her.

Silence stretched between them. Serenity wanted to look up and see if Melchior's expression would betray his thoughts, but she didn't move.

"Leave, Serenity."

She straightened and smiled in his direction but her gaze didn't quite reach his face. "Good day to you, Your Majesty." She left the room.

Lorcan whined at her when she passed him and she smiled down at him. "Let us forget this sadness, Lorcan. There is a countryside to run through... you and Ines."

He yipped at her.

With Alexa's help, she changed quickly and they were off. Serenity, Chigaru, and Nym ran their lysidis until they were tired. Serenity called a halt at the top of a hill that overlooked the valley village below. Chigaru set up the picnic lunch Alexa had packed for them.

Serenity laughed at Lorcan when he collapsed onto the blanket and promptly went to sleep. She scratched him and gave him a few thumping pats to his side. "Did I tire you, my love?"

He rolled his eyes at her before he returned to slumber. Lorcan wasn't the only one who was tired. Ines lay next to her fellows under the shade of a tree, looking equally exhausted.

Nym said, "Ines and the others have never run so far or for so long in years." She looked out over the land to the palace. It resembled a dollhouse in the distance. Worry entered Nym's voice when she added, "Though I don't think it wise to be so far away from the palace."

"He said no and it would be treason from this point on to consider it," Serenity said quietly. She looked up to Chigaru and mouthed an apology. He brought her hand to his lips and she stroked his cheek. "I am not evil enough to tie you to me, Chigaru, if we cannot..." She looked away from him and retrieved her hand. "You should find a companion."

Chigaru said in a quiet voice, husky from lack of use, "You are the only one in my heart, Serenity. I stay by you even if our relationship is not physical. You shall not suffer alone."

Nym stared at him with her mouth open. "You spoke, Chigaru," she said finally. "In front of me."

Chigaru smiled at her.

Serenity said, "He needed a witness, Nym. You heard me relate Melchior's final decision and Chigaru's answer to it. If Melchior asks, then you can answer." She put her hand on Nym's knee. "I don't wish to put you in the middle—"

"I will be wherever you wish to put me, my sweet girl," Nym said.

Serenity smiled at them both with genuine love. Truer friends a person could never have.

CHAPTER TWELVE

IT WAS NEARLY SUNSET WHEN THEY RETURNED. Melchior was not happy about that. He pulled Serenity into his study to tell her so.

"You were out too long. You left half your guard here in the palace, which was reckless. I will not have you killed and we have not been married even a week."

"You insult my guards, Your Majesty. I was perfectly safe with Nym and Chigaru. Not to mention, I had Lorcan with me." Too late Serenity realized her tone could be construed as defiant. She softened her voice and said, "If it will alleviate your worry, my king, I shall take Haige with me next time."

"And what of Theyn?"

"Theyn is Alexa's guard now. I will not have my maid slain in order to get to me."

Melchior studied her for a long moment. "It would be so much simpler to forbid you from leaving the palace grounds," he stated in an off-hand voice.

Serenity couldn't stop herself from growling. His intention was to make her go insane by keeping her locked up in the palace. In Cheslav, she didn't have time to think about leaving the palace for anything. This was Nexeu and she had tasted freedom. She didn't want it taken away.

This seemed to be Melchior's idea of fun—introduce her to a new pleasure only to forbid her from doing it. She ducked her head to hide her hurt at this new development. She forced herself to utter, "If that is what you wish, my king."

"You give in so quickly, little Serenity. Where are your arguments and persistence?"

His endearment made her shiver. It was said in the same tone and the same way as the night of their first and only time together. She didn't want to be reminded of such things and she was only a few feet from him. Their physical relationship was over. The sooner she accepted that, the sooner she would stop hurting inside.

Serenity answered in a meek tone, "I am whatever you command me to be."

"Get out," he said in a deathly quiet voice.

Serenity curtsied and left.

৵৽৹

The brightly dressed bhresya nobles lightened Serenity's mood. They danced a simple folk dance and Serenity ached to join them. It was a beautiful dance and

Theyn had taught her the steps. She sat forward on her throne as though to get up, but she didn't.

This ball may be in her honor but no one acknowledged her, especially not Melchior. Haige and Nym stood behind her throne dressed in their finery, while Chigaru stood at the doors of the ballroom. Serenity had urged them to mingle and have fun in her place, but they had staunchly refused to leave her side. After half an hour of arguing, she had given up and thanked them for keeping her company.

In spite of herself, Serenity's eyes went to Melchior. He danced with Keran and they were beautiful together. Keran's shade of pink made her look all the more delicate against Melchior's dark blue. Serenity looked down at her dark blue ball gown, made to match Melchior—like all of her wardrobe. She felt like a fool.

She decided to have the palace seamstresses start a new wardrobe for her. Everyone knew she belonged to Melchior. There was no need to proclaim it with her clothing.

As though he could hear her thinking about him, Melchior looked at her. Serenity held his gaze, not knowing why he even bothered to look at her. Did he want to make sure she hadn't left, so as to endure the torture of watching but not being allowed to participate?

No one physically held her to her throne and Melchior hadn't commanded she stay. No one cared about her presence and Serenity didn't want to descend into the crowd only to be shunned. She stayed put.

Melchior had to break eye contact with Serenity when he lifted his arm and spun Keran. The movement brought Serenity's attention back to the female. She didn't miss Keran's smug look. Serenity hated her because Keran had something Serenity never could have again.

She looked at Chigaru, who watched her, and she smiled for his sake. The jovial atmosphere made her happy, but she knew it only as a spectator, not a participant. An all too familiar feeling she had hoped to leave in Cheslav.

After two hours, boredom crept over her. A few of the nobles had deemed her worthy of conversation at the ball in her honor, but the chats hadn't lasted long.

She sighed.

Nym leaned forward and said, "King Melchior is occupied with his advisors." She gestured to the side of the room where Melchior stood.

Serenity followed Nym's gaze. Melchior stood with his back to her and looked to be in a deep conversation with his advisors over something important. He made offhand gestures every once in a while. The advisors seemed to adamantly refuse whatever it was Melchior proposed.

Serenity didn't care what the conversation was about. It took his attention off her. She rose from her throne and knew instant disappointment. No one noticed.

The music didn't stop and no one paused to bow to her as they should. She held her head high and descended from the throne dais and exited. She half expected Melchior to follow and demand her return, but he didn't.

She hadn't allowed the maids to clean up the bed from the night before. She, Alexa, and the Hell Hounds used it this night, too.

Alexa was less uptight but she remained nervous. That was due mostly to Lorcan's presence. He had wedged himself between Alexa and Serenity. Every time

Lorcan shifted, Alexa squeaked in fear.

Serenity laughed at how close Alexa had gotten to Theyn in order to get away from Lorcan. Theyn didn't seem to mind in the least.

⁂

"Such as you are suggesting would not set well with the bhresya people, my king."

Melchior glared at his advisor. The male, mouthpiece of the five advisors who surrounded him, seemed to delight in thwarting Melchior's every proposal. "Is that your advice then?"

"Nexeu is still growing used to the peace, as are our human neighbors. Your request would only incite needless turmoil and possibly renew the violence you have sought to extinguish."

"It's not extinguished. I receive daily reports of skirmishes and small attacks. My warriors report only deaths but no answers as to the identity of those who inflicted them."

"All the more reason to refrain, Your Majesty. The treaty is still new and you only married your new queen three days ago."

"I need an heir—or the promise of one." He glanced at the crowd. His gaze immediately went to Keran, but he looked away before their eyes could meet.

"It is not done. You have time, my king, to choose a more worthy choice to bear Nexeu's future ruler. There is no need to rush into a hasty choice when it is obvious to one and all you regret the last. Give the people time to realize the war is truly at an end before indulging this plan."

"The war isn't over, but delayed until the humans break confidence with us again."

The advisor sighed heavily and bowed his head. "Your words show your lack of trust in the humans and yet you ask us to trust them, to trust *her*."

Mention of Serenity, even in a roundabout way, immediately moved Melchior's gaze to her throne. He only meant to glance at her then return to his conversation.

She wasn't there.

He turned and scanned the ballroom, then again when he didn't see her. Serenity's Hell Hounds were gone as well. Knowing they wouldn't abandon her, Melchior realized she had left the proceedings.

The music hadn't stopped and the dancers hadn't paused to pay her homage as she left the room. Such as that would have warned him of her departure so he could stop it. Once more, he looked around the room, but Serenity was gone.

Melchior left his advisors and went to the ballroom doors. Both guards bowed to him. "When did my queen leave?"

"She is gone, Your Majesty?" one guard asked.

The other said quickly, "We had not noticed her departure, my king."

"There is only one way in or out of the ballroom and it is through this doorway. Are you telling me you abandoned your posts?"

"We have not moved this entire night."

"Then you are both incompetent!"

Both males went to one knee with their heads bowed.

Melchior reined in his anger as best he could. Serenity's short stature might attribute to the guards overlooking her, but her Hell Hounds would have left with her. The males shouldn't have missed Haige and Chigaru.

"I shall deal with you both in the morning. Pray I'm in a better mood than I am now or your punishment will be severe," Melchior said then stalked away.

He found himself repeating his mistake of that morning. He opened Serenity's door and found her fast asleep in her puppy pile again. Lorcan lifted his head and looked at him while Chigaru only opened his eyes.

Melchior was about to say something when a pink hand caressed his left horn. Keran stood behind him. "What are you doing here?" he whispered.

Keran walked across the hall and leaned against his door. She purred, "Leave the queen to her guards and be with me, Melchior." She unclasped the brooch at the front of her dress. The entire ensemble dropped to the floor and pooled at her feet. She stepped out of it and entered his room, leaving the door open for him to follow.

He looked back into Serenity's room then stiffened. She stared at him.

Nym pushed Serenity's head back down onto Chigaru's stomach. She mumbled, "None of your concern. Go back to sleep, child." Serenity settled herself and closed her eyes. Nym stole her arm around Serenity's waist, pulling her in close, then said a little louder, "Keran is waiting for you, King Melchior. Goodnight."

Melchior slammed the door and stalked over to his rooms. He slammed his door, as well. Keran was sprawled across his bed, stroking her breasts and stomach. She smiled at him.

Normally, she would make his hands ache to be all over her. Not tonight. Melchior felt nothing in the face of her naked glory.

"Get out," he commanded quietly.

His expression left no room for argument, but Keran still tried to garner his interest. She slinked off the bed and rubbed her body against his arm. Pushing the flaps of his iridescent vest aside, she stroked her hands over his belly.

Melchior grabbed her arm and threw her towards the door. "Now."

Keran snatched up her dress on her way out of the room. Melchior didn't watch her go, though her attitude reinforced what his advisors had told him. Rushing his decision to beget a legitimate heir would cause more problems than it solved.

He hadn't given his people proper time to grow used to Serenity. He hadn't given her proper time to grow used to Nexeu. In a few months time, he would broach the subject again with Serenity at his side. She needed to know what he planned as the decision would affect her—for good or ill, he wasn't sure.

Her reactions were a mystery to him, thus making them hard to predict.

CHAPTER THIRTEEN

"I NEVER THOUGHT I WOULD UTTER THE WORDS..." Serenity started.

Nym gave her a questioning look.

"I miss my lessons. I don't know what to do anymore." She looked around at the many servants and nobles who passed them. A few of the servants nodded to her but the nobles didn't acknowledge her. She didn't bother getting upset.

She wasn't truly a queen. Last night's ball proved that. The disregard of those around her made Serenity wonder if she needed to be guarded anymore. She was married and had served her purpose. The treaty was struck. She didn't even think General Guthr and General Tiann would seek her out again. No one hunted them and, so long as they stayed in hiding, they could lead fairly normal lives.

The time when Serenity needed to be guarded day and night was over. But, she didn't voice this opinion to Nym. The female would surely disagree with her.

She said instead, "I'm at a loss, Nym."

"We could go for a ride."

"We could, but we did that yesterday. I dare say that Ines has had her fill of running for the next week."

"You haven't played with Lorcan in a while."

Serenity shook her head in answer. "Lorcan has discovered other thondis. I won't take him from his comrades as I will see him tonight."

"Would you like to watch Haige and Chigaru spar? They should be on the practice field."

"I really have nothing to do all day." She stopped in front of a painting. It featured a barely clad lavender bhresya female who danced in a field of yellow flowers. "Why did I never learn to paint or play an instrument or sew?"

Her question made her look down at her clothing. She wore a red dress with long yellow sleeves. The hem of the dress, which brushed her ankles, was trimmed in yellow, as was the scoop-necked collar. It was then that she remembered her decision from the night before.

Nym said, "You didn't have time to indulge in such pastimes."

"I have just remembered that I did want to do something today, my aunt. Hopefully, it will take the whole day," Serenity said, her mood lifting in the face of this new chore.

"What is that?"

"I want a new wardrobe. It's silly to continue wearing red, yellow and blue all the time."

"I agree," Nym said, her voice taking on a cold quality.

Serenity sensed Nym wished to say more but didn't and she was thankful for that. Her Hell Hounds were angry on her behalf and she loved them for it, but anger would change nothing.

Nym indicated a hallway to the left. "This way, Serenity. I think it's time you were introduced to the Ladies of the Circle."

"Ladies of the Circle?"

"The seamstresses of the royal family. Only the best are allowed to serve in the circle. Within the circle, three are chosen as the most gifted. Those three hold the titles of Duchess of the Circle, Marchioness of the Circle and Countess of the Circle, respectively.

"Joining the Ladies of the Circle is one way an untitled individual can become part of the peerage. Once a female gains a title from the circle, she does not lose it if another comes along who deserves the title more."

"You've never mentioned the Ladies of the Circle before, Nym."

"Of all that you wanted and needed to learn, it was the least important until now."

They arrived at a set of double doors that had a giant golden circle with silver flowers intertwined around it for a handle. Nym knocked once then pulled the doors open. She said in a loud, clear voice, "Queen Serenity wishes to address the Ladies of the Circle."

Serenity entered the room. There were ten females and one male all seated in a circle at a round table. On the table were various fabrics and threads and sewing supplies.

A soft gray bhresya female stood and curtsied, the others followed her example. "Welcome to the circle, Queen Serenity. I am Setta, the Duchess of the Circle." She gestured to the female on her right and introduced, "This is Lady Volriel, the Marchioness of the Circle, and this—" she gestured to the woman on her left "—is Lady Uleoma, the Countess of the Circle." Setta straightened from her curtsy and finished, "We are here to serve you."

"Thank you, my lady." She glanced over her shoulder at Nym. The female closed the doors and stood off to the side. Serenity turned back to face the occupants of the table. "You look busy. I don't mean to bother you."

"You are never a bother to us, Your Majesty. The Circle exists to serve the royal family," Lady Setta said. "What is it you wish of us?"

"A new wardrobe. I wish to change my color scheme."

"Whatever for, Your Majesty?" asked one of the other females. "It is the old tradition to wear the colors of your husband."

The single male at the table said, "She is human, not bhresya, Mistress Errk. Though, my great-grandmother does not wear her husband's colors. It is foolish to insist Queen Serenity follow a tradition we ourselves do not keep."

Another female said, "Neither do you wear your husband's colors, Mistress Errk. Master Olander is correct to point out the wrongness of keeping the queen in her current attire when you do not practice such."

"My point is made," Olander said. "Thank you, Lady Lihah." He looked down at his rust colored shirt and smiled to himself. "It is coincidence only that I wear my husband's color this day."

"Husband?" Serenity asked in surprise. "You are wed to another male?"

Everyone at the table chuckled.

Setta said, "As is plain to see, Queen Serenity, Master Olander is a lovely shade of powder blue. Such a color is more often seen on females than it is on males. Master Olander—and others like him—is part of a minority amongst bhresyas because he has the coloring of a female. There are females born with the coloring of males, as well.

"Though it is not always this way, those like Master Olander tend to prefer the company of their own gender. We bhresya do not see those types of pairings as immoral or wrong and allow same gender marriages to occur when such an attraction happens."

"Oh," Serenity whispered, thinking on yet another facet of bhresya life that had escaped her education. She'd never heard of the like in Cheslav. There was no law that forbade a same gender couple from marrying, but there was no law that allowed it either. She would have to talk to her mother about it in the future.

She nodded to Setta and said, "Thank you for your explanation. Though my Hell Hounds taught me much, they couldn't teach me everything."

"Insulting," snapped the bright yellow female seated next to Volriel.

Errk hissed across the table, "Hush."

"It is," the female insisted in a louder voice. She looked over at Serenity and then away. "I don't care if she is offended. That title is insulting and demeaning."

"Mistress Taarite, you will show proper respect to the queen or you will leave my circle," Setta said, glaring at Taarite.

Serenity said, "It's all right, Lady Setta. I understand and know that many find my choice of title for my personal guards to be... inappropriate."

"Then change it if you know this," Taarite said.

Setta was about to yell at the female again, but Serenity held up her hand for Setta's silence. She moved closer to the table, which put her across from Taarite. "To call my guards by any other title than Hell Hound would be to dishonor them. It is an insult they wear as a testament for the fear they instill in the humans of the other kingdoms."

Olander grinned at her words. He set aside his sewing and leaned forward. "I hear a story there, Queen Serenity. Tell it to us, please. I love a good story."

Nym walked forward with a chair. She placed it behind Serenity then went back to her post at the door.

Serenity sat, straightened her skirts and tried to think of a good place to start her story. She glanced back at Nym and asked, "How old was I, my aunt?"

"Twelve, Serenity," Nym replied. "It was the day of your birthday."

"Ah."

"Aunt?" Lihah asked.

Several of the others told her to be quiet.

Serenity laughed and made a mental note to tell the ladies of her Hell Hounds' other titles. She said, "Seven years ago, the largest and most well thought out assassination attempt on my life was made. Ten human males had planned an elaborate scheme to get me out of the palace and kill me—on my birthday, of all days."

"It almost worked," Nym added.

"True, true. It would have worked if they had known I had another set of guards besides my Hell Hounds—human guards. My mother was sure my Hell Hounds were more than adequate protection, but she liked to err on the side of caution.

"A spell was used to put any with bhresya blood to sleep. With my Hell Hounds and Lorcan—my pet thondi—out of the way, there was no one to stop those who would see me dead. Or, so they thought. My human guards subdued and captured all except one of the men."

"Were you frightened, Queen Serenity?" Errk asked.

"Very. It was the first time I was ever taken from the palace. All other times my assassins were killed before they ever reached me. I didn't find out about them until I saw the bodies. I was also wounded on that day. Nothing a mage couldn't heal and it didn't leave a scar, but it did scare me badly."

"As it should," Setta said. "So much fuss over a treaty. You would think the humans would welcome peace."

"Not when war is so much more profitable," Nym replied. "Though our kind is just as guilty."

A few of the females mumbled their agreement to that statement.

Serenity continued, "The one man to escape used magic, thus ensuring his safe retreat." She didn't want to get off topic with the many bhresyas who had come to kill her. Her current story had a purpose.

"To his detriment," Nym whispered, then smiled at those who glanced her way.

"Nym used the residual effects left over from the magic and tracked the user to his home in Lev. It was our misfortune the culprit was a favored noble of the king *and* of the queen." She stopped when no one looked surprised at this. "Do you know of the animosity between the rulers of Lev?"

"We don't concern ourselves with the inner workings of the human kingdoms," Uleoma said. She was the only one who continued sewing. Her attention stayed on her project and she didn't seem too interested in the conversation.

"Then of course, I should explain," Serenity said. "Simply put, the king and queen of Lev hate each other. They were a political marriage. After the birth of their one and only child, the king and queen's constant fighting almost sank Lev into a civil war. Finally, they separated. They reside in two palaces that are located on opposite ends of the country from one another."

Taarite snorted and said, "That sounds like my parents. They divorced, however."

"The king and queen of Lev aren't allowed such a luxury. They remain married but their kingdom is split and the nobles must choose sides. There are only a few who are able to court both successfully. My would-be assassin was one of those.

"So, when my mother, Queen Rhiannon, asked that the favored noble be extradited to Cheslav so he could face execution for his crimes, the king *and* queen both refused. It was the first time in twenty years the king and queen agreed on anything. As much as it angered my mother, she could do nothing without chancing a war."

Olander offered, "She should have contacted King Melchior."

The females agreed.

Serenity grinned at his words and she sat forward. The others then sat forward to hear what she would say. In a secretive whisper, she said, "I did—in a manner of speaking." She sat back. "Unbeknownst to my mother, I contacted both the king and queen of Lev and told them if they did not surrender the noble and all those who conspired with him to have me killed, then I would contact King Melchior and let him deal with the situation.

"They were both more than happy to turn the noble over to us. After a brief interrogation, the noble revealed those who had helped him concoct the drug that put my Hell Hounds to sleep. It was our luck those responsible resided in Cheslav, because that was the first time I sent out my Hell Hounds."

Nym interrupted, "That was the first time we were allowed out of the palace and trusted to return on our own, as well. By then, we had resided with Serenity for almost eight years. We didn't want to be anywhere else but with her."

"How romantic," Lihah gushed with a sigh.

Serenity said, "Any and all who had dealings with the assassins and the plot on my life were killed by my order. I didn't want prisoners. I wanted examples." Her look went a little dark. "My mother thought it was harsh, but didn't gainsay me. The people of Cheslav started stories about me. They called me a bloodthirsty demon with a host of hell hounds at my beck and call."

"When Serenity looses the hounds of hell, blood will surely flow," Nym quoted.

"I actually got sick of people saying that. I became insulted on behalf of my guards. It was my right to exact vengeance against those who would see me dead and that's what I did. The more upset and hurt I became, the more people used the phrase to taunt me.

"One day, a few weeks later, another attempt on my life was made. I sent out Nym and the others again. I said to them 'go my hell hounds and carry my vengeance with you.' It was said as a childish joke because I knew more insults would come my way after news spread of the latest deaths at the hands of my bhresya guards. I didn't think anyone had heard me."

"Someone did," Taarite said.

"One of my maids. She reported my words to the entire palace. Suddenly, I really was a demon from the pit disguised as a human sent to corrupt them all, or some other such nonsense. The stories they made up were too silly." There was laughter in her voice as she remembered some of the stories that were relayed back to her. "At first I was angry and I expected Nym and the others to be angry, as well. They merely laughed. Theyn, the joker of my guards, suggested embracing the insult since none of us would ever live it down. From that day forward, my bhresya guards were known as Hell Hounds."

Setta finished, "And, you were known as a demon."

"Demon princess," Nym corrected.

Olander said, "Now, she is a demon queen." He laughed. "Good story, Your Majesty, and well told."

The others agreed with him.

Taarite bowed her head and said, "Forgive me, Queen Serenity. I didn't realize."

"There is no way you could have known," Serenity said. "Bhresyas don't concern themselves with human matters, after all."

She met Uleoma's gaze when the female looked at her. Uleoma's lips quirked as she tried to repress a smile. She nodded to Serenity then went back to her work.

Setta rose from her chair and held out her hands to Serenity. "Well, let us have a look at you, Your Majesty. If you would have a change, we should choose a color that suits you." She helped Serenity stand.

"I don't understand how you humans can function in such clothing," Olander said, fingering Serenity's long sleeves. "Our females have more freedom of movement in their clothing."

Serenity said, "I don't think I would ever feel comfortable wearing so little. If I was raised to it, then I probably wouldn't mind. Queen Rhiannon strictly forbade me from even entertaining the idea."

She looked down at her cotehardie gown. The neckline dipped and showed the swell of her breasts while the rest of the dress covered her completely. Even the sleeves, which brushed the ground, hid her hands if she lowered her arms.

In contrast, bhresyas wore only enough to soothe propriety, which wasn't much. The males wore loincloths with a long vest and the females wore simple skirts and a half shirt to cover their breasts. Some females enjoyed wearing the same vests as the males, but they used ribbons or thin leather strips as a belt to keep the fabric in place.

Though she tried to embrace everything about the bhresya lifestyle, Serenity couldn't conform to their clothing. She had felt naked and exposed. She hoped the Ladies of the Circle wouldn't be put out having to make full dresses.

Setta bent over Serenity's hands and peered at her skin. She turned Serenity's hand this way and that. "Is it true that all Cheslavians are this color of brown, my queen?"

"Not all. Those who reside in the western half of Cheslav tend to be lighter. More tan than brown."

"How boring," Errk said. "You humans only come in shades of brown. I'm glad we bhresyas are more varied."

"You make it sound like she has a choice in the matter," Olander said.

Volriel clapped her hands as she came around to the table and joined Setta in front of Serenity. She said in a chipper voice, "You should choose the color you wish to be, my queen." She clapped her hands more. "Oh, I like this idea. We bhresyas come in a variety of colors but it means we are limited as to what colors we can wear. Your shade of brown would match so many different colors."

"You're right," Errk said, stepping forward. "I hadn't thought of that. We can finally switch from iridescent to more vibrant colors."

Iridescent was the bhresya color of mourning. It signified all colors instead of simply one. It was funny to note while humans saw iridescent as a thing of beauty, bhresyas only viewed it as a symbol of death.

Curiosity made Serenity ask, "Does King Melchior always wear iridescent?"

"Unfortunately," Olander said then blew out an annoyed breath. He picked up the piece of iridescent cloth in front of him and stared at it with distaste. "Our king doesn't want his subjects to think he had a particular female whom he favored over any other, so he has continued wearing the color of mourning."

"He used to wear yellow to match Queen Asha and green to match his son," Taarite said.

"And—"

"Enough," Setta snapped. "Our queen doesn't want to hear about her husband's departed family."

"Actually, Lady Setta, I know very little about King Melchior's family," Serenity said. "I wouldn't mind learning more about them."

"If you want to learn more about Melchior's murdered family then you should have the courage to ask him yourself, not hide behind the palace gossips," challenged a female voice from the doorway.

Setta looked over Serenity's head and her expression turned hard.

Serenity faced the doorway.

Keran warned, "Be careful where you point that look, Lady Setta, or else I will have to inform Melchior of your disrespect. I have as much right to be here as she—" Keran pointed at Serenity "—does. I am Melchior's favorite, after all."

Serenity got the distinct impression Keran didn't mean Melchior's favorite concubine. She also noticed the way Keran dropped Melchior's title. Her form of address was completely familiar. Not even Serenity addressed him without his title, not in public.

"What did you wish of us, *Mistress* Keran?" Setta asked through her teeth.

"It doesn't matter what she wishes," Serenity said before Keran could speak. She stood to her full height and faced Keran. The female may have Melchior, but there was something she didn't have—power. "I am queen, and queens come before lemans, Keran. The Ladies of the Circle will address me and when I am finished with them, I will *think* about allowing you to engage their services."

Keran yelled, "As Melchior's favorite, it is my *right* to use the Ladies of the Circle."

"No, it's a privilege—one that I have just revoked. Leave, Keran."

"You cannot bar me."

"I already have."

"Melchior will hear of this and he *will* make you regret your words," Keran said. She turned and stormed out of the room.

"Bitch," Uleoma snapped.

Serenity looked at Uleoma. As before, Uleoma continued working while the others had stopped.

"I hate that female. It's about time someone put her in her place. Thank you, my queen." She paused in her work and met Serenity's gaze.

"You're very welcome. I'll admit that made me feel better."

Setta reached out and took both of Serenity's hands again. She held them away from Serenity's sides as she looked at her. "I think I know what colors you should wear, my queen. I'm sure you'll be the talk of the entire palace once we are through with you." She released Serenity and turned to the table.

All present waited eagerly for Setta's plan.

CHAPTER FOURTEEN

KERAN SCREAMED AT MELCHIOR, "She disrespected me in front of the entirety of the Ladies of the Circle."

"And?" Melchior asked. He flipped aside the paper in front of him and looked at the one behind it. He'd allowed Keran to storm into his study and interrupt a conference with his advisors because he thought something important had happened to her. When she did nothing but complain about Serenity, his concern had disappeared. Annoyance quickly took its place.

"What do you mean, Melchior? You must go and tell the Ladies of the Circle Serenity does not have the authority to—"

"Yes, she does." He looked up and met Keran's gaze. "Serenity is queen of Nexeu and you *will* address her as such. She has told the Ladies of the Circle not to serve you and they won't."

"You are king!"

Melchior stood, rounded the desk and stood in front of Keran. He grabbed her arm when she backed away and she looked up at him with wide eyes. "Yes, I am king. I have more important things to do than worry about your personal dramas. You have enough clothing when, as my concubine, you need none of it." He opened the study door and propelled her through it by her arm. "Worry about how you will please me tonight—*if* I call you—rather than your petty jealousy of Queen Serenity."

He slammed the door in her face before she could say more. Too late he remembered his advisors waited outside. Melchior rubbed his hand down his face and took a few calming breaths. Keran's infantile complaints were the last thing he needed.

His warriors reported another attack but no news of the perpetrator and the witnesses were dead. Melchior knew the brutality of the killings pointed to bhresya assailants rather than human. He was thankful for that yet confused at the same time.

None of the victims had anything in common and the locations of the killings followed no pattern. His mages discerned no trail, as though the attackers vanished—possibly an erasure spell, though magic such as that was old and nearly forgotten amongst the bhresya. Its use now proved someone still knew how to cast it.

For the safety of his people, he needed to find that person and execute them. The killings would end and he could focus on other matters, namely Serenity.

He opened the door. Keran stood staring at it with a shocked expression on her face. He ignored her and barked at his advisors, "Get in here."

The advisors filed quickly into the room and closed the door after them.

∾∾

Seclusion with his advisors for a full day and most of the night did nothing to solve the mystery of his slain subjects. Sunlight spilling through the windows of his study made him call a recess. All the males were tired, as was he.

He didn't normally sleep during the day, but would make an exception in this case. The matters of court could keep for one day. He stepped out of his study and then stopped.

"Serenity?" he asked with an edge of concern to his voice.

His little wife had her dress bunched in her hands thus allowing her to run faster through the corridor. More than one of the occupants of the hallway stopped and moved out of her way, watching her run past. Melchior purposefully stepped into her path.

She slid to a halt and dropped her blue dress only to pick it up again so she could curtsy properly. "Good morning to you, King Melchior."

"What are you running from?" He looked behind her but didn't see from what or from whom she fled. His gaze returned to her for an explanation.

"Not from, Your Majesty, after," Serenity said. She straightened and dropped her hold on her dress. "I am hunting Lorcan."

"Surely one of the others can find him for you, Serenity. There is no need for you to run through the halls of the palace."

She laughed, then she covered her mouth. "Forgive me, but you mistake my intent. If I let one of my guards find him, that would defeat the purpose of the game." She laughed more.

Melchior found he liked the sound. His lips twitched on a smile he tried hard to repress. To cover the movement, he cleared his throat. "What game?"

"Lorcan and I have played it since I was a child. He hides and I track him. Lorcan always leaves little clues for me to follow. He is very smart." She looked around then went past him and knelt near the door of his study. "I was right. He did come this way," she said with triumph.

"That is Lorcan's," Melchior said. He stood over her and looked at the tiny puddle that had caught Serenity's interest. It had several tiny, reddish-brown scales in it and the scent of Lorcan's saliva. The hound had to have scraped the scales off with his teeth and then spat it in that particular spot.

Serenity straightened and brushed off her dress. "Thank you, Your Majesty. I do not need help with this particular game. I am quite good at it." She looked up at Melchior, then her gaze went beyond him and she smiled.

Melchior felt a moment of apprehension. He knew what Serenity's gaze meant but couldn't believe it had happened again.

"You will lose your prey if you tarry in one spot for too long, Serenity. I have continually told you tracking is most effective when the trail is fresh," said Haige over Melchior's shoulder.

"I haven't lost this game in quite some years, my teacher," Serenity said. She took

Haige's hand and he ushered her past Melchior, who turned to keep her in his sights.

"You haven't lost in some time because you knew the palace of Cheslav better than most. This is the palace of Nexeu. New terrain deserves respect and caution," Haige said. He brought her hand up to his lips. The kiss finished, he released her then turned his gaze to Melchior. "Good morning to you, King Melchior. Does the day find you well?"

Melchior had gotten sick of the Hell Hounds' habit of sneaking up on him. He never heard them or sensed their presence and he knew they wanted it that way. It was their way of showing Melchior his vulnerability.

As much as Melchior wanted to call Haige on his blatant disrespect, the transgression would have to slide. He knew Serenity's guards didn't approve of his treatment of her over the past few days and they showed that disapproval in the only way left to them.

"I'm well," Melchior said.

Haige nodded then turned his attention to Serenity. "Continue, child. You are in danger of losing for the first time in four years."

Serenity nodded to Haige then looked at Melchior. "If you will excuse me, Your Majesty—"

"Have fun," Melchior said.

"I plan to." Serenity picked up her dress again and ran down the hall.

Both men watched her run.

Haige said, "She will never be as fast as a bhresya female. Nor will she be able to use her human nose for tracking Lorcan properly. Despite all of that, she is better at this game than I thought her capable." He looked away from Serenity's retreating back. "For all that Serenity lacks in our eyes, she makes up for it many times over in her own way."

"Does your statement have some purpose, Hell Hound Haige?" Melchior asked. He didn't need the man schooling him. He was not his wife.

"Of course it does, King Melchior." He nodded and started away.

"Hold, Haige. Not even my queen leaves my presence without permission first. I expect the same of her guards."

"As you wish, of course, King Melchior." Haige turned back and faced Melchior with a cold look. "Though every moment you delay me is one more moment Queen Serenity is left unguarded. It would be unfortunate if she became hurt or lost because I was not nearby to render her aid."

"My tolerance of the Hell Hounds' disrespect will only extend but so far," Melchior said through his teeth.

"I'm sure that's not true." He grinned. "We Hell Hounds are Serenity's only guards. She wishes for no others and needs no others so long as we are here, and we are irreplaceable in her eyes. Therefore, there is much we can say and do that will be forgiven as any worthwhile punishment would leave us incapable of doing our job properly." He nodded again to Melchior and left.

This time, Melchior didn't stop him. Haige's point was valid and maddeningly true. Melchior couldn't punish Serenity's guards because she needed them whole. They knew that and used it to their advantage. That was an advantage Melchior planned to take away.

CHAPTER FIFTEEN

"**Q**UEEN SERENITY, King Melchior wishes your presence in his study," said the maid who approached Serenity and the Hell Hounds.

Nym took the dagger Serenity held and placed it with the others. "We will continue your lessons after your meeting."

"There really is no point. I have no aim," Serenity said. "Queen Rhiannon didn't see a need for me to learn how to fight as Alric did."

"Neither did you have time to learn, Serenity," Haige said. "You had other studies to attend. But, don't worry. We will make up for lost time after your meeting with King Melchior."

Serenity smiled at Haige's words and led the way off the training field. She thanked all the warriors as she passed them. Chigaru refused to let them continue their practice so long as Serenity was on the field. He didn't want any "accidents" to occur. The only way to ensure a mishap wouldn't happen was to halt the warriors' practice altogether.

Once she was off the field, Serenity turned back and said, "I'm sorry for the interruption of your training."

There was no answer to her words and she only saw annoyance. She said to Chigaru, "We need to find another place to hold my lessons. Your job becomes harder if I make enemies of the entire royal army."

"The point of the training field is to hone the skills of those who use it. You, as queen, have every right to use the field," Haige said.

"There has to be another way to conduct my lessons without disrupting the warriors." She looked at Chigaru for an affirmative, but he shook his head.

Nym said, "We won't chance it, Serenity. Your safety comes first. That is why we agreed to teach you how to defend yourself."

"I shouldn't have asked. I was bored. The Ladies of the Circle no longer require my presence to finish my dresses, and I wanted to do something besides walk around and stare at flowers all day. I almost wish I had learned to weave or make lace or any number of things the Ladies of the Circle do. Perhaps I should learn to do those things instead."

"I will not allow you to quit simply because your first lesson went badly," Haige said.

Serenity smiled at him. Haige knew her all too well. She tried to bow out of her lessons because she perceived her lack of ability shortly after she started. But, Haige wouldn't let her quit.

They arrived at Melchior's study and Chigaru knocked.

One of Melchior's advisors opened the door. Serenity entered the room with the Hell Hounds. There was no point in making them wait outside if the advisors would be present for the conversation.

Melchior said, "Good day to you, Queen Serenity."

Serenity curtseyed to Melchior. "And to you, Your Majesty. I received your message. You wished to speak to me?"

"I was told you stopped all training on the practice field."

"My Hell Hounds are teaching me to throw a dagger. A silly endeavor to be sure, as I have no aim, but it passes the time."

"Why do you need to learn that, Queen Serenity?" asked one of the advisors.

"I was curious. My experiences with a dagger are few and far between. I wanted to know what the non-pointed end of the dagger felt like." She smiled. "It's heavier."

"Non-pointed?" the advisor asked.

Nym said, "Serenity refers to the few times she's had a dagger pressed to her throat."

"And her back," Haige said. A movement from Chigaru made him add, "And her chest."

Serenity said in a cheerful voice, "Don't forget the one time I caught a dagger in my arm." She touched her upper left arm. "I didn't feel it at first. It only hurt after Chigaru took it out."

"Your guards were lax in their protection of you," Melchior said.

"Only Mael. I was only ever threatened or hurt when I was alone with Mael. I should have noticed the pattern long before the day of our wedding. I didn't want to believe it of her, though. I thought it was only because Mael wasn't a trained fighter like Chigaru, Nym, and Haige."

"What about Theyn?"

"Theyn trained with Chigaru until he was better. His strength alone made him more than a match for all the humans who attacked me, but he insisted on becoming better in case a bhresya attacked."

"Mael is dead, and Theyn now guards your maid. The ranks of your Hell Hounds need to be replenished, Queen Serenity. That is why I called you here."

"With whom, King Melchior?" Nym asked, glancing at her fellows then back to Melchior.

"There are many fine soldiers in the ranks of the royal guard. Any number of them could act as one of Queen Serenity's elite."

"How many did you plan to add, Your Majesty?" Haige asked. He crossed his arms with a knowing look.

Serenity felt a new current of animosity running between Haige and Melchior. It was more than the normal fair. She wanted to ask but didn't think it wise with so many witnesses. Perhaps Haige had some insight as to why Melchior suddenly felt she needed more guards.

"I had not decided yet," Melchior said.

"Well, we can't have the entire royal guard tripping over themselves protecting me. I'm not that important—not anymore. Since I have lost two, then only two should be added. It's simple enough to hold a ranking competition. The top two fighters should be chosen."

"That's too hasty, Serenity," Nym said.

Haige nodded with an affirmative sound. Chigaru bent and whispered in Serenity's ear. She nodded at his words.

Melchior watched this exchange with annoyance. He couldn't hear what the male said. He was sure no one could, except Serenity. Chigaru's talent for silence was unparalleled, even amongst bhresyas. Melchior was sure Chigaru's talent had made him an excellent assassin.

Serenity relayed, "Chigaru has suggested he test those who wish to act as part of my personal guards. He won't entrust my safety to anyone who cannot match his skills. Or, I should say, come close to matching his skills."

"That's a bit arrogant," one advisor said. "The royal army is comprised of the best. Hell Hound Chigaru's skills probably do not even compare."

"You're right, my lord," Serenity said. "They don't compare. Chigaru is better."

"With all respect to you, Your Majesty, you have only your Hell Hounds on which to base your opinion."

"No actually, I do not. I have seen many bhresyas fight over my few years. All of who came to kill me. Chigaru—with no help from any other or any weapon—killed them all. He never uses a weapon. He doesn't have to."

Melchior rose slowly from his seat, searching Serenity's eyes. She looked serious. He asked in a low voice, "I thought your Hell Hounds were the only bhresyas to attack you, Serenity?"

"No. My Hell Hounds were the only bhresyas I kept. Queen Rhiannon indulged my whim only so far. All those after Mael died."

"How many?"

"You know already, Your Majesty. I'm sure you've seen the collection of horns that grace the wall around my mirror. All belonged to those who came to Cheslav to kill me, except the white horn of the male who attacked me on my first day in Nexeu. Twenty-six in all and their owners are all deceased, except Guthr. The last nine came in rapid succession in the last few months before our wedding day."

Melchior looked at her with unveiled horror. He hadn't realized the extent of her danger.

Serenity gave him a curious look then frowned at the Hell Hounds. "I thought you explained all of this to him the day of our wedding."

"Not every detail, Serenity," Nym said. She bowed her head when Serenity glared at her.

Serenity turned back to Melchior. "I'm sorry, King Melchior. I was given to understand my Hell Hounds imparted this information to you already. I would not have treated the topic so indelicately if I had known you were ignorant of my many attacks at bhresya hands."

Melchior shook his head, trying to clear his thoughts. He schooled his features into his normal mask of calm then said, "I am surprised, but that is no reason for you to apologize, Serenity. Your attacks weren't your fault."

"Twenty-six," whispered one advisor. The other advisors were equally shocked.

Serenity's smile returned. "If it makes you feel better, my lords, the humans wanted me dead much more than the bhresyas did. Nearly seven times that number attacked me over my eighteen years. My mother and I thought the news of my Hell Hounds would deter them, but it didn't. However, human assassins never worried me. If they got past Queen Rhiannon's guards, then they didn't make it past Lorcan."

"Leave us," Melchior said. He tried to remain calm but the more Serenity said, the angrier he became. It was an emotion he had become intimately acquainted with over the last few weeks.

The advisors and the Hell Hounds exited. Once the door was closed, Melchior came around his desk and stood in front of Serenity. She smiled up at him. He couldn't understand how she could smile after what she had said, what she had experienced.

Melchior wanted to lash out at those who had attacked Serenity. She and Rhiannon had robbed him of that right when they refused to contact him.

He asked, "How can you speak of your assassination attempts with such ease and disregard?"

"I am alive and they aren't. It was my duty to stay alive so I could become your bride. If the assassins had succeeded, then the fighting between humans and bhresyas would have continued."

She stepped closer to him. He smelled lust on her skin. The familiar scent had haunted him these many nights. Smelling it again was a blessing and torture all at once.

Serenity took another step forward. Melchior turned from her and walked away. Being close to her when he could smell her arousal tempted his control. She wouldn't deny him, but he'd promised himself he wouldn't touch her again.

He said, "We are married, but your duty has not changed, Serenity. You need to stay alive. The treaty only exists because we are married. Though no others have tried to hurt you since your arrival in Nexeu, you need to have more guards."

"I understand, but I agree with Chigaru. He should be the one to test those who would join my Hell Hounds. I trust his judgment and his skills."

"And, if I said I had already chosen those who I would add to your guard? What would you say?"

Serenity frowned and answered in a measured tone, "You have not chosen, King Melchior. You told Haige you had yet to decide how many guards I needed."

"I have not, but that doesn't mean I don't have candidates in mind."

"Then, you would have declared them to me rather than have this discussion to debate their addition."

"Astute as ever, Serenity."

"Thank you, Your Majesty."

Melchior sat on the edge of his desk. "You're right. I have not chosen. My decision was narrowed to thirty, and of those I want you to choose at least five."

"I don't need five other guards. Two, to replace Mael and Theyn, is enough."

"How effective are your guards when they are exhausted, Serenity? They watch you day and night without a break—Chigaru most of all. I'm sure you do not to mean to be intentionally cruel by not allowing them time to have lives of their own."

He preyed on Serenity's love of her guards. If she thought she had wronged them in any way, she would hasten to repair the slight. That was his hope.

Using his logic, she would choose five others, the Hell Hounds would no longer be indispensable and then Melchior could remind them of their stations without fear of leaving Serenity unguarded.

Serenity looked predictably upset at his words and sat on the nearest chair. She whispered, "I had not thought... I don't mean to—"

"In Cheslav, only one of your Hell Hounds was needed against any human threat. Here in Nexeu, that is not true. This is a case of bhresyas fighting bhresyas. Strength alone is not enough. All of your Hell Hounds are with you all of the time because they know of the increased threat."

She met his gaze and he waited for her to speak.

"I will choose."

"Good."

"But, I would ask that Chigaru be the mark my new guards are measured against. I have not changed my mind in that regard."

"So be it."

He had won. He would agree to anything she wanted. "I will start the trials tomorrow."

"I would also ask that I be allowed to be absent, Your Majesty."

"May I inquire as to why?"

Serenity's smile returned to its normal radiance. "I have only recently discovered the Ladies of the Circle. I wish to spend more time with them."

Melchior almost smiled at the way she watched him after her admission. He guessed she wanted to know if Keran had complained about Serenity's treatment. She had to know he would have mentioned the transgression—if he perceived one— as soon as it was brought to his attention, not a month later.

"Your attendance at the trials is entirely up to you, though I require your presence at the end."

"Thank you."

"I'm glad you have found others to interact with, Serenity." Others that weren't the Hell Hounds, he added silently.

"As am I, Your Majesty."

CHAPTER SIXTEEN

CHIGARU AND HAIGE ADMINISTERED THE TESTING during the trials and therefore were too busy to guard Serenity. Melchior placed temporary guards from the royal army at her disposal during their absence. Neither she nor the guards were very happy with the arrangement.

Serenity was proud of the unintentional compliment Melchior paid Chigaru and Haige. The six guards he assigned replaced the absent two. He probably didn't mean the act the way she interpreted it, but she was proud nonetheless.

She didn't want the extra guards trooping after her through the countryside, so she curtailed her need to go riding outside the palace. The trials also meant that Serenity's dagger practice was postponed.

Her only other option was lessons with the Ladies of the Circle. She wanted to learn to sew and the ladies were all pleased to aid her in the endeavor.

Serenity was in the middle of learning how to sew lace to a garment without the thread showing when Melchior had her summoned to the arena. That meant the trials were over and it was time for her to meet her new guards.

She didn't want to go. She didn't want strangers—reluctant strangers—guarding her, but she had agreed.

After she excused herself to the ladies, Serenity stalked out of the room.

"This is a waste of time," she grumbled. Her usual smile was a little flat and obviously forced. It irked her giving in to Melchior over the issue of adding guards to those she already had. She wanted to give her Hell Hounds a break away from guarding her so they could engage in their own lives, but she didn't want guards like those who trailed her now.

Nym asked, "Did you mention that fact to King Melchior, Serenity?"

"Even if she did, do you think he would listen, Nym?" Theyn asked.

He and Alexa had joined Serenity's lessons with the Ladies of the Circle. Alexa wanted to see if the bhresyas' sewing technique was any different from the humans' technique. Theyn's duty required he accompany her.

Alexa said, "King Melchior only wishes you to be safe, Serenity. There is no harm in that. You appointed Theyn to guard me." Her gaze met Theyn's, then she blushed and turned away. "That leaves you vulnerable."

"Whatever his reasons, I don't think my safety is foremost in his mind. If it was, he would have replaced Theyn as soon as I told him of his absence, not nearly a month later." Serenity stopped walking and looked at her companions in turn. All of them stared back at her.

She examined the words that had left her mouth. "Almost a month has past."

"Yes," Nym said.

"Has so much time truly lapsed since my marriage and arrival?"

Theyn nodded.

Nym asked, "You didn't notice?"

Serenity shook her head and looked around again. She whispered, "It seems as though I have lived here longer, and yet, at the same time, I feel as though I have just arrived." She met Nym's gaze. "Does that make sense?"

"Only because you said it."

There was no other way Serenity could explain and she didn't bother trying.

The extra guards Melchior appointed led the way to the arena since Serenity had never gone there before and neither had the Hell Hounds. They stopped at a guarded door. The guards there bowed then held open the door for Serenity.

She stepped over the threshold and almost turned to go back the way she had come. She had never seen so many bhresyas in one place in all of her life. Not even on the day of her arrival were there this many bhresyas.

Rows and rows of stadium-style seating surrounded the large green field of the arena. All Serenity could see was a sea of cheering colors. There was no way to make out one bhresya from another.

"Scared, Queen Serenity?" Melchior asked. He looked over the back of his throne at her.

"Awed, Your Majesty." She walked to the railing of the balcony and looked out over the crowd. "They're beautiful," she whispered.

Melchior's and Serenity's thrones were in a covered pavilion located in the middle of the rows, so there were seats above and below them. With the pavilion's canopy, those seated above them couldn't see the royal couple, and the pavilion extended out over the seats below it, so there was a balcony of sorts.

Nym said, "Bhresyas from all of the nearby cities came to see the trials."

"Surely, they can't be that concerned with my safety."

Theyn said, "Any event held in the arena gathers such a crowd. They are here for entertainment, Serenity, not you."

"Ah. That makes more sense."

She looked down at the field. Chigaru and Haige stood looking up at her. She waved to them. Ten males and females stood a few paces behind Chigaru. Those were the finalists.

"I thought I was only to have five guards added to my Hell Hounds, King Melchior?"

"You shall." He gestured to the finalists and said, "Choose."

The crowd cheered this.

"Choose," Serenity repeated, looking over the finalists. They had to be good fighters if Chigaru presented them to her. She didn't doubt that, but she needed more than a good fighter.

"May I be allowed to speak to them?"

"About?"

"I'm not sure yet. If I'm to choose, I would like to speak with them first."

"If you like," Melchior said.

She thanked him and followed her guards out of the pavilion. The trek to the field didn't take long and the second her feet touched the grass a great cheer went up over the crowd. Serenity stopped and looked at all the happy bhresyas.

"If only every day were like this one," Theyn said. He'd followed her along with Nym.

Serenity looked back at him then beyond him to the pavilion. Alexa stood next to Serenity's unoccupied throne and Melchior lounged on his, watching her.

She whispered, "If only…"

Something unreadable resided in Melchior's eyes. She had missed her chance to ask him his real reason for her forced additions. The question wouldn't help her choose, but it would give her insight into her husband's thinking. Was he worried for her safety? Had there been a threat on her life and he hadn't told her?

She dismissed her curiosity and faced her task. Everyone watched her. She asked the chance to speak with the candidates but had no topic in mind.

Nym said, "Why not find out what they truly think of you, Serenity? That should make your choice easier."

"I simply choose the ones who hate me the least, then?" Serenity asked, a hint of mirth in her voice.

Theyn replied, "You give yourself too much credit, Serenity. The majority of the bhresyas here don't know you well enough to hate you. They have disdain for you, but that's only because you're human."

"Was that said to make me feel better? If so, you failed miserably."

He grinned at her.

Serenity shook her head and laughed. Theyn's words sparked an idea of what she would speak to the finalists about. She approached Chigaru and Haige.

They bowed to her. Haige paced backwards so he stood near Nym and Theyn while Chigaru shadowed her movements. She walked over to the first bhresya, a male bhresya who blended in well with the grass around him.

Serenity asked, "Why did you enter this competition?"

"To be part of the elite guards who are responsible for the safety of Nexeu's monarchs is a great honor," the male answered, his voice carrying over the field. Many cheered his answer.

Serenity digested his words and held his gaze as she considered his answer. The male blinked at her in confusion when she cocked her head to the side.

She finally said, "Good answer. Thank you."

The male bowed.

She moved to the next, a light purple female this time. "If you were to be chosen as an elite guard, what would be your chain of command?"

The female answered without hesitation, "I answer first and foremost to King Melchior and then to you, Your Majesty. As head of the… your elite guards, I would answer to Sir Chigaru and then Dame Nym… that is, until ranking matches are held to determine the true leader and second-in-command of your guards."

The female had her eyes on Nym as she said the last. Serenity guessed the female didn't think Nym worthy of the title of second. As Nym had refused to take part in any endeavor that would take her from Serenity's side, the female wouldn't know Nym's fighting capability. The female probably thought Nym's petite stature made her a weak fighter and Serenity wouldn't correct her.

People underestimating Nym made her an asset to the Hell Hounds.

Hell Hounds?

Serenity realized the female had hesitated then chose another phrase rather than say the title. She now had a line of questioning she could pursue.

She said to the female, "True and well said." Then, she moved to the gray male beside her. "It is common knowledge my personal guards are known as Hell Hounds. Would this title bother or offend you?"

"A title does not dictate how I will perform my duties as an elite guard if I am chosen, Your Majesty."

To Serenity's ears, the male's pretty sentiment translated out perfectly—he felt the title demeaned her guards, not honored them. Bhresya speech was plain to Serenity's ears since she'd had years of learning how to hear what wasn't said instead of what was.

She glanced back at Chigaru and he was blank. That told her all she needed to know. He would give her some indication if he felt the male deserved a chance despite his answer. He did nothing and she moved to the next male, who was a lighter colored orange than Chigaru. Before she questioned him, she said to the gray male, "Thank you for your answer."

The male nodded and tried to hide a look of upset. Serenity felt no sympathy for him.

She asked the orange male before her, "Are you loyal to King Melchior?"

The male rushed out, "I am completely loyal to King Melchior, without doubt or hesitation, Your Majesty."

The crowd, who had fallen into silence while Serenity spoke to each finalist, cheered this. The male waved at the crowd, making them cheer louder.

The male looked smug. He probably thought his question was simple and the outcome easy to predict.

She waited for the cheering crowd to quiet down then she asked her true question, "Are you loyal to me?"

The male hesitated only a second then answered, "As queen of Nexeu—"

"Hold." She stepped closer to the male. "Answer the question I asked you. No more, no less."

"Your station dictates—"

"Try again." She raised an eyebrow when the male gave her a questioning look. He glanced over her shoulder at Melchior, but she didn't bother following his gaze. She repeated, "Try again."

The male's eyes came back to her. He sighed and started, "As King Melchior's bride—"

"Stop!"

The male jumped at the volume and force she put behind that one word. A hush fell over the crowd, even the murmuring stopped.

In a hard voice, Serenity said, "No qualifiers. No preambles. You will answer my question with a yes or a no. Are you loyal to me?"

He held her gaze for the span of three heartbeats. A hard breath escaped his lips before he lowered his eyes and then his head. His silence continued.

"As I thought. You may leave the field." She looked down the line of males and females who awaited her next questions, but there were no more.

She said for the entire arena to hear, "My Hell Hounds are loyal to me. My safety is first and foremost in their minds. Nothing else matters to them and nothing else motivates them but my continued health and well being. Not fame—" she looked at the green male "—or prestige—" she looked at the purple female "—or honor." She looked at the gray male at the last.

All three bowed their heads.

She addressed the line of those who remained, "If you cannot tell me you are loyal to me, then you will not guard me. I refuse to trust my safety to anyone who cannot utter those words." She looked behind her to Melchior. She said just for him, "Never again."

Melchior nodded but said nothing. As before, she couldn't read his mood.

Her attention turned back to the line. "Are you loyal to me?"

No one answered her. Many of the finalists looked away.

Nym stepped forward and called out, "If your answer is not yes, then you may leave the line."

One by one, the competitors filed off the field. Silence strangled the crowd.

Serenity said, "It would seem my guards remain unchanged." She looked up at Melchior. "Was there any other matter to which you needed my attendance, Your Majesty?"

"None. You are excused, Queen Serenity."

"Thank you, King Melchior."

She took two steps then looked back at her six remaining additions. "Chigaru and Haige have returned to their normal duties, King Melchior. There is no more need for them." She gestured to the guards.

Melchior signaled them away with a simple gesture.

The guards bowed to him and exited the field.

Serenity curtseyed to Melchior then exited as well. She said under her breath, "I repeat—a waste of time."

༄·ଓ

Melchior heard her words. Atop the arms of his throne, he clenched his fists. The day hadn't gone at all the way he had planned. First, Chigaru proved himself to be a better fighter than everyone else—except Serenity—had given him credit.

Without a weapon, he had easily beaten all those who matched him. Haige's skills were not as good, but he remained a tough opponent. There were only a few who were able to best Haige. Those few lost to Chigaru.

Melchior was sure he had lost his chance to replace the Hell Hounds. Chigaru surprised him and almost everyone else in the arena when he chose ten of those he had bested. Melchior's hope was renewed and Serenity was summoned, only to have her eliminate that hope with one simple question of loyalty.

He had lost.

Melchior's advisors gathered around him to discuss another way to add to Serenity's personal guards, but he ignored them.

He rose and left the arena without another word. There was no need to belabor a topic that was already decided. No bhresyas, save the Hell Hounds, were loyal to Serenity. She was right to want only loyal guards. So long as loyalty was her only stipulation, Melchior couldn't win.

He accepted that.

CHAPTER SEVENTEEN

THE NEXT DAY CHIGARU'S SKILL WAS THE TOPIC OF EVERY CONVERSATION. Many wondered when the next set of trials would be held.

Chigaru as the main topic of conversation only served to annoy Melchior. The nobles wanted to know about Chigaru—who trained him, if Melchior had sent him to Serenity in Cheslav knowing of his skills, why Melchior wanted to add to Serenity's guards when Chigaru was more than adequate. He didn't want to answer any of the questions and didn't.

Melchior would have never sent Chigaru to Serenity, even if she had contacted him about the assassination attempts. The male was too close to Serenity for Melchior's peace of mind. The palace gossips speculated daily about the possible causes for the amount of Chigaru's scent that had permeated Serenity's skin. All discussion led to the same conclusion—she had taken the male to her bed as her lover even though Melchior forbade it.

It wasn't true and Melchior knew that. Chigaru shared Serenity's bed, but they were not intimate. Chigaru was a smart male and he wouldn't chance an act of treason. That would be a death sentence and leave Serenity open to attack.

Further proof was Serenity's unchanged scent. Everyone smelled Chigaru on her skin, but they ignored the absence of his mark. Constant copulation with a single male changed the female's scent and marked the female as taken. This was a fact true of bhresyas. Melchior was sure the same was true for human females who mated with bhresya males.

He hoped it was true.

To change the direction of his thoughts, he escaped to the courtyard. The nobles followed him there but sensed his mood and stopped their constant questions. They busied themselves with talking amongst themselves or engaging in games of skill and chance with each other. Melchior was able to enjoy the courtyard in peace.

"There he is, Serenity."

Melchior turned and saw Serenity and Nym headed his way. Chigaru was with them but he hung back and that made Melchior suspicious.

"Good day to you, my king," Serenity said. She held out her dress with flourish and curtsied to him.

"Your clothing is different."

The style of her clothing hadn't changed, merely the coloring. It matched

Chigaru's shade of burnt orange perfectly. Melchior was sure that wasn't a coincidence. He was also sure displaying the color change was the reason Serenity had sought him out.

Serenity nodded her agreement and straightened from her curtsy. "The Ladies of the Circle took pity on me and decided I should be adorned in other colors besides constant dark blue." She glanced down at her dress then over her shoulder at Chigaru. "This particular shade of orange is quite lovely."

Her words angered Melchior. It took a great deal of willpower for him not to look at Chigaru. "Some would see the change as... telling, *my* queen."

"Telling of what, Your Majesty? I simply thought I needed a change. I have worn that shade of blue almost all of my life. I devoted myself to the color out of a childish whim. I've found that it's time to leave off such silly notions and grow up." Her smile turned into a grin. "Besides I don't think the color did me justice. The Ladies of the Circle were all too happy—giddy even—to give me suggestions as to new colors I should wear."

Melchior asked through his teeth, "Were they?"

"Yes. Lady Lihah suggested this shade of orange. Lady Uleoma even made another dress from a lovely dark gray. I had a fitting just the other day. Haige accompanied me. He commented we shouldn't stand too close together when I wear the dress because I would blend in with him."

She laughed at the memory. To illustrate his words, Haige had removed his vest and stood behind Serenity while she faced the mirror. True to his words, it was hard to tell where Serenity's dress ended and he began.

She continued, "The third dress they made for me matches his shade—" she pointed to the auburn-colored male with horns that curved around his ears headed towards them "—Sir Erezion, Lady Setta's son. I met him only yesterday."

Erezion bowed to Melchior and Serenity. "My mother has informed me I missed the trials to become part of the royal elite. I was away with my father."

"Unfortunately, yes, you did, Sir Erezion," Serenity said. "Fear not, though. None who entered were chosen."

"Will you hold the competition again, my queen?"

"There is no point. None save my Hell Hounds are loyal to me. I will not trust myself to someone who is not loyal as I want to remain with the living as long as I possibly can."

Serenity darted a look in Melchior's direction while trying to look as though she hadn't. Her actions were obvious and childish. She wanted him to be jealous. Melchior would laugh, but the sound would come out as a growl.

"I'm sure, except for that one stipulation, you would have surely endured to become one of the final ten, Sir Erezion. Your mother has told me you are one of the top fighters in the palace," Serenity said.

"I am happy for the compliment and saddened you will not give me the chance to prove myself, Queen Serenity," Erezion said.

Melchior asked, "Can you say before us now that you are loyal to Queen Serenity?"

"No, I cannot, my king. I wish to be loyal, but I cannot give my trust to someone I have only recently met."

"Then, this conversation is at an end. Queen Serenity has given her only prerequisite and you do not meet it. Good day to you, Sir Erezion."

Melchior wanted the male gone. He didn't like the idea of Serenity having a dress in Erezion's color. She couldn't be ignorant of the bhresyas' tradition of wearing the colors of a lover or spouse. Her Hell Hounds or the Ladies of the Circle would have educated her. That meant both parties purposefully allowed and encouraged it.

Melchior didn't appreciate Lady Setta pushing her son towards Serenity as a potential lover instead of guard. If Erezion qualified as one of Serenity's Hell Hounds, that would make it much easier for the male.

But, he didn't qualify.

Erezion went to one knee and took Serenity's hand in his. "I would ask that I be given a chance, my queen. I know, in time, I would be able to say the oath—before the entire court if you asked it of me."

Chigaru came forward and placed his hand on Erezion's shoulder. Melchior wondered at such an action until Serenity smoothed her hand over Erezion's head, trailing her fingers over the base of his horns. Melchior almost snatched her hand away.

She shouldn't be so familiar with a male she had only just met. Erezion didn't protest and Melchior would look a fool if he called attention to it. He'd also prove to Serenity that he was jealous. He wasn't, only angry at her tests of his patience.

"I refuse to compromise my stipulation for you, Sir Erezion," Serenity said. "However, I will give you a chance to know me. If loyalty does not result, then I hope we can remain friends."

"That is my hope as well, my queen," Erezion said. He stood and nodded to Chigaru. His expression turned puzzled as he looked from Chigaru to Serenity and back. "Is it purposeful that your dress matches Hell Hound Chigaru's coloring, Queen Serenity?"

"So your mother tells me, Sir Erezion. I left the choice of colors to her discretion."

"She chose well," Haige said, entering the courtyard. He joined the group near Serenity's side. "I see the Ladies of the Circle allowed you out of their sights with their precious dress. Well done, Serenity."

"They did make the dress for me, my teacher."

"True, but they were so proud of it. I hardly thought they would let you wear it."

Serenity looked at the dress with a loving eye. "It is different from the normal style of clothing they are used to making."

Melchior, wishing to be part of the conversation that had started with him, asked, "Why do you not switch to the bhresya female style of dress, Serenity? It seems out of character with all the other changes you have made."

"As much as I would like to, Your Majesty, I cannot. I am too shy for such clothing."

"You are very beautiful, Queen Serenity, there is no need to be modest," Erezion said.

"Flattery will not gain you the title of Hell Hound, Sir Erezion. Though, keep it up, and it may gain you a few days in the dungeon," Haige said, his gaze directed at Melchior.

All eyes turned to Melchior.

He said nothing and knew his face was blank. He'd crossed his arms, but the motion meant nothing.

Serenity said, "I was not raised to it and I don't feel comfortable wearing it. The Ladies of the Circle like the style of clothing I wear. They see it as a challenge. I wouldn't deprive them of that."

"Ah, there is a familiar sight," Haige said. He took hold of Serenity's hand and pulled her in the direction of two males facing each other over a long table with holes in it.

The others followed.

Haige asked, "How much time has past since I beheld a true tangzoku table?"

"Only a few weeks, my teacher," Serenity said. "You forget the table we left behind in Cheslav."

"Alric wanted it. And, that was a rudimentary table. I should have crossed the Cheslav-Nexeu border and acquired a real one for you."

"Queen Serenity knows how to play tangzoku?" Erezion asked.

Nym said, "Quite well."

"For a human," Melchior added. It slipped out before he could stop it.

"I didn't say that. I said she plays quite well."

Haige suggested, "You should call for a tangzoku tournament, Serenity. You can see what the game looks like when masters play."

"Tangzoku tournament?" asked one of the males who stood at the gaming table. He placed the metal cup he held on the table and faced the group. "Will you call a tangzoku tournament, Your Majesty?"

"Here, here," cheered the other male. "A tangzoku tournament is just what we need. The people are restless after the elite trials turned up no new guards for Queen Serenity's Hell Hounds. A tournament would restore almost everyone to better spirits."

Serenity said, "I would love to see a tangzoku tournament. When should it be held?"

"Now," answered Haige and the two males in unison.

Melchior, swept up in Serenity's enthusiasm, agreed, "By all means. Now is the perfect time for a tournament."

CHAPTER EIGHTEEN

WORD OF MOUTH SPREAD THE NEWS OF THE TOURNAMENT FAST. The arena was full in an hour and a judge was chosen from amongst Melchior's advisors. The royal tangzoku table was brought out and placed in the middle of the field.

Serenity couldn't wait for the players to take the field. She loved tangzoku because it was the only game she could play against a bhresya and have a decent chance of winning.

Tangzoku was a game about speed and accuracy, not strength—accuracy more so than speed. Two players faced off against one another across a long wide table. Each was given a metal can full of cylindrical metal rods of varying diameters. The rods had to be shaken from the can through a small hole in the top in order to put them into play.

The table had several holes—usually between fifty and one hundred—drilled into its surface. This table had seventy-five. Each rod fit a specific hole. The object of the game was to match as many rods as possible to their respective holes in the given amount of time. Once time was called, the judge would determine the winner based on how many rods were placed correctly.

The game's main element of difficulty was the diameter from rod to rod varied only a little bit. Players had to be cautious and pay close attention to their actions. A player could not have more than one rod in their hand at any given time. If a player found that they had placed a rod incorrectly, they had to empty their hand before they could move it. If the rod in their hand was supposed to go in the hole that was currently occupied by a wrongly placed rod, then the player would have to place the rod in their hand in an incorrect spot so they could correct their mistake.

All that had to be done before the judge called time. Players who still held a rod when the judge called time were allowed to place the rod and then the game play was over and the judge declared a winner. Only the best players were able to accurately place all their rods before the judge called time. That was an instant win.

"First players take the field!" the judge called, looking around the arena.

Several of the audience called out to be chosen and the judge picked at random. The players took the field, bowed in the direction of the pavilion and then readied themselves to play. The crowd cheered as the judge called a start to the game.

Serenity rose from her throne and went to the railing. She watched with rapt attention.

"You'll fall," Nym said in a mothering tone.

"I'm fine," Serenity said. She leaned further.

Chigaru lifted her throne, carried it over to where she stood, and pulled her back so she sat. He nodded with a soft snuff. She grinned at him then turned her attention to the game.

The judge called time three minutes after the start and the players stepped back. He assessed the table before announcing the winner. The crowd cheered and the loser returned to his seat.

"Who will face the winner?" the judge asked.

"I shall," said a female voice that was louder than any other. The owner of the voice made her way to the field before the judge could accept her challenge. She looked over the others in the crowd and dared them to say anything.

The judge allowed, "Mistress Keran will face the winner."

Serenity's enjoyment of the day plummeted. She sat back on her throne with her arms crossed.

Melchior asked, "Something wrong, Serenity?"

"Nothing," she snapped.

She stared down at the field but didn't see the game. All she saw was Keran, who wore a dark blue vest dress that was secured to her body with red and yellow ribbons. The outfit barely covered her pink flesh.

Keran's choice of colors made Serenity angry. She was sure the anger was clear on her face. Whereas Melchior showed not even the slightest emotion over her color change, the sight of Keran wearing Melchior's colors had Serenity ready to send Chigaru after one of the female's horns.

Three minutes later, the judge announced, "The winner is Mistress Keran. Who will be the next challenger?"

"I will," Serenity called. She rose and left the pavilion with Chigaru close behind her.

Melchior asked, "Is that wise?"

"A better question is if she knows a contest of speed between a human and bhresya is no contest at all," replied the advisor who stood behind Melchior's throne.

Haige said, "You underestimate our queen, advisor. Theyn and I taught her this game. She's one of the best players I know—so far as accuracy is concerned."

Serenity stood across from Keran. She nodded to the female when Keran curtseyed to her. "I hope you don't mind. I wanted to face someone who wouldn't feel the need to let me win."

"I would *never* do that."

"I know."

The judge came forward with the can of rods. He held out a can to Serenity, but Chigaru took it for her.

She said, "You will forgive me, but the cup is too heavy. Hell Hound Chigaru will act as my second."

The judge glanced up to Melchior with an apprehensive expression. He said in a hesitant manner, "While a second can aid the player, it has been years... decades since I have seen anyone take advantage of that particular rule." Melchior waved him to continue. "Of course, there is no reason not to allow you a second, Your Majesty."

"Thank you," Serenity said.

Keran took her cup and held it with little effort. "If you cannot hold the cup, *Queen* Serenity, how do you expect to play?"

"Well. Unlike you, *Mistress* Keran, I can use both my hands. The rules do state a player can have a second if they wish to use both hands. Though, it is best if the player and her second are familiar with each other so the second does not slow the player down."

"Yes. Many have commented on how *intimately* your Hell Hounds know you."

The judge rushed out, "Shall we begin?"

"One moment," Serenity said. She placed both her hands on the table with her palms fully splayed then ran her hands from one end of the table to the other and from the top to the bottom. She closed her eyes as she did this.

Haige nodded and said, "Good girl. She remembered."

"Remembered what?" Melchior asked. Serenity's actions made no sense to him. The murmurs from the crowd indicated they were as confused as he.

Theyn said, "To know her battleground before she engages the enemy. Every table is a little different."

Serenity straightened and opened her eyes. "Now, I am ready."

The judge nodded and placed his hand on the table. Serenity placed both her hands and Keran placed her free hand. In this way, Keran and Serenity declared to the judge and the audience which hand—or hands—they intended to use. Once a method of play was chosen, the players could not change it until the next round.

The judge said, "Begin." He pulled his hand from the table and stepped away.

Keran shook a rod out of the can and placed it.

Chigaru shook the can. Serenity caught the first rod when it fell out and then the second. She rolled the rods in her fingers as she scanned the table. After she placed one rod, she held out her hand to Chigaru for another while she looked for the hole of the second rod she held.

The idea was that her hands were never empty. Speed wouldn't win her this competition so she had to have strategy.

"You're behind, Your Majesty," Keran taunted.

Serenity placed her fifth rod. "You slow yourself down when you concern yourself with my progress." With that said, she placed her sixth and seventh rods. She didn't look away from the table once. Curiosity would only slow her down.

The judge called time. Serenity held up the two rods she held while Keran held up her empty hand. The judge said, "Mistress Keran, you may step back. Queen Serenity, please play your final two rods and step back."

Serenity scanned the board then placed the last two rods. She and Chigaru took two steps back in perfect unison.

The judge looked over Serenity's table first. His voice was soft with wonder when he said, "Queen Serenity: Thirty-eight rods placed—all correct."

Haige and Theyn cheered. Soon, the crowd joined them.

Melchior clapped slowly. He was impressed. Serenity hadn't seemed to be doing that well—her movements were slow as compared to Keran's. Even with the high number of rods she placed, Melchior doubted Serenity would win the match.

The judge looked over Keran's table. "Mistress Keran: Sixty-nine rods placed, thirty correct. The winner is Queen Serenity."

Theyn roared over the cheer of the crowd, "Never a doubt!"

Serenity waved to him then turned back to Keran. The female was obviously angry at the loss. "If you had paid more attention to your actions and less attention to your opponent, you might have won, Mistress Keran."

"I will remember that, Queen Serenity. You can count on it." She stalked off the field.

The judge called, "Who will face, Queen Serenity?"

"I will," Haige responded.

Serenity said, "I should concede now while my ego is intact."

"Nonsense, my queen. You have gotten better. There is a possibility you will win."

Chigaru whispered in her ear. She nodded at his words then relayed to Haige, "You will refrain from allowing me to win, correct?"

"If that is your wish, my queen." He ran his hand over the table once he reached it then nodded to the judge.

The game proceeded as it did before. This time when the judge called time, both Serenity and Haige held two rods, one in each hand. Haige had opted to set his can down after he retrieved two rods. Such a strategy would slow him down but it was the way he preferred to play.

The judge allowed them to place their rods. "Queen Serenity: Forty rods placed—all correct."

Serenity asked over the cheering crowd, "What is Hell Hound Haige's total, if you please?"

"Of course, Your Majesty." The judge looked over Haige's table then looked it over again. He stammered out, "Hell Hound Haige: For... Forty rods placed—all... correct?" He looked at Serenity for some kind of explanation.

Serenity crossed her arms, annoyance plain on her face. She tapped her fingers against the curve of her elbow and waited for Haige to explain himself.

Haige said, "I did not allow you to win."

"Neither did you play properly." She turned to the judge and said, "The win belongs to Hell Hound Haige."

"I don't want it." He smiled at Serenity and she glared at him in return.

Melchior called, "Why did you challenge Queen Serenity if you had no intention of playing properly?"

"To speed her up. She can go faster," Haige said. "She's never played for such a large audience. She's allowing her nervousness to impede her gaming ability."

"Be that as it may, you did not play properly. If you do not intend to match me fairly then do not play against me," Serenity said.

"I will play against you," Melchior said. He rose and the crowd clapped. He arrived at Haige's side and stopped, wanting to see if the male would give way or if he would have to make him.

Haige stepped aside with a slight bow. "As you wish, King Melchior."

The judge reset the table and handed out the cans. Chigaru took up his place behind Serenity. He whispered in her ear and she nodded to him then looked across the table at Melchior. His look was cold.

She said, "Chigaru only just informed me you are one of the best at this game,

Your Majesty. I will prepare myself to lose with grace."

"You are quite fast," Melchior said.

"Not as fast as my brother Prince Alric. Should he visit, I think you two should play… if that will not inconvenience you."

"I would make time for the match."

Serenity couldn't think of what to say to his words so she said nothing. They stood in unbroken silence, as the crowd had hushed so they could hear the king and queen speak. She looked over the crowd. Were she and Melchior that interesting?

This wasn't the first time she had noticed all conversation and movement stopped when she interacted with him. The people of the palace seemed to wait with baited breath for another bit of news to relate about the interaction of the royal couple. The scrutiny annoyed her. Everyone should be used to her after so many weeks. And yet, she remained a source of entertainment.

"Proceed, judge," Melchior said.

The judge started the game. The arena continued to be silent. The only sound was the clank of the cans as the rods were dispensed and the sound of the rods being placed in their respective holes.

Like Haige, Melchior chose to use both hands to place the rods. He was a blur of movement. Before the judge could call time, Melchior placed one hand palm-down on the table and lifted his empty can with his other.

The judge called, "King Melchior has emptied his can. Queen Serenity, please stop."

He didn't need to tell her since she had already raised her hands. She held two rods. The judge was about to speak, but she cut him off, "I can see I was right to prepare to lose with grace. You are truly a very skilled player, my king." She laid her rods flat on the table and backed away. She dropped into a curtsey then turned to leave the field.

The judge called after her, "Do you not wish to know how many you placed, Queen Serenity?"

"I placed forty-three and they are all correct. I'm sure I would have placed fifty in the time allotted, except King Melchior ended the match early. It was a game well met. Thank you," Serenity said. She curtseyed again and returned to her seat.

Melchior watched her leave.

The judge said, "Queen Serenity is correct—forty-three rods placed and they are all correct."

The crowd cheered and Serenity waved. The cheering grew. Chigaru brought her outstretched hand to his lips. She smiled up at him and returned the gesture.

Melchior called over the noise of the crowd, "I would face Hell Hound Chigaru."

The gasp that rolled over the crowd was a physical thing. Melchior didn't care how it looked. He couldn't stop himself from challenging Chigaru. A game of tang-zoku was not the field of battle on which he wanted to face the male but he would take it.

Chigaru returned to the field. He bowed to Melchior then held out his hand for the can. The game was started and ended seconds later. Both males finished at the same time with their empty cups in the air.

Serenity clapped. Hers was the only sound.

"Again," Melchior bit out.

The table was reset and the males started. As the first time, they finished at the exact same moment and Serenity was the only one who clapped.

Melchior glared across the table at Chigaru. There was no way the male could match him rod for rod two games in a row. There was no way.

Serenity called out, "Chigaru."

Both males looked at her, but she met only Chigaru's gaze. She said in a stern yet amused voice, "Stop. You'll make King Melchior angry with you if you continue."

Chigaru nodded to her then faced Melchior.

"Reset the table, please, judge. They will play one last time." She met Melchior's gaze. "Unless you wish to stop, King Melchior?"

Melchior growled, "Reset the table."

This time, Chigaru finished first. It was close, but he raised his cup just as Melchior placed his last rod and started to raise his own.

"Hell Hound Chigaru is the winner," the judge announced. He stepped back from the table, his gaze never leaving Melchior. It seemed the judge wanted to be out of striking distance when his king erupted.

Melchior asked in a quiet voice, "Why did you humor me? I am not Serenity. I do not need my ego stroked. You Hell Hounds have never cared what I thought before."

Chigaru remained blank in the face of Melchior's anger.

"You *will* answer me."

Chigaru answered in a voice that was softer than the barest whisper, "She didn't command it, but she wanted you to win. I could not bring myself to lose on purpose. Not to you. Not again. I matched you, instead."

"I'll accept that."

Part of Chigaru's statement confused Melchior. He'd said he didn't want to lose to Melchior on purpose *again*. When was the first time?

Melchior wanted to ask, but kept his curiosity in check. There was a time and place for all things. The arena was not the place and the large audience made it an inopportune time to discuss what Melchior knew to be a sensitive and private topic.

Chigaru bowed to Melchior and left the field. He returned to Serenity's side. She immediately asked him what he had said to Melchior but Chigaru didn't answer. She frowned up at him, then turned her gaze to Melchior when he entered the pavilion.

He said nothing to her questioning look.

"You're not facing another challenger, King Melchior?"

"Chigaru is the first to beat me in some decades, Queen Serenity. I doubt there is another in the crowd. I allowed the tournament so I could enjoy the game, not compete."

"Then I'm happy I had a chance to face you."

Chapter Nineteen

"I WOULD SPEAK TO YOU, MY WIFE," Melchior said at dinner that night.

Serenity barely kept herself from choking. Melchior rarely spoke to her at dinner. When he did speak to her, he always used her name with her title dropped. To everyone, it was an obvious declaration he didn't see her as a queen even though he added the title when he spoke about her to others.

Even more surprising was that he called her *my wife*. Melchior hadn't referred to Serenity in such a way since their wedding day. She wanted to see it as a good sign, and yet she was scared to raise her hopes. Try as she might, she couldn't convince herself that it was a slip of the tongue. Melchior's endearment was intentional.

"Do you wish to hold the conversation now, Your Majesty, or after dinner?" She congratulated herself when she spoke in a normal, emotionally devoid voice. The people didn't need more to speak of tonight. Eagerness in her speech would set the tongues a-wagging. Melchior's earlier match with Chigaru was enough for that day's topic of discussion.

"Once you have finished."

"As you wish."

He nodded and returned to his dinner.

Serenity's appetite was gone. Her entire focus was on possible topics Melchior wished to discuss with her and the way he had addressed her. She played with her food and her distraction was obvious to everyone. She put down her fork and stood.

"I shall be in my rooms when you wish to speak to me, Your Majesty."

"I wish to speak with you now. I shall escort you to my study." He finished the bite of food on his fork and rose as well. He indicated Serenity should precede him out of the room.

She had almost expected him to offer her his arm. That was silly. She read too much into the situation. Melchior abhorred her touch and he wouldn't offer her his arm just to save face in front of the nobles and servants.

She walked out of the dining hall first, but fell into step a pace behind Melchior once the doors closed behind them. Nym and Haige walked five paces behind her. The trek to Melchior's study was made in silence.

Nym and Haige stopped outside the door without being told. Melchior closed the door then faced Serenity.

She wrung her hands. She couldn't think of any reason Melchior would wish to speak to her. "Have I done something to displease you, Your Majesty?"

Too late she realized the mistake she made with such a question. There were many times she noticed Melchior's annoyance with her. She hoped he hadn't waited for her transgressions to accumulate so he could berate her with them all at once.

"No." He walked past her to his desk. "Sit down, Serenity. We need to have an understanding between us. This tension and your childish attempts to make me jealous need to come to an end."

"Of course. You are correct."

"I admit I should have made plain I had no intention of having heirs of you."

"Do you plan to take a bhresya wife to have your heirs, then?"

"I had not given the idea much thought. With all that happened on our wedding day, explaining my reasons for this marriage was forgotten."

"I understand."

"Our marriage is to solidify the treaty between the bhresyas and the humans. I had planned to marry Queen Rhiannon ,but King Kiros went back on our agreement."

Serenity nodded. "My mother told me of this. You had your armies kill the royal family in retribution."

"No, I had Queen Rhiannon's family killed because King Kiros killed my first wife and children. I left Queen Rhiannon alive to offer her the same deal I had offered to her father before her. Both instances were strongly advocated against. My nobles, my advisors, and even my own parents wanted me to rethink the idea of taking a human bride. I knew it was the only way to prove to the humans we bhresyas wanted an end to a war no human remembered the true beginnings of."

"I have never heard of your parents before, King Melchior? Are they... where are they now?"

"They removed themselves from the palace the day I retrieved you. My father and mother abdicated the throne to me over eighty years ago. Until my marriage to you, they resided in the palace of Nexeu. When news reached them the wedding had taken place, they left the palace."

"Why?"

"They do not approve of this marriage. My father sees it as folly and he refuses to set foot in the palace again until you are gone. My mother followed her husband."

Serenity didn't know what to say. She wanted to ask why Melchior felt the need to tell her this.

"I tell you all this so you can see that it isn't only you who has suffered, Serenity. I am separated from the last family I have only because I would not rethink my marriage to you."

"I could return to Cheslav. I am not needed in Nexeu." She didn't want to leave Melchior. Her words were automatic, but she hoped he wouldn't agree with her suggestion.

"Unless we divorced, my parents would not return. It isn't your presence but the marriage they disapprove of."

She whispered, "I am sorry, King Melchior. I didn't know any of this." She didn't know it because her Hell Hounds had never told her. She would ask them later if they had kept the information from her or if they were as ignorant of it as she. Though the Hell Hounds couldn't have possibly known about Melchior's parents' ultimatum, since they had no contact with Nexeu once they were captured and held in Cheslav.

"That is my fault. I did not mean for this information to upset you, Serenity. I thought this would help bring an end to the tension between us. Once alleviated, the people of the palace will stop waiting for us to do something worth talking about."

"Yes, their distraction with us annoys me, as well." She stood and walked over to Melchior, holding his dual-colored gaze as she approached. "However, I don't think this conversation alone will solve the problem."

"Why is that?"

Her dress brushed Melchior's knee when she stopped. She reached out to touch his cheek, but he jerked back. She didn't pursue him. "That is why, King Melchior. You actively avoid my touch. Everyone in the palace... everyone in the kingdom has to know you took me to your bed only once. After that one time, you have shunned my touch ever since."

She dropped her hand and stepped back a few paces to put room between them. "Why did you consummate our marriage if you had no intention of impregnating me?"

"A bhresya marriage is not true until it is consummated. I have heard some human marriages are much the same. And, I was curious what a human female felt like."

Serenity wanted to pursue the natural course of the conversation but to do so would be treason and Melchior had made up his mind. She only hoped he would bring up the topic in the near future and she could ask him again if she would be allowed to take a lover.

Instead, she asked, "Will you allow me to help you rule, at least? Haige made sure my education about bhresya politics was complete. If the people of Nexeu see that *you* trust me, then *they* will start to trust me."

"I respect and admire the measures you took in preparation for your new life here in Nexeu. However, you are not needed to rule."

"Did Queen Asha help you rule?"

Melchior jerked at the mention of his first wife.

"She did, didn't she?"

"Yes, Asha was my regent."

"I do not ask for such an important role. I only wish to aid you. This new peace would be better served if I were there to offer advice on the actions of the other human kingdoms. There is no need to tip the hand of war with a simple misunderstanding."

"When such a time comes that my advisors and I need insight into the minds of those humans we deal with, then your counsel will be sought, Serenity. Until that time, it is best for all that you remain apart from the politics of the kingdom."

"Best how? I don't understand why I cannot be allowed to help you."

Melchior heaved an annoyed sigh. "I cannot trust you with Nexeu's secrets. No one has forgotten whose granddaughter you are."

Serenity stared at him in wide-eyed shock, hurt by his declaration. She wasn't King Kiros. Rhiannon had made sure none of her children followed in their grandfather's footsteps. Or, she tried to. Joah's prejudice seemed inborn and nothing Rhiannon did could alleviate it. In fact, all her efforts to teach him tolerance had only succeeded in making his anger and hatred worse.

"Any human princess from any of the other kingdoms could have filled the role of my bride. I chose Cheslav because the war—the original war—started there. Peace had to start in the same place," Melchior said.

His earlier words had hurt her but this latest statement cut Serenity deeply, only because it proved how foolish she was. She'd spent her entire life falling in love with a bhresya male she didn't know.

All she wanted from the first day Rhiannon told Serenity of her future marriage until now was to be with Melchior. To suddenly hear she wasn't special, that any princess—any *human* woman—would have satisfied Melchior, made her world skew.

Everything was for naught. Years of training and tutoring and never allowing herself to grow too fond of any human man because she was already promised was all for nothing. Destiny had played a cruel joke.

Serenity's voice shook when she asked, "Was that all you wished of me, King Melchior? A legal marriage and nothing else?"

"My intentions were to solidify the peace, nothing else. You said on our wedding day you understood marriages of state, Serenity."

"I understand a loveless marriage where heirs are still expected," Serenity replied in a breathy voice. "I understand a marriage of convenience to unify two kingdoms into one. I do not understand why I needed to leave my home. I do not understand my place in this kingdom."

"Cheslav is more inclined to keep and maintain the peace so long as you reside in Nexeu."

"I'm a hostage."

"If you choose to see the situation that way, then so be it. You are my wife and you are queen because of it."

"I am only the queen of Nexeu because Queen Asha was killed before you wed me. It is within your power to take the title away from me and grant it to your next wife, when you marry her. You will marry another, I know that. Nexeu needs an heir."

Melchior moved away from his desk, turning his back on Serenity. He sat in his chair but didn't look at her. "I will not speculate on the future with you, Serenity. Ruling my kingdom and ensuring your safety have kept me from considering another wife."

"What is there to consider? I'm sure Keran will say yes the moment you ask her. Traditionally, the king would wait for his first wife to bear him an heir before wedding another, but this is an untraditional marriage. There is no need to stand on ceremony in this—"

"Stop, Serenity! Even if I planned to marry another tomorrow, Keran would not be whom I chose."

That surprised her. "She is your current favorite and she occupies your bed almost every night. The whole of the palace thinks it's only a matter of time before you make her your wife and then queen shortly thereafter."

Her gaze searched his for some hint that the rumors were true. She only saw his annoyance.

"The people of the palace also think you go against my orders and take Hell Hound Chigaru *and* Hell Hound Haige to your bed. The change in the color scheme of your wardrobe—" he gestured to her orange dress "—concurs with their suppositions.

Shall I believe them in this as you do in the other?”

“It would be the truth if you allowed me to take a lover.”

“My answer remains no.”

“Why?” Serenity yelled.

Melchior yelled back, “Do not question me in this, Serenity. I have told you already you will not be allowed a lover. Do not mention it again. Ever.”

“Then I wish to return to your bed, Melchior.” Her statement was bold and it shocked her that she had said it aloud. She hadn’t meant to say the words, but there they were.

Melchior seemed as shocked as Serenity. He stared at her.

Serenity took his silence as incentive to continue. She moved closer to him and clasped her hands in front of her in a pleading manner. She whispered, “I love you, Melchior. I want to be with you. I’ve always only wanted you.”

“That is a lie. Your requests for a lover are proof of your lie.”

“I thought to make you jealous. I thought if you knew another bhresya male wanted me then you would return me to your bed... that I would become attractive to you, as well.”

Melchior said nothing.

“I know I may never arouse you as Keran does, but I also know with time I could learn to satisfy you. Please, Melchior. I want only to be with you again.”

He closed his eyes and Serenity thought he might actually be considering her words. Instead of roundabout tactics, she should have confessed herself from the start. Had he known of her emotions for him she could have enjoyed his touch all the sooner.

“I will not take you to my bed, Serenity.”

“Melchior, I—”

“I cannot return the feelings you think you have for me.” He opened his eyes and looked at her.

“I don’t *think* I have feelings for you, Melchior. I *know* I do.”

“You cannot—”

“Yes, I can!” she yelled over his words, hurt by his insult and finally showing it.

Melchior replied in a calm manner, “You *cannot* love me, Serenity. Your ability to lie, even to yourself, hurts you with each passing moment you give this falsehood credence. You haven’t known me long enough to love me.”

“I feel as though I have known you forever. I knew it from the moment I looked into your eyes.”

“Love is not so quick.”

“It was for me!”

He gestured to her. “This is my point. You do not love me but an image of me you made up based on information your Hell Hounds imparted to you over the years. You *prepared* yourself to love me as a way to cope with the new life that would be soon forced upon you.”

While his words made sense, Serenity refused to believe them. She hadn’t imagined the spark of recognition, the meeting of two souls that happened when she met his gaze for the first time. His touch felt familiar to her and she knew his feel even before he introduced himself to her. She knew Melchior to be hers with every fiber of her being. There was no way he hadn't felt the same. She thought she saw it during their wedding ceremony and didn't understand why he denied it.

She said, "Destiny placed us together because she knew of the love we would have for one another."

"Your obsession with Destiny is the reason you cannot grasp reality, Serenity. This emotion you claim to have is not based on any truth. You do not know me."

"Love cannot be rationalized or measured in time."

"Love also cannot endure when it is false. Time is on my side. When enough of it passes, you will come to realize your feelings were nothing but a delusion."

"The only person in this room who is deluded is you, Melchior." She spun around and stormed out of the room.

Her words were said in self-preservation. It was the only means she had of lashing out at him. Melchior's constant denials hurt her. She hadn't imagined their mutual attraction and their first and only night together was her proof.

She had caused Melchior's arousal. Serenity was sure of it. It may have started as mere curiosity but he had responded to her touch as she had responded to his. It wasn't all in her mind. It wasn't.

CHAPTER TWENTY

SERENITY LOOKED AROUND THE COURTYARD. He was there. She had caught a glimpse of him only a moment ago, but didn't want to call out for him through the crowd. No one had noticed her presence and she wanted to keep it that way. If she was careful enough, she could get away from the palace without anyone the wiser.

Her need for caution was exaggerated. No one cared about her comings and goings. Melchior actively ignored her and had ignored her for the past five months. The palace followed his lead. Serenity didn't care anymore. She had her Hell Hounds and that was all that she needed.

That was a lie. But, it was the lie that kept her from crying herself to sleep every night.

"What are you searching for, Serenity?" Melchior asked, stepping out of the shadows.

Serenity looked behind her. It was a little bit of a shock to have Melchior speaking to her and she stared at him for a long while. She had forgotten how hot her body became when she was in his presence. He didn't have to touch her—not that he would—and she was flushed with remembrance of their only time together.

"Nothing, Your Majesty. I didn't know you were here, so I shall leave." She exited the courtyard. She would rejoin Nym and the others in her rooms.

Nym hadn't accompanied her on her errand, in fact, none of the Hell Hounds had. There was no need, though it felt strange without them at her side. Serenity was no longer in danger since everyone ignored or avoided her.

"Didn't you?" Melchior asked.

She stopped but didn't look back. "Didn't I what, Your Majesty?"

"Didn't you know I was here?"

There was an accusation in his voice. She faced him and answered with an edge of annoyance, "No, I didn't know you were here. I thought I saw another enter the courtyard and followed. There are too many here today, so I will search for him another time."

"Him? Is this another of your attempts to make me jealous, Serenity?"

"I cannot make you feel anything that is not within you already, Your Majesty." Her voice sounded tired to her ears and she was. As much as she tried to pretend Nexeu was no different than Cheslav, it didn't work.

She'd dismissed the cruel words and actions of the Cheslavian people since she felt she truly belonged with the bhresyas. But, the bhresyas shunned her as well. She had no place. Everyday that realization pressed upon her more and more and saddened her.

Erezion interrupted their conversation with a happy greeting. Serenity gave an inward sigh of relief at his perfect timing. The conversation was headed nowhere good. It was best to end it before she and Melchior made a spectacle of themselves in front of the entire palace population.

"Your Majesties," Erezion greeted with a bow.

Serenity smiled at him warmly. She wanted to hug him but refrained. "It is good that you found me, Sir Erezion. I need your help, if you aren't too busy."

"I am yours, my queen," he said and bowed again. "You know that."

His words weren't said idly. Erezion had given Serenity his oath of loyalty over a month ago. He recited it on bended knee in front of the Ladies of the Circle instead of the nobles of the court, but it held just the same.

Serenity was glad for his oath. It made her feel a little better about her outcast existence, but she didn't name Erezion a Hell Hound. Setta and Erezion both were deeply hurt and angry at her decision. Serenity didn't see the point of another guard when she barely had a use for her current ones. Not even Melchior broached the subject again, though that would require talking to her.

Erezion had still wanted the title, but Serenity continued in her refusal. He eventually accepted her decision, even if he didn't agree. Though he didn't have the title, he adorned himself like the Hell Hounds in Serenity's shade of brown and he stayed close to her so he could aid her if ever there was a need.

Like now.

"At this moment, I only have need of your nose," Serenity said. "I saw Lorcan enter the courtyard and then promptly lost him. Could you find him for me?"

"Of course, my queen. I will only be a moment." Erezion inhaled deeply then made his way through the crowd.

Melchior said, "You could have called for him. Lorcan would have answered."

"I chose not to bring attention to myself." She faced the way Erezion had gone and hoped he hurried. The afternoon was almost gone and she wanted to get in a good long ride before the sun set.

There was no need for her to rush. Since she took most of her meals in her room, no one would miss her at dinner. She had given up attempting to eat with the nobles. After her argument with Melchior, he refused to sit next to her. She came to dinner that night and he left.

The act was obvious and noticed. That was all anyone could speak of all night. Serenity had to quit the dining hall early because her appetite had vanished. That caused the nobles and servants to talk even more. The whole situation enraged Serenity like nothing else before it.

She thought Melchior's action was a fluke. The next day, she took her throne and prepared herself to sit through the court proceedings as a silent observer. Melchior called a recess the moment she sat down. The entire throne room adjourned, leaving Serenity sitting alone with her Hell Hounds.

That had hurt.

Rather than stay where she wasn't wanted, Serenity had retreated to her rooms for the rest of the day. Not even an invitation to spend the day with the Ladies of the Circle could cheer her after such a slight.

It didn't take long for the nobles and servants to realize Melchior didn't want to be around his queen. All eyes followed her wherever she went. She would enter a room only to see Melchior's retreating back because someone had warned him of her approach. That was enough to make her avoid anywhere she thought Melchior might go.

That was also the reason why she hadn't called out to Lorcan when he entered the courtyard. The gathering meant Melchior had to be there somewhere. She didn't want anyone to notice her and alert him. Serenity didn't want to watch Melchior leave another room because of her.

She held herself rigid as she waited for Erezion's return. Tension thrummed through her entire being because Melchior hadn't left. He stood only a few steps from her but said nothing. She didn't dare look at him. He probably wanted her to leave so he wouldn't have to. She would accommodate him soon.

Erezion came back through the crowd with Lorcan in front of him. "Here you are, my queen."

Several people turned and looked at Serenity. She held her chin high under their scrutiny. This was no time to show weakness. She held her hand out to Lorcan. He came to her with a happy yip and nuzzled her hand.

Serenity thanked Erezion and nodded to him when he bowed to her. She turned reluctantly to Melchior and curtsied. Though she faced him, she didn't look at him. "I shall take my leave then, Your Majesty. Good day to you."

She didn't wait for his reply before leading Lorcan away. She knew all eyes were on her as she left. For the first time since her arrival, she wished to be back in Cheslav with her mother and brother. She couldn't live the rest of her life like this.

At least, for now, she had the release of the countryside. She stroked Lorcan's head and he barked at her. "Do you wish to run with Ines again, my love?"

Lorcan barked in response.

"Let's go find Chigaru and Haige then."

Serenity picked up her skirts to run alongside Lorcan. She didn't make it two steps before Theyn and Alexa came around the corner directly in her path. She pulled up short, but they didn't notice her.

Theyn yelled, "I'm not talking about this with you, Alexa. My answer is no."

"Why won't you at least hear me out?" Alexa demanded. She stepped into Theyn and he stood his ground. "Why?"

"I don't belong in Cheslav. I will see you to the border and your family can take charge of you from there. You do not need me to guard you at your nephew's wedding. They won't want a bhresya there, Alexa. Your family would hate my presence."

"They wouldn't."

"Just because you have forgotten your father's and brother's deaths at bhresya hands doesn't mean they have."

Alexa jerked away from Theyn with an outraged gasp. "How dare you? I haven't forgotten anything."

"Good, then that's settled." Theyn turned and then stopped. He looked surprised to see Serenity watching him and Alexa. "How long have you stood there, Serenity?"

"Serenity?" Alexa asked in surprise. She looked around Theyn at Serenity and squeaked. The sound made her slap her hand over her mouth. She took a step back and then she turned and ran.

Theyn watched her go then turned back to Serenity with a sigh. "We didn't mean to argue in front of you like that."

"I understand your hesitance, Theyn. But, it would make Alexa happy if you were there." Serenity didn't know what right she had to give anyone advice. Her life wasn't an example to live by.

Theyn shook his head. "I remember all too well the scorn for my kind of those who reside in Cheslav, but Alexa's memory has faded. If I were to escort her to her nephew's wedding, the celebration would be ruined and Alexa would be upset. I won't do that."

"Your kind." She sighed. Would bhresyas and humans ever get along?

"Where are you headed, Serenity? May I accompany you? I haven't escorted you in so long. I feel left out."

Serenity rushed over and hugged Theyn. He returned her hug. "I never meant to make you feel that way, my joy. You had only to say so and I could have assigned one of the others to watch Alexa."

"No, it is my duty and I don't dislike it. I only miss our time together."

"Then come with us today. We can be together again—all of us—like we used to be. I'm sure Sir Erezion can watch Alexa for a few hours. I'm equally sure nothing would happen to her in that time."

Serenity turned to return to the courtyard and tell Erezion of their plans. Her feet froze to the floor. In her excitement to have Theyn join her and the others, she had almost forgotten about Melchior. Running into him once was a coincidence. She couldn't do it again.

She said, "Sir Erezion is in the courtyard. Tell him of our plans and then meet us at the stables."

"*He's* there as well, isn't he?" He glared in the direction of the courtyard.

Serenity laid a hand on his arm, heartened at his anger on her behalf. "Leave it be, Theyn."

"How can I? The way he treats you is—"

"I don't want to make this life any harder than it already is," she whispered. She looked away from Theyn's gaze when he looked down at her. His arms tightened around her and she took comfort in his strength.

Theyn blew an angry breath through his nostrils. "I will do as you ask, but things cannot go on like this."

"You're right. I will think on a way to change it later. For now, let me have this time."

"Anything for you, Serenity." He laid a kiss on her cheek then released her to go retrieve Erezion.

Serenity waited. She was glad she hadn't changed into her riding clothes before she went to look for Lorcan. Melchior might have stopped her from going out if he had seen them.

She couldn't think of why Melchior would stop her. Leaving the palace would ensure she didn't run into him the entire day. Somehow, deep in her heart, Serenity knew if Melchior had found out about her plans he would have forbade her to leave.

Theyn returned with Erezion and both men escorted Serenity back to her rooms. Alexa helped her change. The woman still seemed flustered about something, but Serenity decided not to pry.

The rest of the Hell Hounds met Serenity in the stables. Ines was already saddled and impatient to be off. Serenity couldn't wait to feel the open air as Ines raced away from the palace and all of Serenity's troubles.

CHAPTER TWENTY-ONE

NYM STUMBLED INTO THE THRONE ROOM. She fell to the ground with a groan of pain. There was dead silence.

The people in the throne room stared at her in stunned horror. Her right leg was bent forwards and she dragged it behind her. One arm was shredded to the bone, lying limp and useless against her side. She pressed her other arm into her side in an attempt to keep blood from gushing out of the sword wound there.

A female in the crowd screamed then fainted. This caused everyone else to awaken from their stupor.

Melchior jumped off his throne and ran to her.

She rolled to her side so she could look up at him. She spat blood before she croaked, "We have failed as her guard." Her eyes closed and she succumbed to oblivion.

"Mages!" Melchior roared. He left Nym's side when the mages arrived and ran out the way she had come.

There was a trail of blood leading out the front gates of the palace and nothing else. Her mount was nowhere in sight. Nym had walked from wherever the attack had taken place to the palace. There was no sign of anyone else.

Melchior returned to the throne room.

"Where is Serenity? Where are the other Hell Hounds?" he yelled.

Nym regained consciousness and blinked up at him then winced. One of the mages curved her leg to the right direction. She answered in a whisper, "Serenity was taken by Tiann. Chigaru and Lorcan followed. Haige, Theyn, and I tried to subdue Guthr and failed." She looked down at herself.

Alexa ran to Nym's side, Erezion following close behind her. She knelt beside Nym and placed a hand on her shoulder only to pull back when the female winced. She asked in a small voice, "Theyn? Is Theyn okay?"

Nym shook her head. The motion made her gasp in pain. "I was the only one able to return for help."

Alexa started crying.

Melchior glared at the woman. How could she be more concerned about Theyn than Serenity? He turned his anger on the mages. "Hurry up and heal her." To those who stood around, he shouted, "Prepare the lysidis!"

He reached down and hauled Nym to her feet. She gave a cry of pain because the mages hadn't finished healing her. "Bemoan your wounds later, show me the battle-ground now." He dragged her in his wake to the stables, not waiting for his guards to follow before he thundered off in the direction Nym indicated.

She lay across the saddle in front of him, weak sounds of pain coming from her lips every time the lysidi's hooves struck the ground. Despite her pain, Nym was able to direct Melchior to the place of the attack.

Theyn and Haige lay on the ground in a pool of their own blood, but they were breathing. Melchior rushed over to them but turned his eyes away. Nym's wounds were paltry compared to the damage these two sustained. The mages and guards caught up and Melchior motioned them forward.

Nym sank to her knees near her compatriots. "We would give our lives for our queen, King Melchior," she whispered.

"You nearly did," he replied in an equally quiet voice.

Melchior looked around. He could smell Serenity. He could also smell all of the Hell Hounds and their mounts. The hoof prints on the ground showed five lysidis had scattered—the Hell Hounds' and Serenity's mounts. Two other lysidis' tracks, side by side, left the area. The tracks disappeared a few feet after they started.

"They used an erasure spell," Melchior growled. The same erasure spell that had plagued him these many months. Its true purpose had revealed itself.

Melchior smelled no other scents except Serenity and the Hell Hounds.

He followed the side-by-side lysidi hoof prints to their end. Serenity's scent dis-appeared when the prints did and he vowed to find and kill whoever had supplied Serenity's attackers with such a strong and thorough impediment. His first priority, however, was to rescue his wife.

"Tell me what to do, my king," Erezion said. He had followed Melchior step for step when Melchior left the palace.

Melchior glanced at Erezion and then away. He closed his eyes, unable to face the male's obvious pain and helplessness. His treatment of Serenity had facilitated this happening. He regretted his actions.

He had thought his way was best. Serenity would see, in time, she never truly loved him. Once that realization was had, their relationship could progress towards mutual understanding and possible friendship.

It would be good to see Serenity's smile again, as he had missed it. He tried to imagine it. The image that came to him was his first meeting with Serenity when she dropped into his arms, seemingly from thin air. Her entire being was relaxed. She was the embodiment of her name in that—

Melchior jerked. He ripped open his eyes and looked around.

"King Melchior?" Erezion asked, stepping forward.

"Silence."

For only a moment he'd felt something. As though he could reach out and touch Serenity if he just thought about her. He closed his eyes again in hopes the feeling would return. Thoughts of Serenity paraded through his mind. He pictured her smile, her scent, the sound of her voice when she declared she loved him.

The feeling returned.

Melchior opened his eyes and it remained. He could sense Serenity and he knew where she was. He mounted his lysidi and turned towards the growing crowd. "Two mages and the guards with me. Nym, when Theyn and Haige are healed, return to the palace."

"King Melchior, I—"

"Will listen to me, damn you! I'll not have Serenity crying at your funerals," he barked. He turned his mount and raced to Serenity's side. He prayed he wasn't too late.

❧

Serenity bowed against her bonds, her breathing labored. "Kill me," she croaked.

Guthr laughed and replied, "I would accommodate you, little queen, but I'm not allowed." He fisted his hand in her hair and yanked her head back so she looked at him. "I spared your little female guard only because I wanted to save myself for you. I understand you have a taste for bhresya males. I plan to find out how well your Hell Hounds trained you in the art of bhresya copulation."

Serenity spit in his face.

He backhanded her.

"Back down, Guthr. He wants her alive," Tiann said as he entered the room. He had Lorcan on a leash behind him. Lorcan wore a full head muzzle that kept his jaws clamped shut, though he still tried to attack. Tiann laughed at him. "Struggle all you want, you devil spawned bastard, the muzzle is enchanted."

"Lorcan," Serenity said. She struggled against her ropes, ignoring the pain in her body from her beating. Tiann and Guthr had tied her more securely this time.

"Leave him alone," she cried when it became obvious she wouldn't be able to get free. "Let him go."

Tiann sneered at her. "Our benefactor wished the mutt as well as you, Queen Serenity." He looked over his shoulder as one of Guthr's followers carried in another and dumped him on the floor. "Chigaru was just a bonus."

Serenity blinked at Chigaru, not recognizing him. He was covered in blood and his face was a mass of bruises and cuts. She glared at her captors. "Why are you doing this? Queen Rhiannon and King Melchior had all but forgotten about you."

"True and not true because Guthr and I are not the most inconspicuous of males. On several occasions, there have been those who recognized us and had to be dealt with. Their deaths proved an excellent chance to test an enchantment our employer purchased. Since Melchior couldn't follow the trail of bodies to us, we assumed it worked and decided to use it for its true purpose—kidnapping you."

Guthr laughed. "That was not a trail of bodies, Tiann. Once Alric restarts the war, you shall see a trail of bodies."

"Alric?" Serenity asked. "Why would he restart the war?"

"You have been out of touch with home, haven't you?" Tiann taunted. "Rhiannon stepped down in favor of her son a month after your marriage."

"Alric is king of Cheslav," she said with wonder.

No letters had come from her family since her arrival in Nexeu. She didn't think Melchior would keep her from communicating with her mother and brother. That only meant Rhiannon and Alric didn't wish to have contact with her. Or perhaps, they only awaited word from her. It never occurred to her to write.

"Once the war restarts, Guthr and I may return to our former jobs," Tiann continued.

Serenity was scared to ask but couldn't stop herself, "Why would Alric restart the war?"

From the shadows came a familiar voice that answered, "Because Alric will be so distraught over your death—by obvious demon hands—he will restart the war in a heartbeat, dear sister." Joah walked into the light. He looked great except for his right arm. The arm Chigaru had broken was in a sling.

He stroked it. "Due to my banishment, I was not able to find a mage in time to heal my arm properly." He smiled at her horrified look. "I heard you ousted your Hell Hounds from the palace over my injury. Was that sisterly love or guilt?"

Serenity opened her mouth, and Joah slapped her.

"Don't you speak to me! Don't you ever talk to me, you little pampered bitch!" He slapped her again. "When you die, I will return to Alric with news that Melchior's neglect of you caused your death." He smirked at her look of surprise. "The very upset and somewhat jealous Mistress Keran was very open with news of your life with Melchior and about your habit of leaving the palace to ride through the countryside."

He turned away from Serenity and looked at Lorcan and Chigaru. "Poor Alric will be so heartbroken over your death that he will restart the war. While he's distracted with his revenge, I will have him killed and take his place on the throne." He glanced at her. "You, even as a puppet queen, are still a queen, and Mother stepped down so Alric could ascend. To the third born nothing." He clenched his fist. "Once my siblings are out of the way, I will get everything."

He walked over to Chigaru who glared up at him. "You want to get at me, don't you, silent giant?" He signaled Guthr forward. "Rip off his arm. I owe him that."

"No," screamed Serenity. "He only broke your arm, Joah. I'm sorry it didn't heal properly but—"

Joah cracked his hand across her cheek again. "I told you not to speak. Besides, Chigaru is a demon. A simple broken arm would heal in no time. You cannot heal what isn't there." He gave Guthr a nod.

Guthr gripped Chigaru's right arm. He planted his foot against the male's chest and yanked. Chigaru roared in pain. It was the first sound he had made since his abuse had started.

Serenity cried for him. This was her fault. She insisted on riding outside of the palace and she had angered Keran many times over because it seemed there were no ill repercussions, from Melchior or any other. She was wrong and this was her punishment.

Joah laughed at her tears. "Cry all you want. I'm not done." He turned to Tiann. "As promised, Tiann, the hound is yours."

Serenity's gaze flew to Tiann as he pulled a sword. "Don't do this," she whispered. She renewed her struggles against her bonds, ignoring her own pain in her bid to get free. "Please, Joah, not Lorcan."

"Do it," Joah said with satisfaction.

Tiann raised the sword and buried it in Lorcan's chest. The hound screamed. Tiann repeated the motion over and over until the hound's heart stopped beating, then he cut off Lorcan's head.

Joah laughed uproariously.

Serenity screamed.

CHAPTER TWENTY-TWO

MELCHIOR JERKED HIS HEAD UP at the sound of Serenity's blood curdling scream. Everyone looked at him. He spurred his mount faster, telling himself one thing over and over again—Serenity wasn't dead, but if she was, her murderer would wish for death.

He jumped off his mount when they reached the house from which the scream had originated. He could hear Serenity crying, which meant she was alive. He pulled his battle-axe off his back and charged the door.

He was sure his eyes blazed with the anger he felt when he witnessed the horror before him. His gentle Serenity was tied to a chair. Her face was covered in blood and several open wounds and one of her eyes was swollen completely shut. Serenity's dress was shredded and laid bare her beaten and abused flesh. Near her feet, Chigaru was bound from head to toe and lying in a pool of his own blood. And Lorcan...

Melchior understood Serenity's scream.

Guthr spat, "Melchior."

Joah took a step back. He asked in an agitated voice, "How did you find us? The spell I used... She said you wouldn't be able to track us... not by scent or sight. You shouldn't be here!"

Melchior advanced on them with a growl. "You should have killed Serenity immediately if you didn't want me to find you."

Erezion and the guards rushed into the house and the battle was met. Guthr fought with a sword in one hand and a warhammer in the other. Four guards were injured in the battle. He was finally stopped when a sword pierced his back and exited through his chest—Haige's sword.

Tiann was no match for so many bhresyas. He died as soon as the guards were made aware of his presence. The Hell Hounds, now fully healed, stood ready to kill Joah but Melchior stopped them.

Despite the travesties Joah had committed, he was Serenity's brother. Melchior was surprised to see the Hell Hounds as he had commanded them to return to the palace. He should have known they wouldn't listen.

He went to Serenity. Her head was bowed and she cried silently. He undid her bonds and helped her to her feet. He whispered, "Serenity? Are you—"

Serenity shoved past him with a scream and tackled Joah. She clawed at his face and beat him with her fists, screaming the whole time. She stopped her attack long enough to grab Joah's dagger from his belt. She roared, "Die, you twisted bastard!"

Her blow was stopped before it reached its mark. Melchior grabbed her around the waist and hauled her off Joah. She struggled against his hold.

"Release me! He killed Lorcan! Release me!"

"You wish him dead, Serenity?" Melchior asked quietly. He held her against his chest with both arms and found it a hard task. She struggled wildly. He didn't know she had this much strength.

"Yes! Kill him! Kill him!"

Melchior released her into the hold of one of his guards. The male looked scared of her but held her. Melchior lifted his battle-axe. Joah opened the eye that wasn't gouged out as wide as he could and he croaked out a denial moments before Melchior severed his head from his body.

Serenity stopped struggling and sank to her knees in silence. The male who held her looked unsure whether he should let her fall or keep Serenity on her feet. He stood stiff as Melchior looked at them.

Melchior dropped his battle-axe beside Joah's body. He knelt in front of Serenity and put a finger under her chin, urging her to look at him. There was only pain in her eyes.

"You may have ordered blood but you have never taken it. If it is within my power, I will make sure you never do," he whispered to her.

Serenity clutched her arms, her nails digging into her flesh. Blood curled out of the wounds she made. Her breathing came faster and faster until she screamed, "Lorcan!"

The cry originated at the bottom of her soul and the pain in her heart fueled it. Melchior knew everyone in the room felt it to the depths of their souls just as he did.

She fainted and he caught her. He lifted her high on his chest and buried his face in her stomach. He had almost lost her. His stupidity had almost killed her.

Everyone stood watching him.

He straightened.

"Send Tiann's and Guthr's bodies to Queen Rhiannon and Prince Alric," he said. He looked at Chigaru.

The mage who worked on him shook his head and said, "The arm is dead. I cannot reattach it." Chigaru seemed unconcerned. His gaze was only for Serenity and Melchior.

Melchior said, "Gather Lorcan's remains. He will be given a state burial."

❧◦❦

Serenity stared at herself in the mirror. The mages had healed her and she had no scars as a remembrance of her ordeal, only the emotional pain. Her dearest friend was dead and all because of her willfulness and need to lash out at her reluctant husband. If she had stayed inside of the palace walls, Lorcan would still be alive and Chigaru would still have his arm.

Behind her Chigaru and Nym watched her. Shame prevented her from looking at Chigaru.

Thankfully, Nym and the others had healed with few problems. Serenity later heard from the Ladies of the Circle that Alexa had kissed Theyn when the mages finished healing him. That confirmed Serenity's suspicions about their relationship.

Serenity wished them happiness in their marriage. Theyn had blushed when Serenity relayed her sentiment, then stammered out denials. Alexa had threatened to give him another beating if he didn't marry her.

Haige, once he heard a full recounting of the incident from Serenity, had located Keran and punished her for her part in the abduction. Melchior later denied Keran the help of a mage. Her wounds healed but not without scars. She was also banished from the palace and the capital.

Haige presented one of Keran's horns to Serenity and it represented the only horn with a living owner since Guthr was dead. If Serenity ever saw her again, Keran would die too.

Serenity stood. She wore a dress of iridescent cloth for the state funeral Melchior had insisted on having for Lorcan. Though she was human and human tradition demanded she wear black, this was Nexeu and black was not considered a color of mourning. Every bhresya in the palace and many of those in the cities beyond were similarly swathed in iridescent clothing. The entirety of Nexeu was put into mourning, though Serenity had told Melchior not to bother.

Nym stepped forward and held out Serenity's veil. "Dowager Queen Rhiannon and King Alric have arrived," she whispered.

Over the last few days, Serenity had noticed her Hell Hounds had grown as quiet as Chigaru. She knew that was her fault. She hadn't smiled since the day of her abduction three days before. Even Theyn was somber despite his newfound relationship with Alexa.

It had taken two days to convince her Hell Hounds she wasn't angry with them. She even insisted Alexa and Theyn go through with their wedding as soon as possible. Alexa wanted to wait until the mourning period was over and Theyn had agreed.

Chigaru opened the door to the room. Haige, Theyn, and Alexa waited for Serenity. Alexa fixed the veil then took up her stance next to Theyn.

They made their way to the throne room. Serenity entered to silence. Everyone immediately bowed to her but she ignored them all and walked over to her mother and brother.

Rhiannon rushed up to her and folded her in a hug. "My baby."

Alric took Serenity's hand in both of his and held it to his chest.

"We should have enacted the true punishment instead of banishment. This wouldn't have happened if I was strong enough to—" said Rhiannon.

"Mother," Serenity interrupted, "he was your son. A parent should never have to order their child's death."

"A sister should not either," Melchior said.

Serenity nodded but didn't look up at Melchior. She stepped back from her mother and retrieved her hand from Alric.

In the days that followed her attack, Melchior tried to speak to Serenity, but it was her turn to ignore him. She accepted her partial blame for the events that transpired, but she blamed Melchior, as well. She didn't want his apologies, if he planned to give any. She wanted him to go back to ignoring her and leaving her alone.

Alric said, "I understand Hell Hound Theyn intends to marry your maid Alexa.

You are setting a new standard, my sister. I should marry a bhresya female just so I don't feel left out. Perhaps Nym?"

Nym stiffened and gave him an astonished look. "You are jesting, Your Majesty."

Alric winked at her but smiled, showing his words were meant as a joke. "Unfortunately, mother betrothed me to a nobleman's daughter. The wedding is next year." He turned to Serenity. "You will attend, of course, Serenity?"

"I would not miss it, my brother. No matter what my king says."

Melchior stiffened. "I would not deny you your brother's wedding, my wife."

Rhiannon gave a delicate sniff and looked from Melchior to Serenity. She looked ready to ask something but kept her silence.

CHAPTER TWENTY-THREE

SERENITY DIDN'T CRY as Lorcan's coffin was lowered into the ground, and she didn't cry as the dirt was piled on. She had cried all she planned to cry three days ago. She took in the entire ordeal in numb silence. She reasoned Alexa cried enough for both of them.

Though she didn't wish to, Serenity attended the banquet after the funeral to appease her mother and brother. Alric tried his best to make her smile and she was saddened further when she disappointed him.

As usual, conversation flowed around Serenity. Not because the nobles avoided talking to her, but because she refused to speak more than two or three words at a time. She wasn't the only one giving monosyllabic answers. Melchior didn't seem to be in a talkative mood, either.

Alric slammed down his drink after an hour of watching this display. "Serenity, I know Lorcan's death has saddened you, but he wouldn't have wanted this depression. He loved your happiness more than any other." He turned to Melchior before she could form an answer. "Why do you not comfort your wife, King Melchior?"

Serenity spoke quietly then, "Comforting me would involve touching me. Melchior has made it quite clear, touching me is the last thing he wants to do."

The hall fell into silence, all eyes on the royals.

Rhiannon gave a soft chuckle of nervousness and dabbed her mouth with her napkin. "King Melchior has to touch you in order to beget heirs, Serenity."

"If you ask anyone at this table, Mother, they will tell you Melchior has no intention of impregnating me. No one in this kingdom wants a half-human heir to the throne. We have not copulated since our wedding night."

Alric choked on his drink. He pounded on his chest and coughed to clear his airway. He croaked, "That was five months ago."

"This isn't the conversation to be held at dinner," Rhiannon scolded. She gave Alric a look to drop it and then turned the look on Serenity.

Alric ignored his mother's look and asked, "If not for heirs then why did you insist on marrying my sister, King Melchior?"

"To solidify the peace treaty. I mean as much to him—to everyone in Nexeu—as Tiann's and Guthr's corpses," Serenity answered for Melchior.

"You know you are more important than a couple of corpses, my daughter. You are queen," Rhiannon said with a chuckle. "I am not ashamed to say I am happy you will not bear King Melchior's children. I can forget that worry. The endeavor might have killed you. I would cherish a grandchild but not at the expense of my daughter." She gave Serenity's hand a pat. "You will leave your mark on Nexeu through your keen insights, which—I might add—I had a hand in honing."

Serenity slipped her hand away from her mother before she said, "I am not permitted to attend meetings of state."

Rhiannon blinked in surprise then looked at Melchior. He didn't meet her gaze. His hand was fisted on the tabletop and his nostrils flared with each breath he took. She offered, "King Melchior, I don't know if Serenity neglected to tell you, but Hell Hound Haige made certain she would be prepared to help in the rule of—"

"He doesn't care, Mother," Serenity interrupted in a frustrated voice. She ripped the veil from her head, taking her crown with it. She gripped the symbol of her station as she continued in a stoic voice, "I am a figurehead in the truest sense of the word. I have no power and hold no sway. They are waiting for me to die so he can seat a *bhresya* female on the throne as queen." She threw her crown and veil on to the table as hard she could. The gold circlet hit the table and bounced up before it landed in front of a surprised noble.

Serenity didn't care where it landed. She also didn't care if she ever wore it again. She rose from her seat, curtsied to Melchior and Alric, then left the room. The Hell Hounds followed her. They mirrored her angered mood.

She shouldn't have said what she did, but she couldn't stand lying to her mother and brother any longer. They thought of her relationship one way when it wasn't and to let them continue was wrong.

It didn't matter anymore. Nothing did.

෧⚬෨

Alric stared after Serenity in shock then looked back at Melchior. "She is mistaken. There was a misunderstanding, correct?" he asked.

Melchior didn't answer.

Alric looked at the discarded crown. The noble it had landed in front of seemed confused as to what he should do with it. "I thought to find my sister happy except for the death of her beloved pet. Instead, I find the true cause of her depression and I don't like it," Alric said after five breaths of silence. He stood. "Serenity will leave with my mother and me tomorrow."

Melchior pushed back his seat, rose and faced Alric. He said in a low voice of warning, "She is my wife. She will stay in Nexeu."

His show of anger didn't seem to daunt Alric. Melchior attributed Alric's courage in the face of bhresya rage to the boy king's time with the Hell Hounds.

Alric glared at Melchior and accused, "She's your trophy. She's going home to Cheslav."

"Nexeu is her home."

"No, Nexeu is her prison. I have never seen Serenity this upset. My mother tried to hide the assassination attempts but I'm not stupid. I saw the bodies and the blood. Through it all Serenity smiled," Alric said in a cold voice. "The people of the palace called her a walking sacrifice and worse. Still she smiled. Mael, her sister amongst the Hell Hounds, betrayed her. *Still* she smiled." He stopped, clenched his fists at his side and stared at Serenity's discarded crown. "Seven months living with the man... I'm sorry... *demon* she thought she loved and she may never smile again."

Rhiannon stood. "Alric, stop this."

Melchior agreed. The situation had gotten out of hand. They shouldn't have this conversation in public. The nobles and servants stared at them with rapt attention and there was no other sound or movement.

"No, Mother. I've made up my mind. Serenity returns with us tomorrow. If they—" he pointed to the nobles at the dining hall table "—are waiting for her to die, then they can wait for news from Cheslav. That's final." He walked over to the noble who held Serenity's crown. Without pardon or explanation, he snatched the gold circlet from the male and left the room.

Rhiannon stared after her son then looked at Melchior. She moved to his side. He didn't want her touching him and she seemed to sense that because she clenched her hands together, twisting her napkin in her hands instead.

She whispered, "King Melchior, I did not keep my word to you because of our treaty. I wouldn't have put Serenity through the horrors I went through on the day of my ascension for anything, but nothing, not even the threat of death, would have made me force her to marry you if she had objected." She shook her head as her eyes strayed from him to the twisted napkin in her hands. "You may not love her, you may not even like her, but as your wife and queen I thought you would respect her. Or at least, respect the measures she took to help you rule."

She turned away from him to leave the room. She was two paces away when she turned back and added, "I knew you hated my father, but I had hoped you wouldn't take that hate out on my daughter." She exited.

Melchior stood through it all. He could say nothing to gainsay Alric and Rhiannon because everything they said was true. It was a strange feeling to know the words that came from a human's mouth were true. He looked at no one. His fists were clenched at his side. He hadn't expected the day to end this way. He had prepared himself for Serenity's tears and their absence surprised him.

A noble at the table cleared his throat then said, "Perhaps it is best Queen Serenity return to Cheslav. She would be safer—"

"Your continued good health depends on you not finishing that sentence," Melchior said with menace.

The male snapped his mouth shut and cast his eyes down, staring at his plate.

Melchior was more upset with Serenity for having started this conversation in front of his nobles than he was at Alric and Rhiannon. His embarrassment at the words Serenity said made his old anger resurface.

He knew Serenity hadn't planned the confrontation, but he also knew she had in no way hindered it from happening. He found himself thinking back on what Theyn told him the first day he met Serenity—*Don't get her angry though. That girl can be a real bitch...*

Melchior now realized why Serenity hadn't cried at Lorcan's funeral and why she had avoided him. She wasn't depressed, she was angry—at him.

CHAPTER TWENTY-FOUR

TRUE TO HIS WORD, Alric had Serenity packed up and ready to go the next morning. He looked over at the Hell Hounds and asked, "I will not command you, but if you would return to Cheslav to act as Serenity's guards—"

Chigaru placed his hand on Alric's shoulder. Nym said for him, "You don't have to ask, King Alric. We were prepared to follow our queen whether you wanted us or not."

Haige and Theyn nodded at this. Theyn was already atop his mount with Alexa seated comfortably in front of him. She smiled up at him and gave his arms a pat where they circled her waist.

Two lysidis approached the group. Erezion was mounted on one and Lady Uleoma on the other. They pulled their mounts close to Ines. Serenity sat atop her mare with a puzzled expression on her face.

Erezion dismounted and went to one knee beside Ines. The mare shied to the side and pawed the ground. Serenity quieted her mare and turned her attention to Erezion.

He said, "Allow me to accompany you as well, my queen. My place is at your side."

Serenity reached out her hand to him. While he was on his knee, she couldn't touch him. "Rise."

He stood.

Her hand landed on his shoulder. "I would be honored and proud to have you with me in Cheslav... Hell Hound Erezion."

His mouth fell open in shock and he stared at Serenity for a long while. He tore his gaze from her and looked at the other Hell Hounds for confirmation of her words. Chigaru nodded to him.

Erezion turned back to Serenity, taking her hand in his. He kissed her palm. "I will serve you loyally, my queen. You will never have cause to regret your decision."

"Enough!" Uleoma snapped in annoyance.

All eyes turned to her.

She glared back at everyone. "What?"

Nym asked, "Was it your intention to see Hell Hound Erezion off in Lady Setta's stead, my lady?"

"No. I will go to Cheslav. I didn't make all those dresses so a bunch of no-talent humans could ruin them with ill treatment and improper care. She's my queen. I plan to see her dressed properly—even if it isn't in bhresya fashions."

Serenity said, "I would be honored with your presence as well, Lady Uleoma."

She looked towards Cheslav. It was time to go. Serenity looked down at Chigaru, who nodded to her then looked at Nym.

The Hell Hounds mounted up and led the way back to Cheslav. Chigaru went to Ines. He mounted behind Serenity and spurred the mare forward.

Rhiannon looked back at the palace. The nobles watched through the windows and doorways of the palace. Melchior wasn't among their number. She turned in her saddle and faced front, then signaled her horse to follow the others.

Serenity said over her shoulder, "We shall meet you there, Mother." She nodded to Chigaru and he snapped Ines' reins. The mare leapt forward and ran at her top speed. The other Hell Hounds and Lady Uleoma sped up their lysidi mounts.

Rhiannon shook her head at her daughter's retreating form. "I could never ride one of those monsters. The speed at which they move..."

Alric snorted, "She turned herself into the perfect bhresya bride only to be scorned." He kicked his mount forward.

Being back in Cheslav didn't help alleviate Serenity's depression. If anything, it made it worse. Over the course of eight months, Serenity reacquainted herself with Cheslav life. In doing so, she established a pattern of only talking with her Hell Hounds, eating in her rooms and generally avoiding any and all stimulation.

Alric had given her space at first but now didn't know how to cover the ground to bring her back. He sighed heavily and looked at Rhiannon. "The last time I saw her smile was at Theyn and Alexa's wedding two weeks after we arrived back. Even then it was a ghost of her true radiance." He clenched his fist. "I shouldn't have allowed her to seclude herself."

"You are not her king, Alric. She wouldn't have listened to you. She doesn't have to," Rhiannon said in a matter-of-fact tone.

"She is in my kingdom. She's my sister."

"She is a visiting dignitary and may heed your suggestions out of respect for your kingdom. That you are triplets is of no consequence. You are both rulers of very powerful kingdoms and you must remember that above all other things."

"We brought her here because she didn't truly rule Nexeu, Mother."

"True. That doesn't change her role as Nexeu's queen. You cannot force Serenity to do anything she doesn't want to do. You are not her king." She looked up from her knitting and smiled at Alric's furious expression. "She will not stay depressed forever, my love. She has lost her dearest pet and her first love. Allow her time to mourn properly."

"Eight months have past already," Alric whispered.

Rhiannon shrugged. "I was only given eight months to grieve over the passing of my father, brothers, and husband. I wished for more time but couldn't have it because I had to be whole for my children."

"Mother—"

"Out of everyone, I understand her pain more than any other, Alric. Leave her be, if you truly love her."

Alric gave his mother a rueful smile and asked in a joking manner, "Who is ruler? You or me?"

"You, of course, my son," Rhiannon said matter-of-factly.

ᔥᔤ

Melchior threw the papers away from him and growled in frustration.

His advisors shrank from his anger. They all exchanged glances before one said, "Mayhap this would be better discussed at a later time, my king?"

One advisor straightened his stance and stepped away from his fellows. "Bring her back, my king."

Melchior looked up at the male in shock. "You cheered her leaving."

"I thought it was for the best. You cannot rule like this."

The others nodded in agreement.

The advisor said, "We know the signs of a mated pair. Though we had hoped it was merely lust on your part, you have mated with your queen. That is life for our kind. You cannot continue on without—"

Melchior swept his hand across his desk and sent the contents flying. "I touched her only once!"

The advisor shook his head. "Mating isn't about touch, my king. It's about souls. You were mated to her the moment you saw her. It is possible you sensed her as your mate while she was still in her mother's womb."

Another advisor said, "Bring her back. Have your heir with her."

That got Melchior's attention. He stopped destroying his study and stared at the males. "At the ball held in her honor, you said it would be impossible for a half-breed to take the throne. You said a half-breed heir was too soon of an adjustment after a human queen. Have you changed your minds?"

The advisors looked at one another before they looked back at Melchior. The one who had started the conversation answered, "We thought it was a whim, my king. We were not aware you were a mated pair. Had we but known—"

Melchior laughed. All his anguish, all of his pain, all the pain he had caused Serenity was because he refused to admit to anyone, including himself, that he loved his wife. He faced the room of advisors with determination and a new sense of purpose. "When she returns, she will be a true bhresya queen and her children will be my legitimate heirs."

"True—"

"But, my king—"

"*True* bhresya queen! I will have no more secrets from my wife!"

All the men nodded. One asked, "Will you marry others?"

Melchior made his way around his desk. On his way out of his study he said to them, "That will be up to Serenity."

He made one stop before he gathered his nobles and his guards to make the journey to Cheslav. These were the same nobles who had accompanied Melchior to his wedding. He would take her by force if Alric would not return her. He would have

Serenity back and she would be happy at his side.

He laughed at himself and his thoughts. He had once boasted to Rhiannon no human woman was worth war. He was wrong. Even now, Melchior contemplated breaking a fifteen-month peace in order to reclaim his wife.

CHAPTER TWENTY-FIVE

"ABSOLUTELY NOT! In fact, get out of my kingdom," Alric yelled.

Rhiannon gave him a stern look. "Alric, your attitude is unbecoming a king. I have taught you better than this."

Alric sliced his hand through the air. "*He* is not welcome here. Serenity has finally started smiling again, even if it is a little. I will not jeopardize that because he has a whim."

"Alric—"

"Am I king?" he asked in a rough voice.

Rhiannon nodded. "You are king, my son."

"Then, I have made my decision." He looked at Melchior and the other bhresyas behind him. "Leave."

Melchior gave the barest of nods. He had known this would be difficult. Alric loved his sister and didn't want to see her hurt. He could respect that. On his way there, he had boasted to himself of waging war, but killing her brother to get her back would only drive Serenity farther away.

He signaled his guards and they left. The nobles awaited them outside. Melchior would have to find another way to get Serenity back.

He mounted his lysidi and turned it towards Nexeu.

Rhiannon came rushing out of a side door. Melchior wouldn't have taken notice of her if not for the fact that she wore a cloak with the hood pulled over her head so it covered her face. He dismounted and met her halfway across the courtyard.

She signaled him into the shadows. It seemed silly since Melchior was so big and everyone would know he stood there, but her need for privacy and his curiosity compelled him to comply.

"I don't do this lightly, Melchior," she whispered.

Melchior whispered in response, "I understand."

"I thought your scorn was because of her ancestry," she said as she searched his gaze.

"I do not hate Serenity. I wouldn't be here if I hated her."

"My son is proud and almost as protective of Serenity as her Hell Hounds." She heaved a painful sigh. "She is depressed and it goes far beyond losing Lorcan, though he was beloved above all things to her."

She placed a hand on his arm, surprising him. "She treasured Lorcan always because he was a gift from you. She had never met you, only knew horror stories about you, and yet was forever happy at the thought of marrying you. That and only that is the reason why I'm going against my son in this."

Before Melchior could form a response to this speech, Rhiannon stepped away from the wall they spoke near and pushed a tiny knot. A door appeared and slid to the side. Rhiannon disappeared inside. Melchior signaled his guards and nobles to wait, then he followed her.

It was a tight fit. Clearly, the makers of the escape route didn't have bhresyas in mind when they built it. Melchior wouldn't hold that against them at this particular moment if it took him to Serenity.

Rhiannon poked her head out of the passage, then she exited and stood to the side so Melchior could exit the cramped space. She faced Serenity's bedroom door and gave a strangled gasp.

The Hell Hounds stood guard when, moments before, there was no one.

Chigaru nodded to Rhiannon and Melchior. The other Hell Hounds followed suit then disappeared into the places they had come from.

Melchior suddenly had a new respect for the Hell Hounds. He hadn't even known they were there. It was a credit to how much danger they had protected Serenity from that they could appear at a moment's notice and disappear just as quickly.

Rhiannon recovered herself and nodded to Chigaru, who remained. She opened Serenity's door without knocking. Serenity sat in a window seat with her back to the door. Rhiannon signaled Melchior through, but didn't follow, then closed the door after him with a snap.

Melchior jumped at the sound after all the silence. He watched Serenity but she didn't move, didn't acknowledge him.

He finally broke the silence, "My presence doesn't seem to surprise you."

Serenity turned slowly and looked at him but said nothing. Her voice was soft as she said, "I have found surprise to be an emotion I'm not quite capable of at the moment. I force myself to smile just to appease Alric. I don't want him to worry."

Melchior couldn't understand how Alric thought she had gotten better. She looked worse to his eyes. In the time she was gone, she had lost weight. Was this what depression did to a person like Serenity?

"Why are you here, my unwilling husband?"

Melchior approached her. He held out the bundle he had carried all this time. "I had hoped to see you in better spirits, Serenity."

Serenity eyed the bundle but didn't make a move to take it. When the bundle squirmed, she frowned at it. The bundle squirmed until a tiny black nose poked out. Serenity removed the covering totally and revealed a swamp-green thondi pup. She touched the little puppy's head. It snuffled at her then pushed its head into her hand.

Melchior said, "Lorcan mated with a female while in Nexeu. She had her pups shortly after you left." He pushed the puppy onto her lap and stood back. "I know this pup isn't Lorcan, but I also know Lorcan would choose no other to raise his offspring."

Serenity petted the puppy absently. It alternated between licking her hands and lightly gnawing on them. "You came all this way to deliver a puppy. That seems a little…" She shook her head with a little frown of confusion. "No messenger brave enough to overcome his scorn of humans to deliver it?"

"No messenger I trusted with the message I had to go with the pup."

"It couldn't be too important. In all the time I was in Nexeu, you hardly spoke to me. If I entered a room, you left. If I tried to touch you, you pulled away. A girl only needs so many hints, Melchior. I just assumed living out the rest of my life in Cheslav would save you the trouble of avoiding me."

Melchior sat down. All the chairs were across the room from the window seat and he wanted to be near Serenity. He sat on her bed.

He didn't know where to begin. Always telling the truth made life easier for a bhresya, but it didn't alleviate the problem of where to begin an explanation.

"I didn't avoid you out of scorn, Serenity. You surprised me. I imagine Chigaru felt the same way the night he came to kill you. You weren't scared of me."

"Of course not. Chigaru and the others practically raised me."

"That is what I mean. You went to great lengths preparing yourself to live with me in Nexeu. No other female—bhresya or otherwise—would adopt her would-be assassins to serve as her teachers."

"For all the good it did me."

Melchior stood. He wanted to pace, but decided against it. He gave a short growl and sat back down. "I admit I avoided you, but I didn't avoid you for the reasons you think."

"Then why?"

"I wanted you," he said helplessly.

That simple confession stripped him bare and cost all of his pride. He could say it no other way. Confessing to the lust that had gripped him since the moment he laid eyes on her eased the turmoil he'd carried these long months.

Serenity gave a short mirthless laugh. It was the first laugh since the death of Lorcan. She would give Melchior this—he had gotten more emotion out of her in the last minute than anyone else in the last eight months.

She snapped, "You have a funny way of showing it."

"I'm not supposed to want a human. I'm a bhresya!"

"I know that!" She swung back towards the window.

Melchior shoved his hand through his hair. "I'm saying this wrong. Serenity, I'm three hundred and forty-seven years old. I have seen thousands of human females... hundreds of thousands, in fact. When you danced for me, the night of our wedding, it was the first time a human female made me feel lust."

Serenity looked at Melchior in astonishment. She was tempted to call him a liar, and if he were human, she would. The emotion was in his gaze and plain for her to see, as was the vest and loincloth he wore. They were brown, more specifically her shade of brown.

With that simple gesture, he acknowledged her as his wife and family—someone cherished.

The very thing she'd wanted from Melchior from their very first meeting until now was before her and all she could do was stare. He looked away and that snapped her out of her stupor.

Rising from the window seat, she set the little puppy on the ground and it bumbled around the room. Then, she made her way to Melchior. She wanted to touch him but was scared he would pull away like so many other times. She looked up at him and waited. He still didn't meet her eyes. Tentatively, she placed a hand on his arm, ready to pull back if he rejected her.

Melchior looked down at her hand. "You distract me, Serenity. My first wife never invoked such strong emotions in me. After our wedding night, I wanted to bed you every night."

"Then why—"

"I didn't want the feelings I had... *have* for you. I knew the bhresyas of Nexeu would never accept a human queen. If I didn't love you, once you died, there would be no grief," he said in a rush. He sounded like a recalcitrant child who tried to explain why he had done something bad.

"The day in your study, when we argued, you said you didn't return my feelings."

"*Could not.* Not *would not.* I wanted to and it hurt me not to. But, I have a duty to my crown. That duty didn't allow me to give in to my feelings and love you properly."

Serenity stepped closer to him, moving her hand to his chest. She willed him to look at her. When he wouldn't obey her silent plea, she turned his head so his gaze met hers.

"Love? Not lust?" she asked.

Melchior turned his face into her hand and closed his eyes. "I never wanted to pull away from you. Your touch reminded me how badly I wanted you. I envied Chigaru because he slept next to you each night." He shook his head. "No, I wanted to rip Chigaru's head off for sleeping with you each night. He doesn't care that you are human, and he would have gladly become your lover if I had given my permission."

"You never did, though. I thought you were incredibly selfish for that. You had your concubines."

Again he shook his head. "No, I didn't. After our one night, they no longer satisfied me. Keran came to me and occupied my bed but she no longer aroused me. The few times we came together, I was only able to perform because I imagined I was with you instead of her. Even that didn't satisfy me long. As much as I wanted to bring you to my bed, I couldn't because—"

"You didn't want to admit you love me."

Melchior brought her hand to his lips. "Yes," he said against her palm.

"What of your parents?"

"Though I miss them, I will not trade them for you. My hope is my father will see reason in time because the situation between us is different.

"My people call this feeling between us mating. It is more than love. It is two destined souls finding each other. A couple can be married and bear offspring but not be mated—as with my first wife. I cared for her but it ended there. My one night with you and I knew we were mated. A mated pair is life for bhresyas. I couldn't reconcile such a thing happening to me for a human. I hurt you during my denials."

He smoothed the hair away from her face with his other hand. "I was able to find and rescue you because I stopped denying my feelings for you. When I heard your scream, I was afraid you had died. I wanted to cause your murderer pain and horrible death."

His hand clenched around hers as he spoke, then he jerked in surprise and loosened his grip. Serenity didn't utter a sound. She felt no pain, only the strength of

Melchior's feelings for her.

Melchior's gaze searched hers and what he saw there made him want to beg forgiveness for the pain he had caused her. Not because of the way he had gripped her hand, but for the months he had avoided her. Her eyes showed only love. The very same love he had seen in her eyes on their wedding day and every moment thereafter until he drove it out of her. He had never dreamed he'd see it again.

He pulled a dagger from his belt—one similar to the silver ceremonial dagger used at their wedding—and held it out to Serenity. She gave him a questioning look, but she took it.

Melchior guided her hand so the blade rested on his palm. Her hand shook but he made her apply the pressure needed to break his skin. He then guided her hand so she made a similar cut above his left nipple. Blood welled out of the cut and rolled down his chest.

Serenity opened her mouth, more than likely to question him, but he silenced her with a finger over her lips. She kissed his finger and he smiled.

He took the knife from her and took her scarred palm, reopening the wound. She winced and he was sorry for the pain, but it was necessary.

Next, he opened her robe and revealed her breasts. The sight of them after so long distracted him. He gave himself a mental shake and returned to the task at hand. Below Serenity's collarbone, he made a cut. He waited for the blood to well out then dropped the dagger.

Melchior placed his bleeding palm against the cut under her collarbone then he moved her bleeding palm so it rested over the cut above his nipple. She looked at him in utter confusion.

He released her hand and drew Serenity closer, bowing over her until their lips barely touched. He whispered, "Our lives be bound. So long as I live, so too do you. My power is your power, as your happiness is mine. As our blood is mingled, so you become my true bhresya queen." He lowered his lips that last fraction.

Serenity gasped against Melchior's lips. She felt magic all around her and pulled away from the kiss so she could see what he'd done. A slight glowing caught her eye and she looked at her hand. It glowed where it contacted Melchior's skin. Likewise, his hand glowed. She felt the beat of his heart and knew her heartbeat sped up and matched the rhythm he set.

She looked up at him and asked, "What have you done?"

"You will not die in seventy years. So long as I am alive, you will be alive."

"But—"

"You are the bhresya queen, Serenity. It's about time everyone else realized that as well—including me." He pulled her to him and crushed his lips to hers.

Serenity wound her arms around his neck. She squeaked when her feet left the ground. Melchior scooped her into his arms then laid her gently on the middle of the bed. She was smeared with blood and smiling.

Her smile—as always—was radiant.

જ∾⊱

"How could you, Mother? I told you Melchior was not to see Serenity," Alric said as he stormed down the hall to his sister's room.

Rhiannon walked quickly but sedately after him. One of the palace busybodies had informed Alric of Rhiannon's actions. She had thought to return to the throne room and pretend nothing was amiss. Alric had met her halfway there and forced her back the way she had come, berating her the whole way. Rhiannon knew her son would be mad and she couldn't bring herself to care.

Again, the Hell Hounds popped out of their hiding places, but this time they didn't give way when they saw who it was. Alric glared at all of them. He yelled, "I don't care if he's your king. You are living in my kingdom by my invitation. I can force you to leave. Now move!"

Nym opened her mouth but Chigaru stopped her. He opened the door. Before he could get it even part way open, a little puppy hopped out. It snapped at them and growled to the best of its puppy ability.

Chigaru scooped up the puppy and bumped the door open. The puppy grabbed on to his thumb and tried to rip it loose. Rhiannon cooed at the puppy's antics and gave him a pat. The attention distracted the little creature from its goal of ripping Chigaru to shreds. He smiled at the little puppy but watched Alric.

Alric rushed into the room only to be brought up short. What greeted him was his sister and Melchior on the bed, both naked and both smeared with blood. Had they battled? A sharp moan from Serenity caused Alric's face to flush with embarrassment. He hid his eyes and backed out of the room without a sound—not that Melchior or Serenity had heard him come in—and closed the door.

Chigaru spoke softly, "There is love between them, King Alric. There always was. Even before they met, they were mated to each other, fated to each other. Destiny as Serenity called it. King Melchior has made Serenity his true bhresya queen at last."

Everyone gaped at Chigaru in astonishment. He continued, "As true bhresya queen, her life is bound to his. She will be sad to see her brother and mother die... possibly their children and their children's children, as well, but she is happier this way."

Rhiannon's eyes widened with shock. "I didn't know bhresyas could do that."

Nym shrugged and stated in an offhand voice, "It's been done before. Not amongst the royal line, but there have been bhresya and human mated pairs. The sharing of life spans can only happen between a mated pair. The people will have to accept Serenity as their queen now. There will be joy amongst our people once they do."

Theyn added, "Only if they don't piss her off. Serenity may be happiness incarnate, but she can be truly scary when she's mad."

The Hell Hounds nodded as one. They had seen their queen's anger firsthand the day of Serenity's attack. All knew as one they had never felt Serenity's true anger before that moment. They had felt her disapproval and irritation and they were happy that was the extent of it.

Epilogue

Nine Months Later

Hell Hounds and family and a host of palace mages surrounded Serenity to oversee the birth of Nexeu's new heir.

Melchior sat behind her, bracing her back and giving her strength as she bore down to push the babe free of her womb. She leaned against him between pushes, breathing heavily.

"I do not like this, Serenity. I would spare you this pain," Melchior whispered into her ear.

Serenity smiled back at him. "Fine. Next time, you have the baby."

Rhiannon gasped in motherly shock. "Serenity," she admonished lightly, "I taught you better."

Serenity leaned forward and pushed again. "You also taught me," she said with a groan, "that women have their children in private." She leaned back against Melchior once the contraction let her go. "Mother, brother, husband, maid, five Hell Hounds, and six mages are not private."

One of the mages smiled at her. He scolded gently, "If you have enough energy to count and complain then you have enough energy to push, my queen."

Serenity stuck her tongue out at him before she complied. She gripped Melchior's hand and pushed for all she was worth. She was rewarded with the sounds of a baby's cry a minute later.

Rhiannon gave a joyous cry and she cuddled the babe close. "You have a daughter, Serenity. She is precious. She is perfect. And, she has her father's eyes." She offered Serenity the child.

Serenity cuddled her daughter to her breast and leaned back into Melchior so they could see their new daughter at the same time. She smoothed the blanket back and stared.

Her shock had to be evident on her face. She looked up at Melchior and noticed he too looked as shocked as she felt. Their daughter looked human. The only evidence of her bhresya blood was her red and yellow dual-colored eyes and her dark blue hair.

"What does this mean?" Serenity asked finally.

Melchior was at a loss for words. He touched the tiny bundle. She cooed up at him. How did a child of mixed blood look more human than bhresya? He wondered if Alexa's first born would exhibit the same propensity. They would find out in four months.

Alric came forward and hugged all three of them at once. "It means I have a niece. What will you name her?"

Serenity stroked her daughter's blue curls away from her face. "We'll name her after what she is, Alric, just as mother did with me. She is my precious blue gem. Her name is Nilam."

"The heir to Nexeu's throne," Melchior added.

Serenity smiled up at him. He kissed her forehead and whispered thanks to her. In the face of their love, everyone in the room cheered.

THE END

Immortals Lucien and Ranulf have survived to see the modern era to be with the woman they both love once more. Equally anticipating and dreading the reunion, they've vowed to let her decide which of them she wants to be with. But are they prepared to let one woman end a friendship that has lasted centuries?

Eris has just started her dream assignment. She's not looking for an office romance, but her new bosses aren't making it easy for her to avoid it. And right when she gives in to their joint seduction, she ends up tossed back in time to the medieval era where the men she loves have no clue who she is. What's worse, they think she's the enemy.

The Lucien and Ranulf of the past are rough and dangerous. Eris is doing everything she can to survive them while searching for a way back to her time. But returning home means confronting an undeniable truth, one that could end their relationship forever. It's up to her to decide if her heart is strong enough to handle the love of two men and the reality of their enchanted existence.

❧◦❦

FAVORED DRAGON'S RELEASE
He wants her for his bride to end the dragons' curse
but his love for her is ruining his plans.

In the aftermath of a senseless war that claimed many lives, the gods have punished the dragons for causing the conflict. The next generation will not hatch until Prince Shurik finds a human female willing to put aside generations of animosity to become his bride.

Yolette goes to sleep on the side of a mountain, the odd woman out on a couples' camping trip, and awakes in a field outside the home of a dragon. Transported to an unknown world very different from her own, she must depend on Shurik for shelter and guidance.

Shurik doesn't anticipate his growing feelings for Yolette, making the task of proposing that much harder. Danger looms from those who want the punishment ended and from those who want it to continue until the last dragon is gone. Shurik must decide whether he will save his people or his love and pray to the gods his choice is the right one.

❧◦❦

KRISTAR

Destined lovers don't always have it easier.

Chigaru is captain of the guard and he loves his queen more than he should. He is loyal to the royal family but knows his desire for one he cannot have is an issue. He needs a woman who will distract him before he commits treason.

Kitty is a classically trained dancer turned stripper. Her life is perfect except for the shadows of her past catching up with her. She needs to get away before she becomes a prisoner of her destiny.

Five years ago, Silny enacted a plan to regain her lost memories. The last piece of the puzzle is Kitty, and Chigaru is the only one who can cross dimensions to retrieve her. Kitty is not right for his world. Chigaru is not what she expected. They are soul mates, but knowing that might not be enough to overlook their pasts for a future together.

About D. Reneé Bagby

D. Reneé Bagby, or simply Reneé to her friends, is an Air Force brat turned Air Force wife. Born in the Netherlands, she has traveled all of her life and called many places home. She's an avid world builder who loves torturing her characters on their paths toward happily ever after. When not concocting new ways to give her characters a hard time, she enjoys crocheting, reading *shoujo* manga, watching anime and Asian dramas, or bingeing a series on Netflix.

Find her online:
http://dreneebagby.com

KRISTAR

A GEZANE UNIVERSE NOVEL

They are soul mates, but knowing that might not be enough to overlook their pasts

for a future together.

CHAPTER ONE

Five Years Ago – Night Creature Forest

Blue liquid plus red power equaled black flames that spread quickly, burning everything it touched to ash, flammable or not.

Silny blew through her workshop like a hurricane. She upended tables, shattered every glass product within her reach, and shredded every book. None of it made her feel better.

Trent yelled, "Stop this, Silny!"

She ignored him as she threw a giant quartz globe at a cabinet full of bottled powders and liquids. The resulting rainbow of color helped the black flames spread faster and burn hotter.

Trent grabbed Silny's wrists, forcing her to face him. She struggled against his hold, but he was stronger. Silny sometimes forgot that, even though she was taller.

He said in a low, soothing tone, "Enough, my love. This madness serves no purpose."

"How am I to end the curse on myself when nothing around me gives me answers?"

"You will find a way."

"My way resides in the mind of a female who exists in another reality, on another Gezane. I cannot cross the threshold of dimensions. I cannot."

She stopped struggling. Hopeless tears tracked down her cheeks and she slumped into Trent. He closed his arms around her in a comforting embrace she returned.

Trent said, "Let the curse remain, Silny."

"Never. I must know. I must."

"The curse was placed on you for a reason. Only pain can result from breaking it."

Silny jerked away and paced around the room. The black flames kept her from going far. In another few minutes, the whole room would be a giant fireball. She didn't care. Let it burn. Nothing in the room had helped her.

Trent walked over to the one surviving glass jar of Silny's tantrum—the proof she wasn't incoherent in her rage. The white powder of restoration being unharmed meant she could still be reasoned with.

He opened the jar, scooped out a handful of powder, and then returned to Silny. Holding out the powder to her, he said softly, "If you wish the curse broken so badly, my love, you will find a way. I will not stop you. Know I won't shield you either."

Silny cupped her hands and held them in front of her. Trent let the powder sift through his fingers. He stepped into her, cupped the back of her head, and urged her to bend to him so his lips could brush hers.

The tiny kiss and Trent's show of love and understanding calmed Silny like nothing else. She smiled at her husband then mouthed a thank you after he stepped back.

"Shall I send dinner to you or will you join me in the dining hall this night?"

"I will come down to dinner."

"Thank you." He kissed her lips once more. "I shall see you there." He exited the workshop and closed the door after him.

Silny faced her mess. Black fire engulfed the entire room. Only the spot where she stood and the path to the door remained untouched.

She looked down at the white powder she held. With a sigh of resignation, she lifted her hands in front of her lips and blew. The white powder spread in the air, blanketing the room. Everything the white powder touched extinguished and started mending. The tables and cabinets righted themselves, broken glass melted together and reformed its original shape, and containers jumped onto their respective shelves with their contents following after to be stored once more.

The last thing to be fixed was the last thing Silny broke—the giant quartz globe. The seams fused as though it had never been shattered. The globe bounced into the air and hurtled across the room, planting itself directly in front of Silny.

She blinked at it, not knowing why it reacted this way when she hadn't cast a spell beyond the restoration powder.

The globe glowed and showed a burnt-orange bhresya male. He spoke to someone outside the globe's sight. Silny guessed the individual was much smaller than the male based on the angle of his gaze.

"Why are you showing me this?" She touched the globe and the glow intensified. The image inside changed to a human female. She danced on a stage before a large seated audience. Silny knew the girl.

"She is the one from my dreams, the one who eludes me. Why do you show me her?"

The image of the female became smaller and the image of the bhresya male appeared next to her with a silver cord stretched between them. The sight made Silny stumble and cover her mouth as she stared in shock. "It can't be."

She reached for the globe but stopped shy of touching it, not wanting to disrupt the spell with her turbulent emotions. Laughter passed her lips, low at first and then loud and triumphant. Her anguish had enacted a spell that found her solution.

"I have only to get this male to that female and then he will bring her here. She will give me what I need to break my curse."

The image of the male expanded and filled the globe. As it did, the person to whom the male spoke came into view. It was another human female. She wore the crown of the bhresya queen. A red cord stretched between the two.

Silny screamed, "Why do you show me the solution only to take it away from me? I cannot—"

Her tirade ended when the globe showed a third male entering the conversation. Silny recognized Melchior, king of the bhresyas of Nexeu. She heard he had married a human female to solidify the peace between bhresyas and humans. A silver cord stretched from Melchior to his queen, but Melchior acted distant from her, which seemed to upset the female.

"Why does he deny the cord?" Silny whispered. "If he were to accept their relationship, then the red cord of love would entwine with the silver cord of fate. This other male would be left and I could approach him to retrieve his own true mate and thus break my curse."

She stared at the three for a long while. No solution presented itself. So long as Melchior denied his true relationship with his queen, her love would remain with the other male.

Silny yelled, "Show me something useful!"

The globe bobbed and the picture changed to a human male. His right arm was in a sling. He spoke to another human male and a red bhresya male who had one missing horn. The first human male spoke in an angry manner, gesturing ever so often to his broken arm.

Silny stared at the exchange. Her ability to read their lips meant the lack of sound didn't bother her. All three males wanted the bhresya queen dead. A thwarted desire because her guards accompanied her day and night, especially when she left the palace.

The broken-armed male wanted the queen to suffer, but the time required for the amount of pain he wished to inflict upon her was much more than the time it would take Melchior and his guards to track down the queen once she was taken.

An unladylike snort left Silny's lips. "Is that your only worry?" She placed her finger against the globe above the forehead of the male. She whispered, "Come seek me in the Night Creature Forest, little displaced prince. I will help you, and you will help me."

He would hear her words as a whispered suggestion most humans mistakenly called inspiration. As such, he would think he had conceived the plan. Silny only had to wait for him to come to her. She waved her hand in a dismissive gesture. The globe blanked, returning to its original purple color, before it floated away to return to its rightful place on a pedestal in the middle of the room.

Silny exited her workroom with a new spring in her step. She was the happiest she had been in decades, maybe centuries. At long last the curse would be at an end. Once all the players entered her game, she could set herself free.

܀

Present – Nexeu

Chigaru smiled at the sight of his king and queen. Melchior sat at his desk surrounded by his advisors, who awaited his judgments on matters of state. Serenity sat on Melchior's lap. She had one of her breasts bared so she could feed Nilam, her and

Melchior's daughter and the heir to the Nexeu throne. Mother and father enjoyed the act of nourishing their first and only child.

The wholesome sight didn't bring happiness to all who beheld it. Chigaru cast his gaze around the room. None would harm the royal family but Chigaru still perceived each person as a threat so long as they showed irritation about Nilam's lunch arrangements.

Serenity insisted Melchior be a part of every feeding. She sought him out no matter where he was. If Melchior happened to be in the throne room surrounded by his advisors and nobles addressing matters of state, then Serenity fed her child there. She didn't care if others found the sight of her breastfeeding scandalizing or her interruptions annoying. Melchior didn't call a stop to it, which meant no one else could complain.

The nobles had to be happy it would end soon. Nilam was four and the feedings happened less and less. Serenity prolonged them. She didn't want to give up the closeness she shared with her child and husband, but she knew Nilam's dependency on her for nourishment had ended long ago.

Chigaru had suggested she have another child. The words had tasted bitter as they left his mouth, but he'd said them. Before Nilam, Chigaru had thought Serenity would be his. She had married Melchior to ensure the peace between bhresyas and humans, but her heart had belonged to Chigaru. He hadn't minded the idea of being a lover. Royals were not expected to be faithful, especially in political marriages.

His assumption had been a mistake. Serenity loved her husband with her whole being. They were a true mated pair—two souls meant to be together. Serenity and Melchior's marriage had started out rough but Serenity's near assassination had opened Melchior's eyes to his true feelings for his wife.

Once reunited, Melchior had declared Serenity a true bhresya queen. The announcement had had a mixed reception, as they all had known it would. Some still grumbled about having a human for a queen and a half-breed as heir to the throne and future regent, but no one acted on the emotions. None would so long as the Hell Hounds—personal royal guards to Serenity and Nilam—stood in the way.

Chigaru clutched at the air where his right arm should be. His motion made Erezion, a fellow Hell Hound, glance in his direction. The younger male had a question in his eyes that Chigaru silenced with a glare and a soft grunt. Erezion returned to scanning the room for potential threats, as he should be. Chigaru didn't want the male fretting over him like so many others.

He had lost the arm the day Serenity was almost killed. Chigaru had been overpowered, severely beaten, and had his arm ripped off as he lay bound on the floor, helpless to aid his queen as their assailants beat her as well. For his failure, he should have been stripped of his title and cast out of the royal employ. Many called for such a punishment, but Serenity wouldn't hear of it. Only Melchior's agreement that Chigaru retain his position quieted all naysayers.

The loss of Chigaru's arm hadn't impeded his ability to act as captain of the Hell Hounds. A few of the royal guards, who now professed loyalty to Serenity and hoped to gain positions as Hell Hounds, thought Chigaru remained captain because he held Serenity's favor. Those who had challenged him, found out otherwise.

He rested his hand on the hilt of the sword strapped sideways across his back at his waist. He hated the weapon. He hated all weapons. They slowed him down. Or they used to slow him down. Until the loss of his arm, he'd never had to use one. He had been deadly with his bare hands. But remaining leader of the Hell Hounds meant proving himself the strongest fighter. Thanks to the weapon on his back, he remained such.

"The room will come to order," Melchior called.

Chigaru snapped out of his inner musings to focus on his duty. Serenity set Nilam on the ground before resituating her dress so it covered her. After leaning over to kiss Melchior's cheek, she started to edge off his leg. Melchior pulled her back and whispered in her ear. Whatever he said set Serenity giggling as she played at getting away from the kisses he planted on her neck and shoulders.

Serenity said between her laughter, "Yes, my king. Yes. Enough."

Melchior laid one last kiss against her lips and then released her. "I shall see you then, Serenity."

"Me too," Nilam said loudly, showing both her parents an annoyed expression. "See me, too, papa." She balled her fists into her sides.

"Yes, my princess. I shall see you later, as well, though not in the way I plan to see your mother." Melchior patted his daughter's head.

"Is it mama and papa stuff?"

"Yes."

"Ew." Nilam pushed his hand away. "Never mind."

Melchior chuckled and forced another head pat on his daughter, ruffling her blue hair that matched his skin so well. He hooked one of his fingers around her short blue horns and used them to wiggle her head side to side.

"Papa, quit it. I don't wanna shake my head."

Though she protested, Nilam soon giggled like her mother. Only then did Melchior stop. He leaned forward and gave her loud kiss on her forehead. "I shall see you later, my princess."

"Yes, my king." Nilam curtsied, or tried to curtsy. She bent her knees and squatted a little before straightening. Considering she used to jump in place, thinking that was what a curtsy should be, it was an improvement.

Serenity smiled down at her daughter with a mother's love, making her normal visage look more ethereal and beautiful. The sight caused Chigaru's chest to ache. Serenity's happiness was his happiness, but her expressions of love only extended to her daughter and husband now. Whatever love she had once felt for Chigaru had changed to the love shared between close family, not of lovers as he'd hoped it would remain.

He meant no disrespect to his king and knew Melchior had more right to Serenity's love than Chigaru. That didn't make the jealousy gnawing at Chigaru's insides any less painful.

Serenity curtsied to Melchior and blew him a kiss before turning to leave the room. She ushered Nilam with a hand behind the girl's head. Erezion met them halfway and escorted them across the room while Chigaru opened the door, made sure the hall was clear of any threat, and waited for them to exit.

Once Serenity was at his side, a little of his jealousy subsided. A quick glance at Melchior revealed the emotion had found a new home. The male glared at Chigaru in open hostility. The whole of the country treated Melchior and Chigaru's cold war over Serenity's affection as a favored topic.

One and all knew Chigaru loved his queen, though had never acted on it. They also knew that same love was the reason Melchior allowed Chigaru to retain his position as captain of the Hell Hounds. Chigaru would lay down his life for Serenity. All the Hell Hounds would. They all loved her that much. For Melchior to fault Chigaru for his love would mean faulting the other Hell Hounds as well, so they remained at a stalemate.

Chigaru closed the door to the audience chamber and Melchior's anger. The male showed his insecurity when he acted like that. Chigaru would not touch Serenity until she asked it of him, and she would never ask.

Serenity said, "Shall we visit the Ladies of the Circle? They have new clothes for you, Nilam, since you are growing so quickly."

The little girl sighed and rolled her dual-iris red and yellow eyes. Only descendants of the royal family had eyes of red and yellow. If not for her eyes, blue hair, and blue horns, many would wonder if Melchior had fathered Nilam because she looked human otherwise. She had Serenity's brown skin and could be mistaken for a normal human if she wore a hooded cloak and kept her eyes to the ground.

The obvious dominance of human traits in a mixed child further served to anger those who didn't want a half-breed on the throne. And it wasn't a fluke. The three boys born to Theyn, another Hell Hound, and Alexa, Serenity's head maid, showed the same traits—hair, horns, and eyes that resembled their father's within a human body that resembled their mother's.

"Head's up."

Chigaru hadn't needed the warning since he heard the three energetic boys stampeding toward them long before their father called out, but did Theyn the courtesy of looking in his direction.

The boys, a set of twins and their older brother, ran full tilt toward Chigaru and his party. The oldest boy, who brought up the rear, yelled, "We're playing tag and I'm it."

Nilam bounced in place, looking from her mother to the boys.

Serenity sighed but still nodded. "Go on then. You can be fitted later."

Nilam beamed up at her mother before she took off running. The boys blew past them.

Theyn yelled, "Hold it."

All three boys skidded to a halt and faced their father.

"Manners." He gestured to Serenity.

She blinked and smiled sweetly at the boys.

The boys each bowed at the waist and said in loud unison, "Good day, your majesty."

"Good day, Taysn, Ciro, and Dion."

"Thank you," Theyn said. "Go on then." The boys resumed running and Theyn blew out a tired breath. He patted Erezion's back and said, "You're on princess duty. Have fun."

Erezion appeared as though he would argue but heaved a sigh of his own before bowing to Serenity and running after the boys.

Serenity laughed. "That was mean, my joy."

"That may be but I'm tired. The boys have been waiting for Nilam to come out this whole time. Alexa banned them from returning to the nursery until the sun goes down."

"Mother always said children return in kind the same mischief we visited upon our own parents."

"That's what I'm afraid of. I terrorized my parents when I was around my boys' ages. And there was only one of me. My parents waited three decades before attempting to have another child."

Chigaru snorted, agreeing Theyn in childhood had to have been a handful since the adult hadn't matured much. Theyn was the joker of the Hell Hounds. He had played with Serenity more than protected her when he joined her bhresya collection. Because of that, she had started calling him her joy. Only in the last few years before Serenity's marriage to Melchior had Theyn taken an interest in learning how to fight so he could be a better guard.

And though Theyn loved Serenity, it was a familial love. His wife showed no signs of the jealousy that plagued Melchior. In fact, Alexa's love for Serenity equaled her husband's. She alone had followed Serenity to Nexeu, the kingdom of the bhresyas, when Serenity's other maids had abandoned their posts. The two had become like sisters, raising their children together. The children only learned proper forms of address because it was expected.

The Hell Hounds, Alexa, and Serenity were friends first.

Theyn clasped his hands behind his back and glanced between Serenity and Chigaru. "What are we doing?"

"Staying within the palace walls. I have an appointment with my husband later this day." A small amount of heat crept up Serenity's cheeks as she imparted that news.

Chigaru had a good idea what the appointment entailed. Serenity had taken Chigaru's advice concerning her wish to continue holding a baby in her arms. She and Melchior were trying for another child. They had been trying for some time. The palace mages were at a loss as to why Serenity wasn't pregnant yet.

The failure to conceive had started to worry Serenity more in the last month since Alexa had announced her third pregnancy. Only Chigaru knew of Serenity's feelings of unease. He alone shared her deepest confidence—another source of Melchior's jealousy. Serenity came to Chigaru with her innermost thoughts. He was her confidant. She hid nothing from him. He alone laid claim to that intimacy and Melchior hated it.

Chigaru bent down and whispered in Serenity's ear, "Sword practice."

Serenity sighed. "If we must."

"Must what?" Theyn asked.

Chigaru didn't answer and wouldn't answer. When he spoke, he did so to Serenity and in a voice loud enough for her alone to hear. On rare occasions, he spoke to Nym, his second in command. He captained the Hell Hounds in silence. They had all grown used to that and learned to interpret his quiet commands.

Serenity said, "Sword practice."

Theyn made a sound of understanding. "You've gotten better."

"Are you practicing how to lie, my joy?"

"No and you know I speak the truth. You can hold the sword and have learned to block. That is better than in the beginning when you could barely lift the sword."

"I did better with dagger practice." She blew out an annoyed breath. "I don't know why I practice any of it. Melchior has already decreed I will never shed blood."

Chigaru whispered, "You learn for defense, not to fight."

"No, I learn to keep from being bored." She glanced the way the children had run. "Nilam no longer needs me. It's lonely again."

Theyn said, "You could help Melchior."

Serenity's blush returned. "No. We distract each other. The advisors grew tired of our flirting during meetings and suggested we distance ourselves or else nothing would be accomplished. Given the evidence, we both agreed. True queen I am, but my place is not always at my husband's side."

Chigaru placed his hand on Serenity's back and urged her toward the training fields. She hesitated for two breaths before walking. Chigaru didn't mind. It allowed him to indulge in the feel of her gentle heat against his skin. When she started walking, he moved his hand away.

This torture couldn't go on. He couldn't continue lusting after another man's wife, knowing the day he could have her would never come. Perhaps the time had come for him to find a female to distract him and possibly marry him. But where? And who? What female would marry a man whose heart belonged to another?

※

Present – Florida

Kitty wouldn't and shouldn't bang her head against the table in front of her. She chanted that command to herself over and over. The temptation to try and knock herself out was high.

"Next," Vincent called.

"Why?" Kitty grumbled under her breath.

"Hush."

She let her head fall back and wished for plagues, natural disasters, anything to keep from watching another woman embarrassing herself. How many bad dancers existed in Florida? And had they all come to audition? If so, could Kitty order her bullet now?

A bleached blonde made her way to center stage.

"What's your name, sweetheart?" Vincent shuffled through his papers before the woman answered.

"I'm Candy."

"Uh huh. What's your real name?"

The girl frowned and huffed before she said, "Diana Mordane. But I want to be called Candy on stage."

"Sure. Whatever. How about you dance for us before we start talking stage names?"

Kitty rested one elbow on the table and her chin on her hand as a way of preparing herself to not be blown away.

The lights dimmed to the same level they would be on a normal night while the DJ cued up a club mix with heavy bass. Diana gyrated as she stripped. Kitty couldn't describe her level of boredom at the girl shaking her butt and snaking her body while moving in time to the music. A typical club bounce. The first mistake most women made was thinking strippers strutted to music while taking off their clothes. It wasn't art, but there was a technique to it that got men to give up money.

Diana had no technique. In fact, Kitty would pay the woman to stop dancing. Kitty's eyes got big when Diana flounced her way to left stage before she turned and ran at the pole. Kitty held her breath, knowing what the girl was doing and knowing how bad it could be if she messed up.

The worst happened.

Diana missed. She had tried to build up momentum so she could swing around the pole. Most amateurs had to do that since they didn't yet know how to control the spin. She jumped at the pole, managed to touch it, but the speed of her approach jerked it out of her hands and she went flying. Her butt skipped along the stage in time to the music.

Kitty laughed. She didn't pretend to hide it like the other girls sitting in on the audition. After the pain of the last three hours, Kitty deserved this laugh. Even Vincent laughed, though he covered his with coughing and throat clearing.

The music stopped and the lights brightened. Kitty didn't stop laughing now that Diana could see her. In fact, when Kitty saw Diana's red butt cheeks after the woman stood up, she laughed harder. Diana stomped around the stage, snatching up her clothes all while glaring at Kitty.

Diana snapped, "It's not that damn funny."

"Yes, it is." Kitty pointed at the entrance to the club. "Did you see those plaques on your way in? All those pole dancing awards? Red here"—she gestured to the redhead sitting on her right—"has placed in the top three of every competition she's ever entered. She trained all the women in this club. We have a reputation of being the best pole show in town, possibly the state. If you don't know how to work the pole, you say that up front and we could set up training. That is, if your dancing didn't suck so bad. Instead, you chose to embarrass yourself. I, in turn, chose to laugh at you."

Vincent said, "Don't call us. We won't call you. Next!" He balled up her résumé and tossed it over his shoulder.

Diana cursed them out as she left the room.

Red leaned over to Kitty and said, "You know we should be on a reality show. We could call it Stripper Idol or something."

"That's a good idea, Red. Thanks." Vincent scribbled out a quick note on the pad next to him. A huge grin split his mouth, making him look like a jack-o-lantern. "Put that on pay-per-view and it could be a gold mine."

Kitty bounced the back of her hand off Red's arm. "Big mouth."

"The only one with a big mouth around here is you, Kitty-honey. Keep it up and you're going to get yourself in trouble one day."

"You got my back, Red, 'cause you wuv me." Kitty rested her head on Red's shoulder and stared up at the woman with big, batting eyes.

"Get off." Red shrugged her shoulders to displace Kitty's head.

Kitty sat up and looked at the stage when the next woman entered. Nervous energy oozed from the woman's every pore. This was definitely her first time at the rodeo. Kitty gave the woman the once over—athletic body, large breasts that looked natural, and a nice round behind that her jeans couldn't fully contain. Three pluses.

Vincent asked, "Name?"

"Rhedyn Brantley." She looked down the line of people sitting in judgment of her and then back to Vincent. "I know this is an audition to show my skills, but does that include stripping as well?"

"Duh," Vincent snapped.

Kitty asked, "This is your first time stripping, right?"

"Yes. I'm a dancer. I mean, I went to school for dance and was a pro cheerleader for a while before I got married."

Vincent whistled under his breath. "Get out. What team?"

"That doesn't matter," Kitty said, glaring at the man. "Show us what you got, with your clothes on, and we'll go from there."

"Sure." She looked behind her and then faced front again. "I heard what you said to that girl Diana, so I wanted to say upfront I have no experience pole dancing."

"Noted."

Rhedyn smiled. It transformed her whole appearance. The woman was gorgeous. Perfect, white teeth sparkled in the bright lights. Kitty loved everything about this woman. If Rhedyn could dance, Kitty wanted her. The men would flock to this woman. That meant Kitty could step down. She prayed for skill.

The lights dimmed and the DJ cued up the same club beat from before. Rhedyn got into the rhythm and moved like there were already men waiting to tip her. Kitty had to applaud when Rhedyn managed to make her butt clap while wearing jeans. The woman had more than skill. She had talent.

When the music stopped and the lights came back up, Kitty and the others clapped. Vincent put his fingers in his mouth and whistled, which meant Rhedyn got the job. They just had to tell her.

Kitty opened her mouth to impart the good news when a man in a suit ran up to Vincent's side and whispered in his ear. Vincent cursed under his breath and grumbled to himself before asking, "Really? She's the best we've seen."

The suited man said, "That's what he said, man. You got a problem, take it up with him." He jerked his thumb over his shoulder at the VIP lounge.

Kitty looked at the second-floor, glass-enclosed room that acted as the VIP lounge when the owner wasn't on site. Today he was there, choosing to help with the auditions as part of some hands-on initiative.

He had taken over the club a little over a year ago and fired half the staff. He'd then left the club to its own devises, abandoning those still working to overtime and double shifts while they searched for replacements. A search that had been slow going until a few weeks ago when the boss condescended to return and find out why the club wasn't bringing in revenue like it should. Kitty had forgotten he was there since she hadn't heard a peep out of him all day.

Vincent sighed then faced Rhedyn. "Sorry, sweetheart. I think you're great. Even with your clothes on, I was ready to start giving you money."

"Okay." Rhedyn twisted her hands, her nervous energy returning.

"The boss says no. Since he owns the place, his word is law. Sorry."

"I understand. Thanks anyway." She started to walk away.

"Hold up," Kitty snapped. "His word is law my ass. She is fantastic. She's the best we've seen. I want her. Why the hell—"

A loud bang followed by the sound of cracking glass stopped Kitty's tirade. She looked back at the VIP lounge again. The middle of the glass had splintered into tiny cubes. The bang must have been the sound of something hitting the glass. And it had to have hit hard because that was tempered glass meant to be bullet resistant.

Kitty growled before throwing herself onto her seat with her arms crossed over her chest.

Vincent said to Rhedyn, "Sorry again, sweetheart. Thanks for coming out. I'll keep your résumé handy in case the boss changes his mind."

Rhedyn nodded and left the building.

Kitty sat fuming for several breaths. This was unacceptable. More than that, she refused to let it stand. The man didn't get to leave them high and dry for months on end and then come back to play lord and master when it suited him. She snatched up Rhedyn's résumé.

"Leave it, Kitty." Vincent tried to get the paper back but she whipped it out of his reach.

"Kiss my ass." She glared at the VIP lounge. "Open the door. I'm coming up. And tell your goons to stand down."

She stomped her way to the door of the VIP lounge and was actually surprised to find it open. The two men standing on either side of the door winked at her as she passed. One of them pulled the door shut behind her.

Before the boss could say anything, she yelled, "Ice, what the hell is your issue? We need her." She waved the résumé to emphasize her point.

"I wanted that." Ice plucked the résumé from her fingers and looked it over. "Thank you for bringing it up. Now good-bye."

"Shove that bye up your ass. You're going to tell me why we couldn't hire her. I'm not leaving until you do."

Ice glanced at her in a bored manner. "Leave through the door or the glass. Since I've already weakened the glass"—he waved his flushed knuckles at her—"going through it shouldn't hurt much but the fall will. Your choice."

"Try it." She put her hands on her hips and looked down at him, waiting for him to touch her. At six foot two, Kitty didn't intimidate easily. Ice was seven inches shorter than her and at least ten pounds lighter.

She knew him to be a badass, which had nothing to do with him being Asian, though it helped, and head of one of the strongest crime families in Florida. He'd made the original owner of the club disappear. She doubted the police would ever find the body, if one still existed. While all that should scare her, in her current mood, she dared him to start something.

"I like you, Kitty. It is rare for me to like anyone. That sentiment alone is why you are still breathing."

"And?"

Ice went to a large overstuffed chair in the center of the room and sat down. "She's wrong for the club."

"And?"

He glanced at the résumé again. "What comes next is between her and me."

"Let me get this straight. We can't hire her because you're about to take her to bed."

"Something like that."

"Well, shit. I'll give you points for ethics, if nothing else. You still suck though, Ice. Why couldn't you go after that other chick? The one who landed on her ass. She's more the type I've been seeing you go with."

"You're not wrong. Rhedyn Brantley caught my attention."

Kitty walked over and planted herself sideways on Ice's lap. He sat back while resting a hand on her lower spine. Of all the employees, only Kitty braved being around Ice and treating him the way she did. Everyone else treaded on eggshells. He wore scary like cheap cologne and got off on the fear he caused. A sadist through and through, but that helped Kitty figure out where she stood with him.

So long as she didn't show fear or question his authority too much, he would treat her normal...for him. The little power struggle of earlier was a reminder he didn't scare her as much as the others. The day she backed down would be the day he would lose all respect for her, if he had any to begin with.

"Ice, I'm tired. You promised to bump me down to server once we hired three more girls. So far, the bottom of the barrel has auditioned. We are never going to find anyone if you keep picking them off for your to-be-fucked list."

He flicked his finger against her back, hitting her in such a way that made her startle with a small intake of breath at the tingling sensation crawling up her spine. It hadn't hurt but it was uncomfortable. Kitty had no doubt Ice had intimate knowledge of the human body and all the places to hit someone so it would cause the most pain. He'd given her a warning.

She snapped, "Well?"

Ice chuckled, similar to something one would hear from a young boy who liked to torture small animals. The sound made Kitty want to shiver. She quelled the urge since she got the feeling that would be construed as a sign of weakness. He said, "I definitely like you, Kitty." He stood, dumping her off his lap, and stepped over her.

Kitty stared at him from the floor.

After folding Rhedyn's résumé and stuffing it into his back pocket, he said, "I'll put in a call to my contacts up north. They'll send some girls our way. Girls with experience." He glanced over his shoulder at her. "Happy?"

"Thank you." She picked herself up off the floor. "How soon before I can be on server duty?"

"One month. You won't be a full-time server. I still want you dancing. The six-foot pussy is one of the big draws of this club."

"Fine. I want to pick the days though."

"We'll see." Ice walked away, leaving the room and Kitty.

That was a small victory, at least. She would rather be a full-time server, but compromise wasn't always a bad thing. If Ice let her pick her days to dance, she would consider it a win.

After four years on stage, Kitty wanted to keep her clothes on. The money was fantastic. She had even managed to save a chunk of it, but the fun had worn off. She used to love to dance for the sake of dancing. Taking her clothes off hadn't bothered her. She loved working the pole and had enjoyed learning how. She couldn't compete on Red's level, but Kitty wasn't that ambitious. Her lack of ambition was why she was stripping rather than strutting and fretting her hour upon the stage.

Kitty had been destined for greatness. The invitation to a prestigious dancing school was testament to her ability. But all Kitty had seen was the life her mother wanted but couldn't have. She'd been living through Kitty and Kitty had gotten fed up and run away. Literally. She'd packed up her car and drove to Florida.

Waitressing tables paid nothing. Office work didn't suit her. And her attitude made any job in retail or working with the public in a customer service capacity a big mistake. Kitty decided to try stripping as a whim and hadn't thought she would get past the auditions. Vincent had snatched her up, seeing her potential and willing to train her.

He'd gotten her into Ice's club. Vincent had heard of the switch in ownership and thought it might be a good opportunity for him to move up in the world. With Kitty as an incentive, since she'd gotten a good reputation by that point, Vincent managed to land the club manager position.

Though he was a hard-ass of a boss, he still thanked Kitty on the odd occasion for helping him get the job. To this day, Vincent still called her the best investment he'd ever made. Considering how much money the man had made playing the stock market, that was saying a lot.

Speak of the devil…Vincent poked his head in the lounge. "You didn't come down after the boss left. Thought I would come up and make sure you were still breathing."

"Just thinking."

"You've got big, hairy brass balls to be talking to him like that. He freaks me the hell out every time I see him."

"He knows. Don't you know if you run from a dog it's going to chase you?"

Vincent laughed. "Yeah, you're right. That don't change that Ice is one scary SOB." He jerked his thumb over his shoulder. "We open in an hour. Get ready."

Kitty saluted and then headed for the dressing room. On her way out the door, she heard Vincent grumbling about the cost of fixing the glass and having to close the VIP lounge for the night for safety reasons. She would work at bringing in extra money tonight since the broken glass was partly her fault.

Work. When had this job become work? It had started out as a party every night. She danced and flirted while taking her clothes off. She made more in a week than most in an entire month. On a good night, she pulled down nearly a thousand, if not a little more. On a slow night, she pulled four or five hundred. That was still better than any other job she could think of—any legal job anyway.

She entered the dressing room and started removing her street clothes so she could change into her first outfit of the evening. She would switch three or four more times depending on how her night went. A tired sigh almost made it past her lips, but she stopped it. She'd been awake for five hours and already she wanted to go home to bed. The feeling plagued her more and more.

She used to like her job. An odd feeling had started creeping over her the past few months. She felt restless and ill at ease without knowing why. Her first response was to run before bad got worse. If something didn't change soon, she just might. The only thing keeping her here was her. Her bank account could take her anywhere in the big, wide world...except she didn't know where she wanted to go.

"I need a man."

Red laughed behind her. "What the hell for? To steal your money, knock you up and then knock you around?"

"Not all men are like that, Red."

"All the men we'll meet are. Hell, half of them are married. You're smart, Kitty. Don't screw that up by putting a man in the mix."

"You're right."

"I know I'm right." Red turned around and licked her lips as she slid her gaze down Kitty's body. "Now a woman, on the other hand, might—"

"So very not interested, Red. What's wrong? Did your girlfriend dump you?"

"Don't even get me started on that thieving skank."

"Okay. Leaving that one alone. I'm strictly dickly, otherwise I would jump you in a hot second."

"You never know unless you try."

"I need to make sure the DJ knows my song selection." Kitty bolted for the door.

"Scaredy cat," Red said in a sing-song.

Kitty replied in the same manner, "Damn straight."

She headed for the DJ booth, throwing greetings at the other employees she passed. The men all gave her blue-sequined negligee with matching bra and panty set appreciative looks. At one time, Kitty had loved the reaction she got from the men. Now it annoyed her.

They all liked to look but never touched. Of course the company's no-fraternization policy, which was now strictly enforced thanks to Ice, contributed to her problem but she blamed her height for remaining dateless. She was too tall.

Most men didn't like tall women, and her type didn't extend to men shorter than her. The few taller men she had met thought she was too tall. She hadn't been laid in weeks. Maybe the source of her unease came from that. Could it be something so simplistic? If it was, fixing it wouldn't be hard, and she wouldn't have to run away to do it.

Get laid. She had a goal and she knew just the man to see the deed done. Her ex loved it when she called in favors. Thinking about how she would spend her morning made Kitty's night look a lot better.

If her anxiety remained after some therapeutic sex, she would worry about it and the cause for it then.

࿇

KRISTAR

Available in digital and in print

http://dreneebagby.com